The DENSHAM DO

BRUCE HARRIS

The Book Guild Ltd

First published in Great Britain in 2022 by
The Book Guild
Unit E2, Airfield Business Park
Harrison Road
Market Harborough
Leicsestershire, LE16 7UL
Freephone: 0800 999 2982
www.bookguild.co.uk
Email: info@bookguild.co.uk
Twitter: @bookguild

Typeset in 11pt Adobe Garamond Pro

Printed and bound in the UK by TJ Books Limited, Padstow, Cornwall

ISBN 978 1914471 087

British Library Cataloguing in Publication Data.
A catalogue record for this book is available from the British Library.

For my mother
Irene Ettie Harris
née Walker

Contents

FRIDAY MORNING AND AFTERNOON, June 14th

Matthew, bride's uncle

It was one of those gremlins in the works things, I suppose, which doesn't make it any less irritating. My niece Kate is now a smart London lawyer, and tomorrow she would be marrying another smart London lawyer called Robert. I have always had a real soft spot for Kate, and I only sketchily know her intended, so when my brother Peter and his wife Helen decided that they would make block bookings at the hotel on both Friday and Saturday nights, Mary and I decided there and then that we'd devote the entire weekend to Kate. We were both a little vague as to what we would do if we didn't like the intended, but we feel duty bound to have a good look at how things are and then decide whether Kate is to be congratulated or earmarked for protection.

So, naturally, with both of us planning to get to the hotel by not too late in the day, two problematic work calls came along for me before ten o'clock in the morning. Firstly, one of my sub-editors, Ken Slater, was on to me at twenty past nine concerning decisions about next week's issue, and I had to remind him that I was on leave for a family do this weekend; Tony Fenwick was in charge. All of this he knew perfectly well, but Slater is one of these guys who forgets selectively, as it were, meaning anything he doesn't choose to remember for political or work evasion reasons. He doesn't get on too well with Tony, who once described him in my hearing as a 'neurotic little pedant', with the insertion of another adjective which shall remain nameless just before 'neurotic'. I worked out how to say 'no' some time ago, so I told him he would just have to manage; sometimes, family has to come first.

Fifteen minutes later, Mary was on to me in a panic, or as near to being in a panic as she ever gets, which is speaking a bit faster and sighing here and there. She's head of English in a big school, and if bad news starts arriving on Friday concerning how many of her department are going to be in on Monday, she needs to do something about it.

'Wendy Shaw's aunt has died, and the funeral is on Monday. Apparently. The death rate amongst Wendy's relatives is alarming; I can think of at least five who've popped off in the last six years. I keep meaning to ask her to at least invent one or two other contingencies. John Phillips is on another course all week; he says he told me about it ages ago, and maybe he did, but I don't remember. Perhaps it is me – can you be going prematurely senile at fifty-two?'

Mary's my darling, as ever, but delegation isn't her strong point, and having met her number two, the intense, doe-eyed Baz – who can put much reliance on a guy who goes around calling himself 'Baz'? – it probably wouldn't work anyway, so arrangements have to be made before she comes away this afternoon. Otherwise, her head, Sheila Golding, will, in her trenchant phrase, 'have my guts for garters', and I can believe it. I've met Sheila.

In the event, I negotiated a cease-fire and promise of mutual co-operation between Tony and Ken, with a few well-chosen words also involving gartered innards, and Mary managed to find an agency not entirely staffed by bandits or morons or both, and we got away before five. The hotel was in Devon, and probably not more than forty minutes' drive from us, but on Friday afternoons, the Devon mile along two-way country roads can stretch like elastic. I sometimes imagine lurking tractor drivers, twirling their villainous moustaches, who wait until 4pm precisely and then trundle out to go their seven or eight miles at about one mile an hour on roads so crowded that no-one except cyclists can get past them.

However, we got by, and Alanscombe House, once the almost stately home of a rich marine merchant, came into view through the hedges at no later than ten past six. It was a showers and sunny intervals type of day, but we approached it in one of the sunny intervals. It was big, but not too big; posh, but not too posh. An architectural mongrel, Mary called it, and certainly the red bricks jar a little with the double-glazed to hell windows and bunged on balconies of a rather later vintage.

We'd seen it before, but we'd never yet stayed in it; too much on the doorstep, I suppose.

As we approached, we saw the balcony rooms dotted along the façade, and guessed that their height must provide beautiful country views. This weekend might prove to be interesting in more ways than one.

Celia, bridegroom's grandmother

After my usual breakfast, a little toast and some item of whatever fruit is in season, I took my remaining tea into my conservatory. Almost all apartments in our Greenhaven Retirement Village – 'an oasis in the twilight of life' – have their own conservatories, generously spaced and intelligently designed, affording spreading views of the village's lawns and carefully tended flowerbeds. Mr Call Me Bill Douglas, the general manager of the village – a title which rather gives away the whiff of corporatism which attaches to the whole venture – is always advising us all to 'relish our good fortune', and I do so relish, whilst bearing in mind the three hundred and fifty thousand onecers my good fortune set me back and the further three thousand per annum maintaining it costs me. Fortunately, my late husband Derek and I tied up our affairs so convincingly that the hyena packs who sniff around the retired had not even the merest off chance of drawing blood, and my good fortune remains affordable.

To be entirely honest, much as I take a wholesome pleasure in the neat landscape before me, there are mornings when I do have an ulterior motive for my post-breakfast conservatory sit, in the pleasing shape of our new young gardener's assistant Rory. His easy smile and twinkling eyes would be nice enough in themselves, but Rory, in his brief time with us, has already shown a penchant for stripping off his shirt and displaying his splendid torso to the world, thereby shooting up the numbers on several blood pressure monitors dotted around the village. He did so now, bless him, tying the sleeves round that unfeasibly trim waist, and waved to me happily, following it with a big thumbs-up sign. This presumably meant he knew about my approaching wedding weekend when my lovely grandson Robert would finally make his way down the aisle. Rory is such a genuinely good-natured boy, quite like Robert himself, in fact, in nature if not in torso. Robert is long and lean, and of a more sinewy build, though I seem to recall that the last time I saw him in a swimming costume, probably at his parents' gîte, I should think, he would have been about seventeen, an age given to sinewy boys. I was uplifted; a smile and a wave from a beautiful half-naked young man is not a bad way to get the weekend going. I returned the wave, trying to share the simple optimism of youth, much as my reservations about the forthcoming nuptials threaten to engulf me.

I had until noon to pack and prepare myself, and then it seemed a car was to come and take me all the way to Devon; as the Greenhaven Retirement Village is in Wiltshire, this is a journey of some length and expense, which caused me to make a token protest to my son Malcolm. I use the term 'token' advisedly, because I was viewing the prospect of getting to the hotel in Devon with some apprehension. I couldn't possibly miss young Robert's wedding; apart from the fact that he is an absolute poppet, the shining star of the family, it may be the last one I ever attend. Consultants have become notoriously reluctant to commit themselves with any kind of precision, I think largely because we live in such a litigation-prone age. If they say someone will pop off in such and such a time and the person does not so pop, they can be accused of imposing unnecessary stress; if they say someone will pop off in a space of time and they pop off prematurely, as it were, they are open to accusations of not taking the illness seriously enough. However, whenever I go for these infernal tests which the man insists on me having, the expression on his face is guide enough, without the accompanying flow of largely incomprehensible technical gibberish. I am currently seventy-eight, and the man's sucking a lemon mouth tells me eighty will be pushing my luck, let alone any prospects of a telegram from the Queen, if they will still be doing that by then. Do they still do that? One loses track.

In the meantime, I seem to be saddled with what always feels to me like a malevolent little individual gnawing away inside me; I think of him as Tom Thumb-like in size, but not with Tom Thumb's generally benevolent, good-natured smile; this little chap carries a miniature power drill and lets it go inside me from time to time, bless him, for periods varying between seconds and minutes, though lately he tends to be at it more often and for longer periods. I have another surname for him other than Thumb, but I will not repeat it here so as not to offend the gentle-natured. Suffice it to say that it rhymes with 'Tucker'.

However, Robert is my solitary grandchild, which is perhaps one of the reasons why I am so fond of him, and it would take a whole regiment of Toms to keep me away from his wedding.

I always wondered whether he would be able to match up to his father's achievements; he is every bit as intelligent as his father, but he lacks Malcolm's ambition, and, I suppose I would have to say, ruthlessness, to some extent. Malcolm 'took silk', as they call it, almost five years ago – the term always makes it sound vaguely criminal, rather than a tremendous professional achievement. As a consequence, he is now a Queen's Counsel, and whether the quieter and more contemplative Robert will ever achieve such a thing I do wonder. Their different choices of specialisms are typical of them, in many ways.

Malcolm has practised mostly in the divorce courts; should you find your husband or your wife, though the former is a good deal more common than the latter, has been cavorting about with male or female bits of stuff as the case may be and you decide the blighter has to go, Malcolm Harrington QC is who you might employ to ensure that the aforesaid blighter pays up for his misdemeanours. You will, of course, have to be quite tolerably well-heeled; Malcolm doesn't come on travelling expenses and luncheon vouchers. He told me not long ago what his total bill came to for extracting one middle-aged wife from a particularly libidinous old sot of a property tycoon not long ago, and suffice it to say it would undoubtedly keep me comfortably in my Greenhaven Retirement Village splendour until the telegram from the Queen arrived, were it not for the fact that I will almost certainly pop off at some point in the interim.

A similar sucking lemon mouth to my dear consultant was exhibited by my daughter-in-law Barbara when listening to Malcolm insisting that a car be provided to take me to and from the wedding. Barbara is still an attractive woman – in a good light she can look a little more Celine Dion and a little less Cruella de Vil – but she remains quite careful with the readies, especially the readies spent on other people; analogies concerning the looseness of ducks' posteriors spring to mind. But Malcolm stuck to his guns, standing there in my conservatory booming away, bless him, as if denouncing yet another miscreant husband, and Barbara was eventually forced into giving me her best rigor mortis death grin in a sad imitation of a smile. Anyway, a car it was to be, with my own choice of picnic lunch taken with me or a stop at a suitable watering hole on the way. I chose the former, with one of those little bottles of champers you get on the planes thrown in; while I don't want to turn up at this hotel blotto and singing Nelly Dean up on a table in my knickers, a little sip of celebratory champers is not unreasonable, I feel, on my way to my only grandchild's wedding, and quite possibly my last anybody's wedding. One of my oppos in my twilight haven is a lady called Alice Curzon, who once said to me that she was so old she no longer buys green tomatoes, and that tends to be how I feel much of the time now.

And from such information as I have, Robert appears to have chosen well. When I was first told that the girl is from Devon, I had visions of some buxom lass with rosy cheeks and arms strong enough for a full milk pail in either hand, but then Robert showed me a photo; the modern girl, of course, very much so, tiny little waist and not a great deal more round the bust, with her hair swept right back like a nun in a wind, but very lovely, in her way, with a sophisticated, knowing smile for one so young and intelligent, assessing greenish eyes. I looked at Robert looking at the photo and decided they probably weren't keeping themselves chaste before marriage, but then nobody does now; many of them don't bother getting married at all, and when all's said and done, why should they, once the whole stigmatic thing about so-called living in sin has been discarded? I remember determining off my own bat to find out the essential gen about men sometime before I married, after one or two startling and mysterious experiences. I had to practically corner my most outspoken aunt, dear Aunt May, the bohemian of the family, and interrogate her in words of one syllable, and then I didn't at first credit what she was telling me.

I knew perfectly well I'd never get any more than a lot of daisy-chain nonsense about storks and bushes out of Mummy. Derek took me skinny-dipping not long before we married, very bold in those days, and I confirmed Aunt May's lowdown and had a jolly good time doing it, too. Derek seemed to know all about it how to do it without issue ensuing, as it were, which both impressed and worried me. I decided, in any case, that since I would shortly be marrying him, if issue did ensue and anyone is nosy enough to do the nine-month maths and come to a wrong answer, well, sod them.

Anyway, young Kate is also a lawyer, it seems, and trained in London, even though she was brought up in Devon, so there's every chance that we will be able to communicate without needing an interpreter. She and Robert work together, and I'm a little dubious about that; much as one loves someone, seeing them all day and every day can dampen the ardour. But I gather they work on different cases, even if in the similar areas of land issues – disputes over ownership, negotiated terms for developments and that sort of thing.

Young Rory and his torso having had their moment, I could turn to more pedestrian issues, such as my packing. I resolutely refuse to wear a hat; unlike many of the old dears in this place, at least half of whom are always bewigged in public, I have a perfectly good head of hair of my own, thanks to meticulous care and a bit of luck. I cannot stand these mad hatty women who turn up at weddings with incongruous contraptions of fruit and foliage jammed on their craniums as if they're on an away day from Bedlam. A good hairdo will do, thank you, and I have already had our itinerant lady, one Megan Crowthorne, to attend to it yesterday. The experience is not cheap, and it comes with a blow-by-blow account of Megan's social life and activities on her Faceweb or Twitterbook or whatever you call them which can reach Force 9 on the tedium scale, consisting, as it seems to do, of electronically spouting a lot of rubbish to people you've never met and probably never will.

The packing was eventually accomplished. The actual clothing didn't present many particular problems; I have several posh frocks suitable for such occasions, both day and evening. A lady of seventy-eight has had time and opportunity to acquire a few handrags and gladrags along the way, and while it's true that my weight has dropped a little over the past couple of years, it has at least provided opportunities to revisit garments formerly written off as ludicrously optimistic.

It is, as usual, the pills which become time-consuming: white ones, pink ones, little duo-tone lozenge objects, ones large enough to ensure a somewhat ironic demise should they manage one day to stick in my throat. I have long since lost track of which ones are supposed to do what, but I am always terrified to stop taking anything, especially on public occasions, in case drastic side effects ensue and I find myself sitting in the wedding venue perspiring like a spent horse or burping in loud sequence like a navvi on a Saturday night.

I still had time enough for the final denouement of *Homes Under the Hammer*, where truly miraculous things had been done to a terraced house in Whitehaven, wherever that might be.

Shortly after eleven, I moved back to the conservatory, and at quarter past, I watched some big silvery vehicle sweep down the drive and was speculating idly on whose affluent offspring it might belong to when I realised it was highly likely that it was for me. I was going to have some attentive chauffeur carrying my modest luggage towards this virtual limousine, and then I would be swept away as every inmate of the village presses faces against windows in wonder that such an elevated personage had come amongst their humble number.

What a wonderful way to start a weekend!

Phyllis Drayton, neighbour and family friend of the bride's mother

Colin and I agreed to differ, as tends to be the case these days. Colin thought two nights in the hotel is 'silly', by which he means 'expensive'. I thought that Helen was probably my closest friend now and entitled to more in the way of support than simply turning up on the day, eating and drinking with the multitude. Colin, with that wife-boosting subtlety for which he is so justly famous, made a noise in the region of a snort, and said, 'God, Phyllis, Helen Densham will manage everything perfectly well without any help from you.' Bearing in mind that Colin's job is to manage a store, keeping both customers and employees happy, his grasp of tact is often quite astonishingly inept. But perhaps the job uses up his entire stock of tact, so that he has none left for home. It certainly uses up his entire stock in other directions, but we will put that to one side for the moment.

He was, of course, as usual, partly right. Helen is everyone's rock of dependency, and what she organises stays organised. I sometimes think a Christmas Eve will come when I will look out to see Santa and his entourage waiting patiently on the Densham front lawn for a signal from Helen to enter on the cue she has devised. I don't doubt hotel, flowers, cars, seat positions, meal, speeches et al are all precisely scheduled and will tick off like clockwork.

None of which, of course, was the point. The point was to be there with the best friend, to give moral support, as Colin would be happy enough to do if it was one of his ghastly golf course chums and they were up for slicing their handicap or topping their niblick or some such bloody thing. Even in the life of Helen Densham, unforeseen contretemps can arise, especially as those around her tend to be less controlled and efficient than she is herself. Her husband Peter is a university lecturer, and that still carries a certain clout, but as the world knows well enough, Peter is still intent on a game attempt at making love to everything female and under thirty which swims into his orbit, and I don't doubt there will be a few lady lecturers and possibly a lady postgraduate or two who have been or who still are on Peter's to-do list, or even Peter's currently-being-done list.

Son Tom can also be a little unpredictable. Poor Tom seems to have missed out on the brains quite generously possessed by the rest of the family; his university career came to an abrupt halt when some collective outrage was committed by the rugby team and Tom personally was convicted on the evidence of about five hundred and thirty-eight witnesses of wantonly peeing in the Dean's Fountain, or some such similar facet of the architecture of the place which had been standing, presumably unpeed in, though one has one's doubts, since about 1475. A quick survey of any local rugby club would rapidly reveal any number of Toms. He makes a kind of living in what is called 'leisure management', supervising people in gyms and doing some personal training and what have you, and he seems to have a genius for finding submissive little women who get involved, find him quite fun for a while, but eventually shy away from a life spent listening to a dozen men singing 'the hairs on her dickey dido hang down to her knee' in their garden and trying to pretend they don't know what they're talking about.

Tom is amiable enough, bless him, and good company for about the first gallon, though things can go rapidly downhill on a long do, and the wedding will be an all-day do.

In any case, I chose to be at my friend's side, fond as I am of her and all the family, even Peter, ageing Lothario as he is. I suppose there is a sense in which I feel a feeble and probably terribly disloyal sympathy with him. Helen is a rock, yes, which is wonderful if you're looking for something to lean on, but perhaps not quite so brilliant if you're looking for something to snuggle up to. Helen rarely talks about her love life, and I suspect it's not just because she's not the sort of incurable free talker on these issues as I am; it's got a lot to do with the fact that there isn't much of it. Helen is very big on duty and obligation, and I suspect once she'd squeezed out the obligatory two, one male and one female, she rather lost interest in the proceedings. Peter, of course, didn't, and one of the great unalterable truths of the middle-aged male, or at least the ones as presentable as Peter, is that if you hide his potty, he will go and find another one to pee in. I have a sneaking suspicion that Helen is not as concerned as she might be, on the grounds that, while Peter is rogering some impressionable young academic, he's not actually bothering her. The whole business of rumpy-pumpy is all far too moist and disorganised for Helen's taste, I think.

Not that she shies away from dispensing advice when Colin and I are going through one of our regular periods of tension in the bedroom area, such as when he got hold of my copy of *Fifty Shades of Grey* and started getting very ambitious ideas, entirely missing the point, i.e. he is not Mr Grey, nor does he stand a dog's chance in hell of getting the gig, frankly. Then there was his 'toys' phase which, when combined with his known iffiness in the DIY department, meant that I felt in constant danger of being intimately electrocuted and spending several of the most embarrassing hours of my life in the local A&E department.

'Turn the tables; use one or two on him,' said the ever-sagacious Helen, and when one contraption shuddered to a halt less than two thirds of the way to what might have been an impressive and memorable climax, the toys phase relapsed, never so far to be reborn, though one or two curious noises from the bathroom suggest he might still be carrying on experiments in auto-eroticism.

But these tête-à-têtes tend to be one way between Helen and me, and while the vision of her occasionally clad in black leather bra and panties and clutching a cat o'nine tails ready to lambast Peter's guilty botty is an entertaining one, I doubt it actually happens.

'We are a partnership of equals,' Helen said. 'It is better for married couples, I think, to preserve their separate identities rather than attempt to merger themselves into some bizarre hybrid creature. Each to her or his own, is my belief.' His is rogering, hers is organising, but I have to say his does sound a lot more fun.

However, be that as it may, I had told the surgery that my part-time receptioning would be even more part-time this week and would not include any part of Friday. This increased their problems, as it is also Helen's workplace – we met at work before we realised we were near neighbours – and the health centre without Helen is like Waterloo without Wellington. They will need to get hold of some locum or other – if they can do it with doctors, they can do it with receptionists – which will mean chaos next week, with doctors pathetically wandering corridors in search of wayward appointments and nurses syringing wrong ears or slicing off wrong varookas, but hell, that's showbiz. Daughters can't marry themselves.

I had a sandwich and set off in my sturdy little Fiesta not long after. Colin would still go on about going down to one car, by which he means me driving him to the golf club so he can get sloshed with impunity every time and not just the times he cons someone into giving him a lift, whatever his stuff about ecological approaches and considering the bloody planet.

The lanes of Devon were even more hellish on Friday than they are the rest of the time, but one does one what has to do. In the name of friendship.

Simon Roche, school and university friend of the groom

The idea was that Duncan's driver would meet him when he got in to Heathrow on Friday morning, then he would come home and pick me up, and we would be chauffeured to the hotel. He'd been in Italy, not so much drumming up business as trying to clear his backlog of it. His IT consultancy was doing well enough even before he added cybersecurity to it, and since then it's been heading rapidly towards the stratosphere time. He keeps flinging statistics at me – typical, just a couple of days ago, 'eighty-seven per cent of small businesses in the UK alone were hacked in 2012'. An epidemic of hackery has been murder for businesses everywhere, except Duncan's and people like him.

He once said to me that there were people who thought of him as a bit 'geeky' because he wears glasses when he's working on about a million screens a day. We were lying naked in a hotel room at the time, and geeky wasn't the word which sprang most readily to my mind.

He's dark, so much so that even though he shaves every day, he practically has a bristle beard at the end of it. He's... well, let's say athletically built, and there's hardly a crevice or patch of him which doesn't turn me on.

He was in touch with me all the way; I knew the plane was on time, I knew when he was in the car, I knew how far away he was and how long he thought it would take. I could have met him at Heathrow, but the place gives me the creeps and I've had several nervous breakdowns getting in and out of it. Orla Fitzgerald, the manager of the hotel which employs me as assistant manager, decided in her wisdom and benevolence that I could have a three-day weekend, though I don't doubt she will have it back in various deadly night shifts or spectacular times of year when London is teeming with tourists. Orla and I are coming to understand each other, slowly but surely; ever since I set up with Duncan five years ago, the option of leaving the hotel business altogether and become something in Duncan's spreading set-up has given me the chance to look Orla in the eye more determinedly when I have to, and I found to my surprise that she quite likes it when people stand up for themselves. It's as if she's setting them some kind of test. We're not exactly buddy-buddy yet, but she's moved from being platinum-grade bitch from hell to mildly annoying authoritarian tartar who is at least around when the going gets a bit sticky, which in the London hotel business, is more or less daily.

Anyway, the benevolence of La Fitzgerald is something I decided to take advantage of, and have a lie-in, a bath and a go at the papers before Duncan returned and we travelled into the West Country along that expletive deleted A303, rather than me struggle around Heathrow and get stressed up before we even set off for Devon.

It might not be the easiest of weekends. Duncan had been suspicious of this wedding ever since the invitation arrived. Duncan is jealous of Robert, irritatingly so at times. It's silly, really, but understandable in its way. Robert is an attractive guy by anyone's standards: the short jet-black hair, the interesting soft hazel eyes, the high-cheeked bone structure which makes him look aristocratic when he's contented, which is most of the time, and horse-faced and lugubrious when he's not. He also has one of those long, elastic bodies, which I suppose comes from all his swimming and squash and what have you, and which give you the impression that there wouldn't be many positions, contortionist or otherwise, which he couldn't arrange himself in if he wanted to.

I once said this to Duncan, and immediately thought, you should learn to get your mind in gear, Roche, before you engage your mouth. Big mistake.

'Oh, yeah, tried a few of them out with him, have you?' he said, with that Northumberland twang rising immediately as soon as he starts getting vexed.

'No, as a matter of fact, I haven't,' I said, and then I thought, to hell with it, Si, let's try and nail this one once and for all, and I went for it.

'Look, Duncan, I've known Robert since we both found ourselves, at eight years old, in that prep school which my parents nearly bankrupted themselves to send me to, whereas his parents would have regarded the fees as loose change. Meaning I had every reason to dislike him, but I didn't. We found it easy to talk and we supported each other doggedly through that hellhole of a place and on into the semi-state outfit we went to afterwards. Through all that time, he's been to me the brother I didn't have. And he is a good-looking guy and nice with it. But I don't fancy him, and I've never fancied him; I've seen him with custard all over his face when he was still such a kid he couldn't eat his dinner properly; I've seen him blubbing his face off because a teacher shouted at him; I've seen him covered head to foot in mud and God knows what else after one of those dreadful cross-country runs we used to do. I've seen him naked about fifty thousand times from childhood onwards; I could tell you the timetable of the acquisition of his and my pubic hair, I could take you through the geography of his body from top to toe. But I still don't fancy him, firstly, because he's not gay, never has been, and never will be, and I sorted out at an early age the stupidity and futility of fancying confirmed heteros. He's still totally at ease with other guys; we've stood next to each other in the showers and discussed our love lives before now, and nothing was ever going to happen, Duncan, because *he isn't gay!*'

Duncan was looking a little shell-shocked by this stage. He was driving at the time, and that set, dour northern thing was coming over his face. I had a sudden idea that he might stop the car and order me out, and we were in a not very salubrious part of the East End at the time. So I calmed down a little.

'Secondly, we do and we always have regarded each other as brothers, and that means platonic, or it still does for us, anyway. Thirdly, I love you and I still do, because you do to me and with me things which Robert never has and never would, and because you are a colossus in my life which reduces everyone else in it, however long I've known them, to pygmies by comparison.'

He did stop the car then, but for a different reason. When we'd reached a bit of Hampstead Heath type land a little further on, he pulled off the road and into a patch of woodland, and there we had what Duncan calls a SAFF, and it's probably enough for me to say that the first three letters stand for Special Al Fresco. Duncan has a particular *penchant* for saffing, and on more than one occasion, while in the process of being saffed, I've looked out of the car windows expecting a vehicle with a flashing blue light to turn into our secluded country lane or an irate warden of something or other to suddenly appear behind the nearest sand dune.

All the same, there are times when the saff position being employed doesn't actually allow much visibility, and with my feet firmly jammed against the roof of the car and Duncan well into that gentle but emphatic rhythm of his, I had nothing else to distract my mind than a reflection that I should maybe try making him jealous a little more often.

So when the wedding invitation arrived, Duncan didn't dare make too much fuss about it, though just a smidgeon of dourness came over him. After one of those smouldering pauses of his, he said, 'I suppose he wants you to be his best man, since you've probably known him longer than anyone else, except maybe his parents.'

There might have been an edge of irony to his tone, but I decided to take the question at face value and keep the whole thing neutral.

'No, Duncan, he doesn't want me to be his best man, or if he does, he hasn't told me about it. The Twittervine says it's going to be one of his lawyer pals, one of those guys he plays two hours of squash with after winning yet another legal triumph, following that up with a trip into the City with to get wrecked on the very best wines and malts. Giles something or other. Probably with a Duke for an uncle and a hize in the country.'

'Goodness, Si,' said Duncan, with that knowing smirk he assumes sometimes. 'Would that be jealousy I see rearing its ugly head?'

Touché, I suppose. And if I'm being honest, the fact that being Robert's best man hadn't even been mentioned does niggle at me just a bit. But, then again, I don't see him too often now, maybe two or three times in the last five years. If it was someone other than Robert, I might think he doesn't much like the idea of what his young bride might think of a gay best man: 'Oh, yes, and has he been leading me up the garden path for all these years? Am I some kind of substitute for Simon Roche, now that high-powered business type Duncan Allen has snapped him up?' But no. I don't doubt Robert's enthusiasm, in getting down to it with the lovely Kate, is all too obvious. Like me with Duncan. We don't have the options the ladies have. Excitement is all too revealingly visible.

Duncan got home, and he was still talking to me while the car was coming up the drive. I went to him, and we kissed and cuddled a little on our own front door, while the chauffeur Alan looked steadily into the distance. Alan's nice, but easily embarrassed.

'Friday traffic. We'd better get a move on, dear boy,' said Duncan as we went to pick up the cases I had so carefully packed. It wasn't all baths and lie-ins, and there are a few things left which we still do for ourselves.

He's taken to calling me 'dear boy'; odd, really, the sort of thing a neighbour or an uncle might say, I suppose, though the uncle probably wouldn't fondle my buttocks while saying it. Well, I suppose it depends on what sort of uncles you have, really.

As we settled into the back seat of the car and he started telling me all about Italy and how deceptive the laid-back *la dolce vita* really is when it comes to business, I reflected on the life we've made and how silly it was to worry about a long trip to Devon when I would hardly notice anything around me until we get there. I suppose I was apprehensive, if I'm honest, as I tend to be when going to places I've never been to before, and I'd never been to Devon. But, when all's said and done, Devon produced Kate Densham, who has captured the heart of my old mate Robert

Harrington, so it must have something going for it, and a few vague impressions from television programmes are not the best ways to judge a place. In any case, it was about Robert, for me, because I love him in a truly platonic, brotherly fashion, and that isn't something I've been able to say for many of the attractive guys in my life.

Friday afternoon
Matthew, bride's uncle

We seemed to have managed to arrive even before Peter and Helen, and I didn't particularly want to disturb them at home. They were no doubt in the middle of various hectic last-minute situations of one kind of another, but Helen would have everything in hand and they would be making an appearance soon enough. It could have been that they were waiting for the happy couple to get over to them from London, thinking an initial meeting at home might be more suitable than all getting together at the hotel. Everyone knew that the happy couple have actually been living together for the best part of two years; Kate isn't pregnant yet, as far as I know, but the only reason for that will be they are the kind of happy couple who only intend to become a happy threesome when they are good and ready, and that isn't yet.

However, we hadn't been forgotten, by any means. They'd done us proudly in terms of the room; it was one of the balcony ones at the front of the hotel which we were admiring as we drove in, and its comfortable living area next to the bedroom made it more of a suite than a room. A vase of flowers, a half bottle of champagne and a card saying, 'Welcome, Matt and Mary; hope everything is as you like it and we're looking forward to your company for the weekend; love, Peter and Helen.'

Mary spent the best part of half an hour just drinking it all in, drifting between the bedroom, the balcony and the living area.

Mary is restless these days when we stay at a place where we've never stayed before, which isn't anything like as often as it used to be. She suffers periodically from insomnia, usually connected to digestion problems, and I think it is still in her mind that she is going to need to move away from full-time teaching before very much longer. I know she can't help seeing it as some kind of defeat. But we are both in our fifties now, when all's said and done, and adolescents, even the non-truculent ones, en masse day after relentless day are not an easy proposition.

Eventually, she smiled at me and decided she will start the unpacking. This was a relief and a relaxation in itself; she had given the place her approval and we would be settled here. At this point, of course, off went my phone and I knew the number well enough. I was about to simply shut it down, but I did need to put a marker down for the rest of the weekend, or the whole thing would become impossible. I took the phone out on to the balcony.

'Ken, this had better be good. We've only just got to the hotel, the hotel where we are about to have a private family wedding weekend—'

Ken rarely wastes time on preliminaries. 'Councillor Joe Needham. Does that name mean anything to you, Matt?'

'Of course it does.'

Needham is chairman of the planning committee and has a reputation for putting contracts neatly in the way of his pals by giving them detailed advice about the best ways to tender applications and the best prices to undercut everyone else. He is also supposedly in the business of taking backhanders, big drinks, for favours done. The local press – even, occasionally, one of the nationals – retains at least a corner of the eye watch on Needham, the theory being that he will inevitably slip up sooner or later. But Ken was playing silly games with me, and I didn't like it.

'I know Needham well enough, Ken. Get to the point. You're gatecrashing my leave—'

'He's there where you are. Well, if he isn't, he soon will be.'

'What? Why on earth would Peter and Helen invite the likes of Needham—'

'Don't ask me. But there are vague rumours of a land deal, which is Joe's usual department.'

'I don't get it, Ken. What's the connection with a wedding?'

'Good question, boss. We've been wondering about that ourselves. The only conclusion we can come up with is that Peter, acting for the university, wants something out of Needham.'

Mary came out on to the balcony, and we smiled again, but this time there was an edge of impatience around her eyes. She knew it was work calling, and I knew all the good start we'd had might be out of the window if I didn't wrap the call up fairly soon.

'Harrington also seems connected with the deal somewhere,' Ken continued.

'Harrington is a divorce lawyer, Ken. Come on.'

'Not Harrington senior. Harrington junior, or at least, the outfit he works for.'

'Ken, you're talking about the bridegroom. You're talking about the guy who is about to marry my dearly beloved niece.'

'Yes, I know. That's why I thought you might like to know.'

'Come to think of it, Ken, how the hell do *you* know?'

'Oh, come on, boss. Big nobby wedding in a top-class country hotel. They're practically putting out press releases.'

In another thirty seconds, he was gone, with a smug 'don't worry about a thing; all is well back at the ranch, boss', and I was feeling a little as though he had just walked up and thumped me right in the midriff. The implications were disturbing, to say the least; Needham is a crook, quite honestly, and so good at being a crook that no-one has yet been able to pin anything on him. The idea that Kate's prospective husband might actually be partly responsible for that, with careful bending and stretching of property and planning permission laws, was not what I want to have to think about here and now.

And, of course, not just Robert Harrington. Kate works for the same outfit as he does. Speculations which put my heart down into my stomach now could not be avoided as to what London might have done to the favourite daughter of the Denshams. Kate was adamant that she would train and eventually practise in London, though her father and her greater family made it clear that they would rather she remained amongst us. Kate, from childhood onwards, has always been a formidable character, a girl who knows her own mind, with both her mother's formidable powers of organisation and her father's eloquence. Had she decided somewhere along the line to ditch her simple Devonian past and make pots of money by teaming up with the bad guys? Had she actually used her knowledge of our vicinity to ease a predominant local crook's way to making pots of money, taking her generous cut along the way? What had finding her way into the wealthy Harrington elite cost her, and how had this relationship with Robert Harrington changed her?

I suppose these reflections made me look rather more pale and depressed than the uncle of the bride should be looking at this stage, because when Mary walked out on to the balcony again, unpacking completed, and smiled in my direction once more, I saw her smile fade into a question very rapidly.

'Everything alright, Matt?'

So now I knew something I didn't really want to know, and something my brother, the father of the bride, might well want to know – need to know – and probably didn't. Knowledge can be both the editor's curse and blessing at the same time, information not privy to others which he must now decide what to do with, and even more so when it impacts on his own nearest and dearest, his own private life. I decided to do what most editors, and probably most uncles, usually do, and play for time.

She was gazing at me with some concern, and I was rapidly working out a form of words which might work, for the moment at least, when it was clear I no longer had her attention. She as gazing over the hotel's stately if rather brief approach drive, and when my eyes moved in the same direction, I saw what had momentarily stunned her. A truly enormous car, as big as a car can be without actually being a stretch limousine, was making a majestic progress towards the hotel. I'm no great car expert, but I can recognise a Roller when I see one, and this one looked like one they usually reserve for heads of state.

When it drew to a halt in front of the hotel's big reception portico arrangements, it was only a matter of yards away from us and slightly to our right. I half expected a chauffeur to dash round and open the back door, but the figure on our side stepped out unaided. He was tall – strikingly so, at least six feet four, I'd say – and though there was a pronounced streak or two across the temples and the hair on the crown was not as luxuriant as it probably once was, he was a man without extraneous middle-aged flesh, clearly in fine shape, and with a commanding presence even without the Roller. I'd never met the guy, but I felt certain that I was looking at Mr Malcolm Harrington QC, father of the bridegroom.

Gazing at him from above, I found it difficult to control the host of questions, both personal and professional, which crowded into my mind at the sight of him. No doubt me and my kind are hicks from the sticks in his metropolitan circles, but we have our fair share of conmen, hoods and political hucksters in the south-west, like everywhere else, and I'd been around now long enough to know some of the give-away signs – the loud, take control of the situation braying voices, the quick meeting speeches denigrating the men and fulsomely praising the women, the hard stares and expansive, watch me gestures. Harrington displayed none of these; I heard no booming voice or twists of irritation – he was, if anything, almost deprecating and semi-apologetic as various staff bustled about to do his will. And yet, even alongside the similarly commanding presence of the tall, immaculately coiffured lady in the expensive blue coat whom I took to be his wife Barbara, Harrington had a kind of aura about him, an authoritative effect which seems to make people concerned that everything should be properly done in his presence.

Perhaps he didn't know that his son is a crook; they clearly work in very different legal disciplines. Perhaps the son's crookedness, if that's what it is, has arisen from a lifetime of being overshadowed by the old man. Perhaps Robert's connections with Needham are of a different nature than they might seem. I was there for what should be entirely social and family reasons, but much as I try to keep work and private life separate, my journalistic antennae on this occasion were twitching right alongside my anxiety for a well-loved niece, and it was an intoxicating cocktail.

Celia

My escort to my grandson's wedding was provided by Malcolm's very own personal driver, an amiable and competent chap called, very firmly, Ron. His second name is Pearson, but the days of addressing the 'servants' by their surnames are long gone, and clearly my son knows the man as Ron. Not Ronald – 'too posh' – and not Ronnie – 'too kiddie' – but Ron. He is one of the few men, in my experience, with whom a restful passenger experience is possible, though the pleasure of the ride was helped substantially along by the car being so large, comfortable and quite astonishingly quiet. I even found myself dozing at one point, which is almost unprecedented for me in a car. Of course, one does reach an age where anxieties about such matters become a little ridiculous. When death is more or less occupying one's entire horizon, rather than being no more than a blip in the distance, the actual method by which one pops becomes a touch academic. However, being pureed across the highways and byways is perhaps not one of the more elegant and dignified exits.

I was afraid the weather may have been too uncertain for our little picnic, though I didn't doubt this car would have various gizmos and thingummyjigs in terms of folding tables and cup holders to ensure the experience of eating inside it did not become a matter of contortions beyond my aged limbs, so that I finished up showering oneself with liquids and foodstuffs and arrived at the hotel looking as if I had just been in a bunfight at a kiddies' party. However, things took a sudden turn for the better, the sun emerged and Ron seized the day, detouring a few miles off the main road to a rather nice little park with which he was obviously familiar from previous trips, with neat grassland, a few carefully tended flowerbeds and clean, dry sort of bench-cum-table affairs. I noticed there was also a ladies' excuse-me within a convenient distance, so bingo generally, I thought, for Ron. I could see why he appealed to such a practical man as my son.

So far, I had only been able to discern two weaknesses in Ron's otherwise blameless being. Firstly, we had to rid him of his habit of calling me 'Madam', which makes me feel uncomfortably like a successful brothel-keeper. 'Celia' is a step too far for the mother of his employer, I suppose, so we compromised on 'Mrs Harrington'. I wondered whether that would clash with the other Mrs Harrington, but he got as near as he dared to pulling a face and announced, 'The other Mrs Harrington does like being called Madam, Mad... I mean, Mrs Harrington. In fact, she doesn't allow herself to be called anything else.'

'Well, let's face it, Ron, she *is* a madam,' I said, and we laughed conspiratorially like naughty children. I foolishly offered him a drop of my champers, but of course he was driving, and the merest modicum of champagne on his breath whilst conveying the boss's mother about could put him in deep water, though I suspected Madam herself wouldn't be quite so put out.

His other odd tendency was to be constantly peering, clicking and fingering the rather large phone thing he carried around, which he referred to at one point as a 'smart phone'. It was black with streaks of green here and there, all of it obviously done in reinforced plastic, and it didn't seem particularly smart to me, but he seemed to be almost obsessed with it. Even while we were enjoying our bits and pieces of food, he was peering at it, and then he suddenly began murmuring, 'Dear, oh dear' to himself, as if the device had suddenly poked its tongue out at him or something.

Within two minutes of his 'oh dearing', his not particularly smart phone went off, and I use that term advisedly. One moment we were enjoying the peace of a rural parkland, the next the little thing was giving off trumpet noises, which I discovered later from Ron collectively form a piece of music called 'Fanfare for the Common Man', and I wondered if the man has secret communist leanings. I almost precipitated a very tasty smoked salmon sandwich into a nearby flowerbed and thought nostalgically back to the days when phones simply rang.

'Yes, sir, I do understand,' Ron said into his device, and I immediately suspected it was my son he was talking to. 'The lady is right beside me, sir. Yes, I will.' He paused and looked at me a little apologetically. 'Your son would like to speak with you, Mrs Harrington. Will you feel happy talking into this phone?'

I took the thing from him gingerly, checking with him concerning which way up it should be, and tentatively spoke into it, still thinking about good old-fashioned ear and speaking pieces. 'Is that you, Malcolm?'

'Yes, Mother. I'm sorry to force one of these devices on you; I realise you probably aren't too familiar with them, but I don't have any other choice, I'm afraid.'

Normally by this time in a phone conversation with Malcolm, I am already holding the phone slightly away from my ear. He often can't distinguish between the sort of tone needed to overawe a crowded courtroom and the one needed to speak down a phone line, and I feel, as Queen Victoria did when addressed by

Gladstone, as if I am a public meeting. However, his tone today sounded much more subdued, almost back to his not quite so assertive adolescence.

'Don't you, dear?' I said, a few apprehensions gathering around me like invasive scents.

'No. I'm afraid the news is out now; it is all over Facebook, Twitter, the gossip columns, the society websites, everywhere. I wanted to make sure that you knew, Mum, before you arrived at the hotel and find out what everyone else already knows, it seems.'

'Already knows what, dear?' I said, as I began to wonder whether the loss of his dear son to marriage had precipitated some kind of mental brainstorm, though that isn't really something I would associate with Malcolm.

'Barbara and I are in the process of divorcing, Mum.'

My breath momentarily left me and I found myself staring in mesmeric idiot fashion at little bits of green and black plastic.

'Lost for words for once, Mum? Not all that surprising, I suppose.'

I couldn't explain to him that I was not so much lost for words as discovering that the word which was most urgently springing to my mind was 'hallelujah', perhaps not the most tactful response in the circumstances. The forms have to be observed if we are to remain civilised.

'Darling. How awful for you. At this time, of all times.'

'Well, exactly,' he said, and his indignation brought back something of his usual megaphone form of speech. 'Barbara and I had hoped to complete the whole business as unobtrusively as possible, but perhaps because of the publicity surrounding the wedding, people have been talking to people, journalists have been hanging around our friends and neighbours like hyena packs, and someone has let the secret out. Barbara and I were intent on keeping it quiet at least until the wedding was over, for the sake of Robert and Kate, but the cat's out of the bag and I wanted you, of all people, to have the truth straight from the horse's mouth, if you can follow my meaning through this barrage of animal allusions.'

I had a fleeting impression that I should say 'here, here' or something at this point. I cast around for something sensible to say. 'What has always concerned me most, dear, is your happiness, and I've always felt that you never have been truly happy with Barbara.' Chiefly, I wanted to say, because she has always been a gold-digger with deeply acquisitive tendencies, but of course I didn't. Mothers know when to keep their peace.

'It went well for a while. She was so graceful, so beautiful, and I really did love…' He had to stop for a moment and control himself, and my old heart wrenched. Ron, bless him, was looking at me across the table with real concern.

'Now, of course, there will be all the cheap jokes. Densham might even try to insinuate a few into his wedding speech, I suspect. Eminent divorce lawyer now handling his own divorce. Will he charge himself his own fees? And the media will be writing in similar vein. They are so tediously predictable. And now the fingerprints of it will be all over Robert's wedding. Damn and blast.'

I had to remind him that it's Mummy dear he was talking to, before the language becomes even more injudiciously barrack room, and he was instantly contrite.

'Of course. Forgive me, Mum. It is just so dreadfully frustrating.'

'Absolutely, darling. A little damning and blasting is not outrageous in the circumstances. What will you do?'

'Do? How do you mean? Find someone else?'

'Well, possibly, Malcolm,' I said, and immediately wondered whether he already had and that's what had broken the thing apart. He is a wealthy and very attractive man. But that could wait.

'No, I mean necessary agreements, who has the house, all that sort of thing.'

'Oh, I see. Well, we have discussed all that, of course. It would be too embarrassing to be seen wrangling in public, after all the marriages which have involved me professionally. Barbara will stay in the London house, which will become hers; I will take a flat more centrally, which will be actually be more convenient for working purposes, I have to say. We have agreed on a settlement which is generous to her while not being ruinous for me.'

Meaning, essentially, dear Malcolm will mostly get his way, as he usually does. We continued our conversation, circling around the main issues, as is the family habit, to some extent. I know him extremely well, of course, and whatever the final crisis was, he was a little put down at what feels like a defeat in some way, though my impression was that his main sensation was relief. Even though the news had not emerged in the way he would have preferred, it would at least mean he finally knew exactly where he stood, as did Barbara.

Ron was very careful with me as we finished our pleasant little meal and packed everything away ready to set off again. Little Tom rhymes-with-tucker had started up again, inevitably, I suppose, but I remained determinedly cheerful, and eventually, my manner and general joie-de-vivre got the truth home to him.

'Do forgive me for speaking out of turn, if that's what I'm doing, but it strikes me that you've never been all that keen on Mrs Harrington, have you... er... Mrs Harrington?'

'I can't entirely deny a certain distance, Ron. Mothers are notoriously difficult to please in respect of their daughters-in-law. However, enough said for the moment. There is a wedding to enjoy. Tell me more about what this remarkable smart phone of yours can do, then we must take to the road again.'

As we continued our stately way towards Devon, I contemplated the breakdown of Malcolm's relationship and what I suppose was my disgraceful lack of proper feelings of regret. Perhaps I was probably not as sympathetic towards Barbara as I might have been. Malcolm has, it's true, always been very confident and a little overpowering. Towards the end of his life, even Derek found his own boy overwhelming at times in his utter certainty and supreme self-confidence. It would surprise me more that Malcolm had not had affairs rather than if he had, and in some ways, good family as hers was, he as much overpowered Barbara as courted her. He is possessed of relentless, fierce energy, both in and out of working hours; Derek once described him as 'driven'. The problem was and is that Barbara too, is driven; driven to Harvey Nichols, driven to Fortnum and Masons, driven to Harrods. She has always lapped up the lifestyle while doing precious little to contribute to bringing it about, and she is essentially a cold fish. I have never been privy to their secrets in the bedroom department, nor would I wish to be, but if Malcolm is anything much like his father in his – what shall we call it, appetite? – and I think he probably is, then a cold fish like Barbara is not going to be able to hold him.

I suppose it was both the news and the comfortable purr of the big car which overwhelmed me. I am used to a quiet and sedentary existence in the Wiltshire countryside where no more commotion than a cow or two clearing their throats disturbs the general torpor, and there I suddenly was with a son whose marriage has disintegrated and a grandson on the verge of marriage. I was having a particularly silly dream about Malcolm and Barbara sitting in a park near a motorway throwing cheese sandwiches and sticky buns at each other when a distant voice suddenly woke me and I found we were progressing majestically up the drive of a sort of miniature Blenheim Palace with balconies on the front. I think the distant shout was from one of a couple of gardeners working in the vicinity of the hotel's spreading front gardens, both of them fully clothed, and mercifully so, since neither can boast torsos or posteriors in the Rory league.

The hotel was imposing enough, and my first impressions were encouraging enough, but I was suddenly apprehensive at this gathering of the clan of which I was now matriarch, I suppose, and my need to both live up to their expectations and to see that we are not disgraced in the eyes of the family with whom we are about to be linked in marriage. The abrupt and apparently quite public end of the bridegroom's parents' marriage was not the best of starts, and the relaxing, convivial atmosphere I had hoped for away from the comfort of my retirement village already seemed compromised.

However, even after Derek's departure, I still felt an urgent duty to keep our partnership's flag flying on all possible occasions, and this old girl's nose would not be put of joint quite as easily as all that. While Ron and other people too numerous to distinguish individually bustled around the car, my luggage and me, I maintained a truly Grande Dame hauteur, though even my regal demeanour was unable to withstand expressing a delight in the beautiful accommodation which I had been given, with its spacious balcony looking out over miles of surrounding countryside. I almost felt inclined to step out on to it and wave graciously, though as the rapt and worshipping audience would amount to no more than a couple of dishevelled gardeners and a sheep or two, it was perhaps enough just to sit for a while gazing out over a Devon which seemed every bit as lovely as Wiltshire. In such settings, hoping for the best becomes much easier.

Phyllis

Owing to a good forty minutes behind a male pensioner with a hat on in his car (male drivers with hats on are always, in my experience, bad news), on a road where overtaking is virtually impossible unless you happen to be some kamikaze young clot ODing on adrenalin, it was pushing along a bit by the time I got to the hotel. I had visited the place once before for somebody else's wedding, one of the girls at work, so I knew the general layout.

The fact that I was of the wedding party reduced the booking price sufficiently for me to be able to push the boat out for two nights, though it pushed it too far out for Colin's taste, of course. We even had a little bit of whingeing concerning the personnel: 'The trouble with weddings is one can never really know what calibre of people one might be dealing with.' I had to point out, with enough emphasis to ensure that he actually was listening to what I was saying (he doesn't, on occasions), that the likelihood of Helen or the family Helen is allowing her daughter to marry into containing people who are crazy, or hopeless drunkards, or given to casual indecent exposure, or whatever the hell it was that he implied, was pretty slim and one was going to have to bloody well put up with what one got or cop an almighty flea in one's ear. He pulled that odd disgusted gurn he does when he flops his ball into a bunker, then mercifully shut up.

I hadn't expected to be sufficiently far up the pecking order to merit a balcony room, and clearly I wasn't, but even the lower grades of room at the Alanscombe were very presentable and they had remembered to give us a twin room. My days of having Colin jerking the quilt from my recumbent frame or turning over to breathe the evening's Scotch and soda into my face are well gone, I'm happy to say. The view over the side car park was less than inspiring, but the room generally was clean and comfortable and would do for a couple of nights.

Of course, the image I realised I had probably developed, of being the best friend stalwartly at Helen's right hand, had already been confronted with a more complicated reality, as such ideas tend to be. I found my way to a suitable place in the car park without the 'prang' which would have given Colin chortling ammunition for about the next half century. The slight dent I gave the bumper of a badly parked protruding Mondeo in the year 2006 in Sainsbury's car park is still one of Colin's little golf club anecdotes, I gather, though I firmly squelch any mention of it to my face on the basis of a statute of limitations. Having so parked, I noted the arrival of Judi Curzon, probably Helen's oldest friend, dating back to their schooldays. Judi with an i, that is; her name is actually Judith, but apparently, according to Helen, she 'simply wouldn't answer to it – much too much jolly hockey sticks and school stories', though it seems to me as good a name as any for the woman, who is one of the rather horsey individuals girls' schools do seem to turn out in droves.

Listen to me. Beware the green-eyed monster. Judi Curzon is an attractive and always well-turned out woman, still stoutly resisting any incursions of middle-aged flesh, like Helen herself. She is generally quite loud and hearty, it's true, but I really shouldn't make her sound like some kind of frump in tweeds who is always talking about steeds and fillies and good breeding.

Jealousy, I suppose. I've never been much given to close female friends. I was never exactly a tomboy, but in school boys tended to be less complicated and not necessarily needing to be fed intimate confidences and secrets, or confessions about private fancies, likes and dislikes. I am essentially a superficial soul, but comfortable with my superficiality, which is perhaps why Colin and I still sort of work; it suits me that he goes his own way for much of the time and life in a pair is so much simpler and more affordable than life on one's own, when push comes to shove. But, of course, as I get older, niggles and insecurities creep in, and questions about the rest of life become more urgent when it begins to dawn that there isn't as much rest of life as there used to be. Helen is holding my hand through the nearest I've yet been to a mid-life crisis, I suppose, Helen who is everyone's sheet anchor, both at work and at home. This Judi of hers, who goes back further than I do and is probably a good deal more accomplished and interesting, is rocking my boat a little, adolescent as it all is, and exactly the sort of thing I spent a lot of my schooldays trying to avoid.

By the time I finished such unpacking as is necessary, it was gone four, and tea loomed large on my comfy bourgeois agenda. Of course, drink-making facilities were available in the rooms, but sitting there with my little cup looking out over the car park was not particularly exciting, especially in a hotel where I knew at least a fair smattering of my fellow guests. I established at reception where Helen and Peter were; a suite, no less, one of the resplendently balconied jobs looking out over Devon. With a deviousness and intelligence typical of Phyllis Drayton née Routledge, I resolved to go and lend my friend Helen moral support with whatever facet of the proceedings she was currently sorting out, whilst at the same time satisfying my curiosity concerning their suite and whether or not they were actually throwing things at each other yet.

A long, ornately carpeted corridor ran along beside the top floor where the suites were, and I confess to being a little taken aback simply by the vast amounts of space between one front door and the next, as if these suites were practically independent houses. When I reached the number of Helen and Peter's, the door was already slightly ajar – no more than three or four inches, but enough to suggest that whatever was happening inside was not anything which would require a visitor to knock, so I opened the door wider and went on in, intending to emit a bar or two of wedding march to herald my entry.

The sight which greeted me was one which would almost certainly stay with me for the rest of my life, or at least until if and when memory dissolves. Helen and Judi Curzon were clutched in a deep embrace, their arms around each other and as close to each other as two humans can conceivably be without actual sexual congress taking place. They were mouth to mouth in a long, lingering kiss, sideways on to me and totally oblivious of my presence. I suspect they were entirely unaware of the door being open, with that tendency of hotel doors to either not close properly or sneak themselves back open when you think you've closed them.

I could have done one of several things, but there was only one I could really live with, which was to move back and out of the room, while leaving the door exactly as I found it. The corridor carpets were clearly so plush as to deaden any sound of approach or departure, and I beat a rapid retreat to my more humble quarters without anything else happening at all.

My reaction, I hasten to point out, wasn't one of disgust. If the spectacle of their kiss did seem incongruous in any way, it was, ridiculously, because they are almost the same height, and the conventional picture of such an intimate kiss would almost invariably have the downturned face of the man and the upturned face of the woman.

My instant retreat was also on the basis of being an intruder. Women do show affection to each other, of course, and more so than men, but I have been around quite long enough to be able to distinguish between the kiss of friends and the kiss of lovers, and what I had just seen was, without a shadow of doubt, the latter.

And I didn't need to reflect on it for too long to realise how so much about Helen would instantly fall much more logically into place. Perhaps it began with her acknowledgement of the necessity for heterosexual activity in order to have her children, and have them with a decent-looking man of some intelligence and character, and her subsequent total reliance on the lover she had started with. I could see clearly enough the impossibility of someone with the iron public control of Helen to have the whole of the rest of her life defined by her sexuality, and the ease of her maintaining the trappings and role-playing of wife and mother, as long as her refuge, her release, however she defined it, was available.

Where exactly it left Peter, of course, was another question altogether. Did he know? Was his constant philandering a quid pro quo? And what of Kate? What of, for God's sake, Tom?

My tea overlooking the car park suddenly became desperately necessary, and the reassuringly mundane experience of it calmed me down. Appearances, even apparently decisive appearances, can be deceptive; for all I knew, at the hothouse girls' school which Helen attended with Judi, such elaborate displays of affection were part of school life and continued after it without any great significance being attached to them. I remember setting Colin off on an extravagantly noisy chortling session after suggesting that Ken Palmer at the club was having an affair after seeing him order a round of drinks from the new barmaid.

'Ken Palmer,' Colin announced between renewed chortles, 'is an incurable snob' – this from a man who would never venture into the club's public bar in any circumstances whatever – 'and, even if he dared to have an affair, it wouldn't be with a barmaid.' I was only a few yards away from Ken at the time, and there seemed to be to be a pleading in his eyes, a need to have his secret and have somebody to protect it.

So, of course, it was pull-yourself-together-Phyllis time. Maybe you over-estimated what you saw out of an instant guilt at having just barged into the room. Maybe girls' school stuff, see above, their equivalent of old boys' secret handshakes or badges. Maybe a long-gone adolescent affair which they liked to temporarily light up again from time to time.

Having pulled myself together enough to start my bathing and dressing preparations for the evening, for once in a positive bliss of solitude, one or two inconvenient reflections still intruded like little lumps in the smoothness of my pulled-together gravy. Helen visited Judi Curzon quite frequently – 'trips to town', she called them, as Judi lived much closer to London than Helen did. 'Trip to town next week, Phyllis, catch up on the great metrop, do lunch, etc.' Judi divorced and reverted to her maiden name years ago.

Lying in the bath is conducive to reflection, I've always found, and I hadn't been relaxing in it for very long before I remembered how, after quite some time, it did eventually transpire that Ken Palmer *was* having an affair; not with the barmaid, true, but the barmaid did happen to know about it – an indiscretion in the club lounge when they thought everyone had gone into dinner – hence the pleading eyes and over-affectionate manner from the cornered Palmer.

I concluded, not for the first time, that I am one of those people whose instincts in these matters tend to be accurate with others, even if they struggle with themselves. Helen and Judi were lovers. There was no really good reason why they shouldn't come out, in the atmosphere of the present day, but it somehow didn't surprise me that Helen hadn't and probably wouldn't. Helen is classically the kind of determinedly self-contained individual who would not allow her sexuality to be anyone else's business but her own, and Judi, from a similar background and educated in the same place, almost certainly would feel the same. I suppose there was a pang of regret inside me that my relationship with Helen would never be quite the same again, and the questions still sloshed around inside my brain like an unsavoury soup of speculations and suspicions. Did Peter see in it some kind of justification for his own philandering? Had they made some kind of deal, some mutually convenient accommodation, with Helen prepared to put up with being thought of as the deceived wife and Peter the randy old goat of an errant husband for the sake of not going through the whole complicated and expensive mish-mash of the divorce courts and who gets what? For the sake of keeping the fiction alive for the kids?

And, of course, the inevitable 'you're one to talk, aren't you, Phyllis?' happened along again. What else was my marriage but a basically contrived fiction? For the sake of not rocking the boat? Which is, ultimately, worse – not recognising a truth which appears inconvenient, or making oneself believe a fiction because it's convenient? Should a woman who has some quite outrageous fantasies based on two young men who separately sometimes attend the same early-morning swimming sessions as herself on the relatively rare occasions when she can stir herself to get up and go, really see herself as happily and convincingly married?

At this point, a few other instincts returned, I'm afraid, or perhaps not so afraid, since it seemed to me that I had been being beastly to myself for long enough now. My bath became the scenario of one or two more outrageous fantasies involving both young men at the same time. My credibility gremlin chuntered about the impossibility of all three of us getting into the bath but, not for the first time, I told my credibility gremlin to sod off and settled into an infallibly useful way of relaxing and relieving the strains of the day.

Simon

Well, silly me. Unknown as it was, to me at least, we fetched up in a truly beautiful part of the world, and everyone seemed very friendly and laid-back. We were placed, like gay lords surveying our terrain, in a big room-cum-suite with a balcony which presented you with the Devon countryside stretching away towards the coast. A little presumptuous on our parts, I suppose, since we were hardly amongst the principals of this wedding, but very typical of Duncan, and one of his more engaging characteristics. The fact that Duncan is loaded has made a few of my friends raise their eyebrows a little, and there have even been one or two barbed comments more or less reducing me to rent, though rent rarely goes to the extent of entering into a civil partnership and I suspect there's a certain amount of the green-eyed monster pointing in my direction, to be honest.

No, Duncan could be as loaded as Croesus, as far as I'm concerned, but if he was a crude and inconsiderate pig, I would never have countenanced taking up with him. He's the type of man who doesn't just earn money for the sake of piling it up and looking at it; he earns it because he likes to live well, and for him, living well means taking care of his nearest and dearest as well as himself. I know very well how he has really put himself about to take care of his ailing and, in the case of his father at least, frankly tiresome parents. His father used to have a lot to say about 'poofters' and the evils of 'political correctness', until Duncan told him, in Duncan's inimitable straight-off-the-shoulder way, that the poofters' population included his son, and if he didn't like it, he could do the other thing. He didn't like it and I think still doesn't, but he keeps his opinions to himself and maintains at least an appearance of something like liberalism. Since he and Duncan's mum Mary, a gem of a woman if a little censorious in the alcohol department, now live in a beautiful house at Amble on the Northumberland coast whose acquisition was largely funded by Duncan, his liberalism has more or less been shoved down his throat like a dose of castor oil, but medicine cannot but be a little unpalatable at times.

Duncan is generous to a fault with people he cares about, including himself, and he makes a point of booking the best available in whatever hotel he's staying in. He doesn't much like hotels anyway, but his job makes them more or less inevitable, and, as he says, 'If the confinement has to be, it might as well be comfortable.'

Like a wild beast staking out its territory, I had to take an hour or two when we arrive at a place to have a good look around and locate everything. Duncan has come to accept this. As usual, he had no more than a cursory wander about the suite, sniffed a general approval and settled down at a convenient spot, in this case the long desk underneath the wall-mounted television, to set up his various gadgetry, mainly the laptop thing and the smart phone. I took a turn around the grounds, extensive and well-laid out, as you would expect from a country house, which is obviously what this place was before it became a hotel. I had Robert on my mind again, as I supposed I would have for the whole weekend. I am still very fond of him and it is still on an entirely platonic basis, but sentiments are going to have to be guarded while Duncan is around, which at that moment was saddening me a little, in spite of the splendour of my surroundings. I was remembering a time when I was walking off the athletics field, back in sixth-form days, having just done several practice laps – I was quite good at running, which proved to be useful in keeping the jocks off my back – and I'd gone topless out of heat and fatigue rather than any attempt to show off the wonders of my anatomy. In a reverie about how best to improve my sprint finish – yes, I really did think about stuff like that then – I'd suddenly discovered two of the worst of the jock fraternity walking one on either side of me.

Collins, a big ginger-haired brute of a rugby player, was on my left; Sharpe, who was startlingly ape-like in both appearance of temperament, was on my right; I could even smell his sour sweat.

'She's almost completely naked, Sharpey, showing all her butch shoulders and pecs off,' said Collins in his best mincing accent, at which he was surprisingly and rather suspiciously good.

'Shall we help her go all the way, and let the world see it all?'

Sharpe did his sad sort of deep-throated snigger, really suggesting no more than he thought Collins had cracked quite a decent joke and he would now just crack on. He'd moved slightly ahead when Collins returned to his subject.

'Knickers down for the boys, little Simon Rochey. Wouldn't you like that?' and in an entirely different tone, 'Come on, Sharpey, you twat, it'll be a laugh.'

Sharpe turned and looked back uncertainly; Collins actually made a move towards my waist. Collins was a very odd character in some ways; I'd heard rumours about the coarse things he seemed to like to get up to in the communal bath the rugby lot used, and some boys commenting on the sorts of places his hands would be wandering around in scrums. I suspect Collins was – and probably still is, though I've never been interested enough to find out – about as gay as it's possible to be, but because the prominent stereotype of being gay at the time was about effeminacy, obsession with appearance, effusive speech, etc., Collins was able to camouflage the whole thing very neatly in his hearty rugby-playing persona. The ridiculous thing was that he must have seen me in the showers about a thousand times, but I don't think enjoying the view was really what it was all about; humiliation, specifically mine, was what it was all about, with perhaps a bit of business to follow when he'd got my shorts down.

My heart was accelerating, but I had sort of decided what I'd do. I would make an obscene gesture at him – like most boys, I had quite an impressive range to choose from – and run. Neither Collins nor Sharpe were anywhere near fast enough to catch me before the changing room, and the safety of numbers.

I was on the point of doing the obscene gesture, my hand straying downwards to the relevant area, when I heard a shout behind me on the left.

'Si?' I knew it was Robert even before I turned to look. He'd been over in the long jump area – the field events were more his thing, insofar as any athletic event was his thing – and he was jogging easily over to us. He moved smoothly, in spite of the long legs; Collins seemed momentarily hypnotised by him. Many of the boys found Robert intimidating, I think, partly because of his family wealth and connections, but also because of his often-cutting wit and a kind of self-contained toughness which no-one ever seemed confident enough to challenge.

'What are you doing afterwards?' he said. He'd run right across from the long-jump pit without even beginning to be out of breath. Such is youth.

'I don't know – getting something to eat, I suppose,' I said. Sharpe had already moved away; he wasn't in Robert's league in any department of life, and he knew it. Collins was still stood there, his mouth open and a frown on his face, as if someone had pinched his sweetie.

'Well, look, why don't we...' Robert seemed to see Collins for the first time. 'Was there something?'

A vague question, in the general direction of Collins, phrased and executed in classic Robertian fashion, a little more polite than 'sod off, Collins', but amounting to the same thing. Collins duly sodded off, contenting himself with one or two sotto voce oaths, while Robert and I strolled on to the changing rooms, with him talking animatedly about the perils and pitfalls of long jumping and the very strong possibility that he would pull a thigh muscle or two if he continued to have to keep up this level of training. As he stripped naked in the changing room and went off to the showers, with his customary total lack of embarrassment or inhibition, he was speculating on how well he would be able to get 'his share' while nursing a 'gammy leg', his bright eyes flashing and his mouth constantly parting into its easy smile, and I was thanking, once again, the kindly god who had decreed the miracle of my not fancying him and being able to be his friend.

It was well to the rear of the hotel, in a kind of bower affair that bordered a flower garden and lawn, when I looked up with that vision of the sixth-form Robert in my head and saw the man himself, sitting at a bench in a tieless white shirt, one long immaculately trousered leg thrown over the other, as he looked intently at a bunch of papers in front of him.

For a moment, I was debating whether I'd inadvertently taken anything hallucinogenic recently – yes, I have done that, stupid boy as I was – but I knew I hadn't, because Duncan had made it clear from the start that he didn't and he wouldn't stay around if I did. Perhaps this vision was simply the result of my thinking about the past. But the vision then looked up and the face split into almost exactly the same smile as I'd been remembering.

'Si! The man himself! My main man! How the hell are you?'

We embraced warmly, as we always did when meeting up; I could smell that aftershave of his and the wonderful open air-ness he always exuded. An acid drop about main man obviously not meaning best man trembled on my tongue, but I managed to leave it there.

I glanced at the stuff he'd been examining, dull as ditchwater legalese, by the look of it, though there were a few pieces of paper with a police logo on them, which intrigued me. He shut the folder casually, if just a little too much so, I thought.

'What on earth are you doing, bridegroom man, mooching about with your briefs or whatever they are on the night before your wedding? Why the hell are you here at all, for that matter? Aren't you supposed to not see Kate until the morning, or something?'

'Oh, we're not bothering with most of that obsolete stuff, Si. It's going to be the way we want it, essentially; it comes with the territory when we're the ones who're paying for the thing – well, most of it, one or two voluntary donations accepted. We've got the bridal suite and all that, but we're in it tonight and tomorrow night; we don't go for all this disappearing off for the honeymoon halfway through the thing either. Anyway—'

He suddenly stopped and looked down at the ground. I wondered for a moment whether he was thinking about not going through with it, but it seemed incredible; he and Kate have always been crazy about each other.

'I don't suppose you've noticed, not being into Twitter and all that stuff,' he said. 'The news has broken that my mother and father are in the process of divorcing each other. I knew about it a while ago – they told me, together and separately – but some mean-minded troll has obviously thought to leak it into the social media on the ha-ha basis of the great divorce lawyer splitting with his missus at the same time as his son gets married.'

'Oh, Robert, I'm sorry,' I said, as I had to, though my boyhood visits to the Harrington home, comparatively rare as they were, had always made me wonder why his parents had ever married in the first place. They seemed to drift about the place like two ships deliberately navigating so as not to ever get too close to each other. His father was not at home for most of the time anyway, but when he was, the two of them lived and moved in different areas of the house, which had more than enough space for them to avoid each other if they wanted to. I remember being astonished to find, on a summer holiday visit when I was fifteen or thereabouts, that they not only didn't share a bed, they didn't even share a bedroom. They even, and this really did come as a revelation to someone with my background, used separate bathrooms, and at that time, the idea of two bathrooms in the same house struck my adolescent mind as just about the height of affluence and indulgence.

However, Robert was hurting; he had that stiffness of movement, the neck held precisely, the hands gesturing with a slight compulsive jerkiness, that I knew well enough signified his anxiety. His big weekend was looking as if it was going to be hijacked by his parents' difficulties, and Kate, who reputedly never had got on too well with her prospective mother-in-law and whose confidence was more fragile than it seemed on the surface, was probably already fuming.

I put my hand on Robert's arm and he covered it with his own hand. Then he momentarily turned his face away, and I had the impression that he was making a decision. Whatever the question was, he resolved it quickly, which is another of his endearing characteristics, and I had, once again, the peculiarly gratifying experience of being folded into his confidence.

'Si, there is a very good reason why you're not best man at this do, even though you absolutely should be, after all this time. It grieves me badly enough that there is any kind of reason, but it gets under my skin even more that I'm not able, at the moment, to tell you what the reason is. Don't get me wrong – Giles is a good friend and a deeply valued colleague, but he is here rather more in the second capacity than the first, and even that is more than I really ought to be telling you, for both our sakes. In time, you'll probably work the thing out for yourself, but even if you don't, you have my firm promise that I will tell you as soon as I'm able to do so.'

I was deeply touched and, in a curious way, relieved; something mysterious and a little disturbing seemed to have temporarily loomed up between us and he had now controlled and rationalised it so it no longer needed to niggle at me. I didn't see any point in delving any deeper, and I wasn't about to interrogate him on the subject, since I knew well enough it wouldn't do me any good. It was true that he had replaced one mystery with another, but it was clearly a mystery not connected with me or with a breach in our friendship, so I could live with it easily enough for the moment. I leaned over and kissed him lightly on the cheek, reassuring him that whatever he did or decided was alright by me, and soon afterwards, he was gone, with his files and his gadgets, apparently with a little more work to do before he could relax in the bosom of family and friends.

Back in our suite, Duncan was heavily involved with his gadgets, and did no more than raise his head slightly when I walked back in.

'Got your bearings, dear boy?' he said. 'Marked out the territory?'

Even in the happiest of relationships, it isn't necessary to tell one's partner everything, and while masochism does have a role in our lives, it is more a sexual than a social phenomenon, it would be fair to say. Telling him I had just been sitting privately with the bridegroom, holding his hand and kissing his cheek, might have been the strictly honest thing to do, but honesty is not always the best relationship policy, as I already knew well enough.

'Yes. It's a really nice place; well-laid out grounds, everything where it should be. I'm sure we'll enjoy it here.'

A non-committal silence. Then, for the first time since I'd returned, his face turned up towards me. 'I'm sorry, Si, but the stuff we seemed to be picking up on the way, about Robert and his parents; it does seem to be true. Hell of a time for it.'

See above. A less thoughtful individual would probably have blurted out, 'Oh, yes, I know, he just told me,' but this Simon is not so simple.

'Oh, Duncan. On the weekend of his wedding. What a pain.'

He said nothing for a few moments, and he seemed in deep thought, looking from one gadget to the other. With his gadgets, he sometimes resembles a few of the boys I knew at school who concentrated their leisure time on playing or writing music; he is completely withdrawn from the physical world around him, temporarily but totally absorbed in what the changing screens are telling him, and making careful conclusions from all the information available.

I started feeling a little nervous, as if all his gadgets were telling him that I hadn't been entirely honest with him and he was silent in irritation.

But no. When he turned to me, it wasn't with annoyance, it was with puzzlement. 'Someone's trying to hack into the hotel's records. Guest details, rooms, booking times, the lot. In a country hotel in Devon.'

'Maybe it's something to do with the Harringtons splitting up. The media poking their noses wherever they can get them.'

'That might be true, if the attempts were being made from America or Western Europe, though even then it would be a bit fanciful to assume that the Americans or continental Europeans were that interested in an English lawyer and his wife splitting up, whatever the lawyer's specialist fields were. But these hacks are coming in from Eastern Europe. Turkey, Bulgaria, Moldova.'

We looked at each other blankly. Then he smiled, that mischievous, conspiratorial one of his, like a bad boy planning his next outrage. 'This could prove to be a fascinating weekend in more ways than one, dear boy.'

I couldn't but agree with him, though perhaps for not quite the same reasons. Nevertheless, I felt I'd done enough for the moment in terms of time and effort on what would have been my best-man duties, were it not for Robert's mysterious pronouncements on the subject.

It disturbed me a little that a growing fog of mystery seemed to be settling over what ought to be a straightforward if upmarket family wedding in Devon. But for the moment, the only mystery I was concerned with solving was why we had already been in this hotel for some time, with evening and necessary socialising rapidly approaching without as much as a little fooling about in our lusciously appointed en-suite bathroom. It sometimes isn't all that easy to get Duncan away from his gadgets, but then, I do have my means.

FRIDAY EVENING AND NIGHT, June 14th

Matthew

Mary was preparing for bed, and I was taking the air on the balcony so as to give her space and time. It wasn't particularly late, it was only quarter to ten, but Mary had one of the intense headaches she seems to keep getting, and it was hardly surprising after the challenging and frankly bewildering evening we'd spent. We both knew an early night was now probably the only way Mary was going to stand much chance of getting through tomorrow without further trouble. We have got used to booking twin rooms in hotels now, for exactly that reason. She is increasingly vulnerable, and we are both thinking seriously of her going into a full 'retirement', at least from teaching, until she can recover and become more robust.

'It is irritating, Matt,' she was saying before she started getting ready for bed. 'It seems to feed on itself, and the more I try to concentrate on getting better, all this "mind over matter" business, the more the headaches and the tiredness insist on making their presence felt.'

Mary's fragility would, of itself, unsettle me, but it wasn't the only aspect of this situation which was now unsettling me.

Mary herself predicted that the whole business wouldn't be straightforward 'because weddings never are', and she was more right about this one than I think she herself realises.

Peter came round to our room quite early – it was only just after six. He had already mentioned to us that the probable idea for Friday evening would be a dinner with the main 'principals' of the two families, not including Kate and Robert themselves, who have made very clear that they intend to rest in their room on the eve of the day, after checking around the hotel and talking to the necessary people to ensure everything is in readiness. It's unconventional, I suppose, but they have already been living together for some time and I suspect that they are only marrying at all to satisfy their parents and the wider family. In a sense, I am grateful that we won't be seeing them, because there are a number of things I may have to ask Robert Harrington before this event is over, and it is not inconceivable I may have to ask them in a professional capacity, but I need to be better informed before that happens.

Peter was himself; urbane, smiling easily, effusive in his apparent delight at meeting up with us again. I suppose it's some sibling jealousy or rivalry thing, but I do tend to find his polish and elaborate civility a little galling at times. Fair enough, he likes and cherishes Mary, or at least does a very fair impression of doing so, but we have known each other since we were both snot-nosed kids, and it does seem laboured at times for him to observe the conventions so meticulously. He also has that underlying superiority which he's always had, when even compliments sound vaguely condescending, as if he's laughing behind one hand even as the other is held out towards me.

'You always were something of a master of the written word, Matt,' he said at one point, with that quiet, inscrutable little smile of his. 'If this event does finish up in your professional columns, I don't doubt you will do justice to what a special do it will be.'

Statements verging on the unanswerable, a Peter speciality. After about fifteen to twenty minutes of news and gentle bantering, with Mary joining in readily enough – she likes Peter, even in spite of herself and her disapproval of his philandering ways – Peter suddenly decided, the way he does, to sum it all up and be elsewhere.

'Well, half seven for eight, then, if that's OK. The main restaurant; they can't give us our own little room, but they have promised a decent table a little removed from the central toing and froing, and the hotel isn't yet full by any means. If we can establish some sort of rapport with the Harringtons, in a relaxed setting before everything becomes hectic, I'm sure it will make the whole thing go more smoothly. As you must know by now, the Harrington parents find themselves in a rather embarrassing situation, and I think we need to make clear that we intend to be as supportive as possible.'

And off he went, leaving us feeling that we had our orders. The meal itself was a constrained, rather jittery business. Malcolm and Barbara Harrington were even more physically formidable at close quarters than from a distance, and the air of informality which everyone was attempting to preserve was too studied to be really convincing. The Harringtons were also dressed for formality, with Barbara in a beautiful long light blue evening dress and Malcolm in a dark blue lounge suit, accompanied, of course, with a tie with the crest of some legal organisation or other etched onto it. Peter was a little irritated from the start; he had probably mentioned to them, as he did to us, that with dress formality more or less compulsory tomorrow, this evening could be rather more loose and laid-back. It could be that they had just decided to ignore Peter, wanting to establish from the start that they did not intend to be pushed around, whoever's wedding it was, but I think it more probable that the Harringtons simply don't do loose and laid-back.

We were, somewhat oddly, joined at the table by Helen's old school friend Judi someone or other, who didn't seem to me to correspond to a wedding principal, but the Harringtons are as guardedly charming to her as they are to everyone else. Mary found the whole business rather overwhelming, and I could already see from her eyes that a headache was brewing. I was perhaps a little more tetchy and monosyllabic than normal – it is my business as a journalist to attempt to win people's trust and confidence, but my discoveries, or perhaps more accurately suspicions, about the presence of Joe Needham and the kind of dealings he may be cooking up with my niece and her intended have unsettled me. I really wanted this do to be an uncomplicated family occasion, and it was rapidly turning into a professional assignment.

The Harringtons' impending separation remained a ghost at the feast until we had finally sat down and ordered our meals. As our waiter departed with the details, Malcolm Harrington addressed the table, more or less as if it was a jury.

'It would be ingenuous of us to simply ignore what appears to have been infesting social media all day. We can only apologise if the wedding atmosphere is soured in any way. We are in the process of divorcing, and that in itself is true, but it is our business only and we really were hoping that it wouldn't interfere with the wedding. It is particularly galling to find it released in these circumstances. There are only a limited number of people who know, and we will, I do assure you, find the culprit out. Meanwhile, we will try to keep it away from the business of the day as well as we possibly can—'

'Yes, alright, Malcolm. Speeches tomorrow, darling. We're not in a courtroom to be harangued,' Barbara Harrington said tersely.

A very pregnant pause, with Harrington's long sigh and brave, resigned smile speaking volumes about their relationship.

'Having been there myself,' said this Judi person into the void, 'I do sympathise. As you will know only too well professionally,

Malcolm, if it has to be gone through, it is best for it to happen as quickly and painlessly as possible.'

I would personally see this as a presumptuous intervention in a number of ways, but the Harrington matriarch, Celia, who is already rapidly endearing herself to us all with her exercise of the matriarch's prerogative of more or less saying what she likes when she likes, grabbed the baton in her inimitable way.

'It does have a certain symmetry about it, doesn't it? As one marriage ends, another begins. They are all essentially lotteries, really, aren't they? I mean, how can you possibly know how your partner will look in twenty, thirty, forty years, and how can you tell what twists and turns of character and personality will affect them in the meantime? The charming bride can become the over-indulged harridan, the dashing bridegroom can become the ageing philanderer. Not that I classify either of you two sweethearts in such roles, of course,' she continued, with Helen and Judi scarcely able to hide wicked smiles and Barbara Harrington looking as though she wishes her eyes could suddenly become death rays. Peter was also shifting uncomfortably in his seat, particularly alongside the phrase 'ageing philanderer'.

'It saddens me very much, after so long, but if you really can't stand the sight of each other anymore, my dear Malcolm and Barbara, it's probably best for all concerned, isn't it? There is enough unhappiness in the world, goodness knows, without adding to it—'

'Yes, Mum, I think the point has been made. Perhaps we can move on. Peter might be able to tell us what's happening at the university these days, which I'm sure will be of greater interest to the company at large than the business of Barbara and me, which is, after all, social media notwithstanding, still our business. How are things in higher education, Peter?'

Conversation became general, as the saying goes, and I bided my time. Not long after nine, the meal was finished. Helen and

Judi had taken their remaining coffee and drifted off into the main residents' lounge, after Helen had checked with Peter that, 'Presumably you will want a drink or two with your long-lost brother, won't you, darling?' All three Harringtons had retired to Malcolm and Barbara's suite, where the old lady would no doubt continue her sport until they could persuade her to retire. Mary had gone up to the room and assured me about not worrying, because she was going to take a codeine and watch a little television, and Peter and I found ourselves in a comfy niche in the bar, alongside one of the bay windows which look out over the hotel's grounds.

It does not take either of us long to 'come off it', it being his elegant manners and social discourse, when we are not in company, and I was in no mood to beat about the bush.

'What the hell is Joe Needham doing on the guest list?'

He gave me one of the weary, supercilious glances which he knows very well rub me up the wrong way. 'What's this, Matt? After some kind of scoop or something? Can't you take time off?'

I leaned forward towards him, and he could see I was being very serious. 'You know as well as I do what kind of man Needham is. I have information that he may be embroiled in some sort of land deal with Harrington junior and with, Peter, your daughter and my niece. It also, unless I'm very much mistaken, involves your university. This isn't the time for your sophistry. I want to know, and so should you, whether Kate and Robert Harrington are mixed up with Needham and his friends – and why.'

For a long moment, he looked at me blankly, as if not understanding what I was saying. Of course, I know well enough every trick in his book, and this is a stalling technique, hoping whoever he is talking to will be intimidated or puzzled enough to change the subject or, after a short pause, allow him to. And, of course, he knows me well enough too; he knows the obstinacy and inquisitiveness that partly caused me to be a journalist in the first place, and he knows some tactics work with me and some don't. In any case, after a pause which I think was mostly about him playing hard to get, he leaned right across towards me and his voice quickened and lowered.

'I am going to tell you what I know at this point, Matt, partly because I am finding certain matters worrying and I have a feeling you will be getting involved with the business I have in mind quite soon anyway, but you will forgive me if I insist that I'm talking to you as a brother and not as a journalist I happen to know. I know well enough you can tell the difference, and I have to be sure you will respect the difference, and please don't think I'm impugning your professional integrity. It's just that, in the case of Kate, I have to be one hundred per cent absolutely sure.'

I chose not to be insulted, the issue already seeming to be too important to bother too much about egos, professional or otherwise. I put my hand on his arm briefly, the sort of simple gesture which is the nearest we ever get to physical affection.

'Peter, you have it on my word of honour as both an editor and your brother that not a single word of anything you tell me will ever get quoted in my paper without your clearly expressed permission.'

He glanced around him; there was no-one close enough to us to hear a conversation conducted in a reasonably normal tone, but it intrigued me that he seemed to be genuinely wary of someone hearing him.

'Needham and some developers he's associated with are aiming to buy a huge chunk of university land. Like a few other universities, with successive legacies, historical rights, endowments, etc., mine is sitting on much more land than it really knows what to do with. Many of them hold on to it because of possible future expansion plans, but mine has decided to get rid of a substantial chunk to fund developments elsewhere, determining that if they do add to the buildings, the policy will be more about building up than out.'

He'd got all this out with hardly a breath; now he paused and gathered his thoughts. I think he could see by my expression that I had a good idea of where he was going, and he seemed to gather confidence from my understanding.

'Needham doesn't publicly acknowledge any connection with them, of course, because he's chairman of the planning committee which he has rigged to do what he tells them. When he makes sure the developers get the contract, with lots of stuff in it to make it at least look respectable – ecological considerations, fuel-efficient buildings, affordable housing, all that sort of thing, though what it will mostly be about in reality will be "leisure housing" or second/ holiday homes. If it goes through, he is in for a truly awesome handout which might enable him to retire. After exhibiting what I thought then was innocent interest, he found out Kate's law speciality, which is land and the development of it; she is in a team with Robert Harrington; that's how they met. He then seems to have decided to recommend Kate and Robert's London-based chambers to the developers, largely because of Kate's extensive local knowledge. Kate's chambers will do very well out of pushing the development through; I discussed it with her and she felt OK about taking it on. As professor of politics and economics, I'm on the university board and my say will have a lot to do with whether the university approves the plans. Needham is well known for pressurising via family connections, and now he has two ways to do it. He also has enough "leverage", as he calls it, of all kinds to get the planning committee to do what he wants.'

He had to stop and take a sip from his drink. He glanced at his watch; we both knew time and opportunity was limited in a place where so many friends and relatives were staying.

'Listen, Matt, I think we would do better to take a stroll in the grounds at this point. As I've started explaining the situation, I might as well give you the whole story, and with all the local connections and knowledge you've got, we can start talking tactics, which will make me feel better. I'm already thinking the more people we have "on our side", the better, and especially people with thorough local knowledge.'

We finished our drinks and strolled out into the cool air; it was a still night, and the generous lighting around the main hotel building meant we could put a bit of distance between it and ourselves and still be able to see each other well enough. We found a bench in the grounds where nobody could possibly be in earshot unless someone had actually bugged the bench, which neither of us really saw as realistic even in our now quite conspiratorial turn of mind.

'It all seems so perfect, doesn't it? A badly needed housing development, with energy-friendly dwellings and environmentally careful infrastructure, and including a generous smattering of affordable homes. Responsible use of university land, the university profiting generously and acquiring funds for educational use, and Kate and Robert's chambers enhancing their reputation for handling reputable developments. Everyone's a winner.'

I felt his frustration so keenly now; it was, absolutely, a beautifully neat set-up. But I know Joe Needham.

'But for the kind of people Joe Needham associates with,' I said, and his eager nod had an element of gratitude about it. 'I have people who keep Joe Needham in their brief always. He is very careful, and he knows some people who are very rough indeed; we have to look out for what we're doing, and try to ensure that the nationals don't come blundering in at the critical moment and muck it all up, but sooner or later he will slip up, by phone, email, meeting somewhere where he thinks no-one will see him, and the whole pack of cards will tumble about his ears. We know the so-called developers who give him the big handouts are sometimes money launderers, or drug dealers, or even people traffickers, or maybe a bit of all of them at once. There are plenty with foreign connections who want to get their feet well into the UK for all sorts of reasons, and the likes of Needham are their bread and butter. But all Kate and Robert will be doing is the legal business; when the land is bought and the development starts, they'll be out of it, won't they? I know it's going to hurt you to see such people getting hold of university land, but once the deal is done, that will be it as far as you're concerned, won't it?'

'Matt, you know planning issues better than that. The university can't just sell the land off and forget about it; the university has need of the local planning authorities, and we have had to agree that no sale will take place until a viable scheme has been approved. That's why Needham is coming to the wedding.'

His face set, the way it did years ago on one of the boyish occasions when he realised that his charm and eloquence had not fooled our father, who was about to take embarrassing and painful retribution for his latest little prank. Fathers did that sort of thing then. Peter has always been like that; much too tempted to sail close to the wind and see what he can get away with. Unfortunately, that now seems to manifest itself most clearly in his marriage.

'Joe Needham is my colleague and esteemed friend. Apparently. This isn't the first time the university has had contact with the local planning committee, as you can imagine, and we have a vested interest in keeping him sweet. There are budgets and jobs at stake on these land deals. Raising tuition fees solved some of the problems; it didn't solve all of them, by any means, especially as it was accompanied by government money virtually drying up altogether. Good old Joe and I have met and worked together on a number of occasions, and he has even helped Kate out in the past with information and interviews, etc., on land issues. The board wants me to cosy up to him as much as possible, for the sake of this deal and whatever may follow it, so I cosy up. I invite the man to my daughter's wedding, and even more so now that both he and I know that he has put a whole pile of lucrative work my daughter's way. Unofficially, of course. That's the kind of man Needham is,

Matt. He spreads his web wide and people get inextricably caught up in it. Now, perhaps, including me.'

'Well, you know your way around, Peter. The point is, once this deal is done, Kate will be out of it, won't she? And better fixed to choose what she wants to do?'

His tone suddenly quickened and lowered. 'Matt, Kate is a bloody crusader, isn't she? You know her well enough; you know her as well as I do. I'm desperately afraid that she and Robert are doing this largely because they, too, want to nail Needham and prove that he's fixing things for these people. Needham, of course, has never acknowledged in any way that he had anything to do with Kate's firm getting the developer's business; Kate's background and Devon upbringing is clear enough on the chambers' website, anyway. I think her and Robert are thinking they are good enough to get enough evidence on Needham and his specific connections with these developers to take him down.'

'Oh my God.'

'Yes, exactly. If I'm right, they're playing a very dangerous game, and they could well finish up getting out of their depth. Or worse. I've heard plenty of stories about what's happened to people who got across Needham and his friends, and I know some of them at least to be absolutely true. And that's just Needham. What these drug dealers and traffickers are prepared to do – well, it makes my blood run cold just thinking about it.'

He shook his head. I needed to say something, anything, which might sound upbeat, the way I used to do all those years ago, though I feared even then it might not sound very credible, as my back in the day comment along the lines of, 'You don't need to worry about Dad. He's in a good mood today. He probably hasn't noticed anyway.'

But I did have some more promising material to work with.

'Three points to make, Peter. I'm sure you hear those words often enough in university circles. One, Kate is as smart as a button, and I suspect this London lad is no less, because I doubt whether he would have got anywhere with her otherwise. Two, Needham needs you and the university every bit as much as you need him – probably more so: the university is the biggest potential customer he's got on his own patch, by a long chalk. He could get at you via Kate, but he knows what the consequences will be. And, three, and I'm taking you into my professional confidence this time, every bit as much as you've taken me into yours, my paper already has quite a lot of stuff on Needham, and some of it's quite good. Needham can't carry on the way he does without making local enemies. We haven't got quite enough yet to definitely and beyond all reasonable doubt bring him down, but we're not a million miles away and he knows it.'

'Which puts you in danger as well, I suppose. Bloody hell.'

'Me? Oh, everything we have about Needham doesn't depend on me. It's kept very securely tucked away, I can assure you. If anything suspicious were to happen to me with even a whiff of the handiwork of Needham and his friends, my guys would be at him like never before, and the very least we could achieve would be to drive him well out of this area, and good riddance. He knows that as well. The fact that he's not a fool is part of our insurance, Peter. He's smart. But I honestly think he's not as smart as our Kate, Peter.'

We were silent for a moment, perhaps to consider this proposition apart from our affection for the girl in question. Kate has been a high-flyer from the start, romping through GCSEs, A levels and degrees while hardly turning a hair, and we both know her ability to talk, charm and interest. She has her mother's organisation abilities and talent for retaining information, and her father's charm and gift of the gab. We had few problems with believing that she would be a match for Joe Needham, streetwise as he may be. But fear arrives from the unknown, and we didn't know exactly who Needham was now working with. Or for.

'We'd better go in,' I said. 'Two brothers having a stroll about and a chat after not having seen each other for a while is nothing unusual to anybody, but father and uncle spending the entire evening in each other's exclusive company is probably going to excite interest in quarters where we don't want interest excited. We'll keep talking all weekend, brother. Two heads are better than one. Talking, observing and acting if we have to.'

We shook hands, and he smiled his gratitude, Peter the society man right back in situ.

'I must circulate, charm, ingratiate. Check that all is ship shape and Bristol fashion. Talk with Helen, who most certainly won't be panicking, of course, but may need to consult about something or other.'

'Last time I saw her she was having a riotous time with that old school friend of hers,' I said, as I got up ready to head back into the hotel. 'They seem very close. Nothing lasts quite like the old school, eh, Peter?'

A really odd expression came over his face, a kind of flush accompanied by a narrowing of the eyes. It startled me, as an inexplicable reaction to a commonplace statement.

'Yes, quite. Nothing at all.'

Now I realise with a start that I am still sitting on this balcony and it is not as warm; the night has set in. I go back into the room, and Mary has dropped off, which is probably for the best. The only lights are her bedside lamp and, bless her, mine, meaning it is easy enough for me to use the bathroom and get into my own bed without disturbing her. Twin rooms have become essential in recent years, both at home and away, as she tries to see her life and her work through the constant, sapping tiredness which so relentlessly weakens her. I have a lot to think about, and a fair few bits and pieces to worry about, but it doesn't take very long before the weariness of a very active day demands its dues.

Celia

I was back in my own quarters now, thankfully, and the night was pleasant enough for me to take further delight in my balcony, albeit with a stout coat wrapped around me. I was also grateful for my own company, and I suppose a little afraid that I had become rather too used to my own company these days. A delightful meal was laid on for us earlier in the evening, with the laudable intention of allowing the principals of both families to relax in each other's company before the main event, as it were. I realised quite early in the proceedings that I was somewhat out of my depth in this company.

The bride's father, whose name is Peter, is a tall and rather good-looking man in his mid-fifties, I would guess, with still quite a tolerable head of blondish hair and a certain supercilious sexiness in the cool eyes. His wife Helen is almost as tall as he is; she wears her hair in a rather short, severe way and dresses similarly. The make-up is quite minimal and the manner verging on the authoritarian; I could as well believe her being a headmistress as I could the madam of a house of ill repute specialising in sado-masochism. Curiously, we also have with us a woman who is apparently an old school friend of Helen's, a person called Judi, certainly not lacking in self-confidence and bonhomie but much too much of the Roedean jolly hockey sticks rumbustious horsey type for my comfort, and Peter's as well, I would guess, judging by his decidedly stiff smiles when these two women occasionally indulged in schoolgirlish behaviour and giggles quite grotesque in women of their age.

Barbara, of course, sat monosyllabically through almost the entire meal, looking around her as if someone had just suspended a particularly piquant little pile of dog poo under her nose. This became even more marked when Malcolm, the silly boy, chose to make one of his speeches bravely acknowledging all the fuss about his marriage, instead of just keeping schtum about it as is better in social situations, and certainly the preferred procedure as far as Barbara is concerned. I tried to alleviate the situation by making a few general and, I hoped, conciliatory remarks, but it rapidly became clear that all I was actually succeeding in doing was fanning the flames and even, amongst one or two of our company, causing amusement of entirely the wrong sort. Not for the first time in recent years, I had the feeling that I had wrong-footed myself and lost the social touch I once had. Derek's business did need a certain amount of entertaining, and we also had to keep up our standing in the area, of course, and I had always thought that I had a deft-enough touch in these matters.

The solitude of old age can be something of a mixed blessing. In the immediate aftermath of Derek's death, I experienced feelings of relief at the same time as being enormously guilty about them; Derek was very ill, in the last year especially, and every day seemed to be a repeat of the painful walk through glue of the day before. Only after he'd been gone for several months and I'd finally stopped addressing remarks to him in the next room before remembering he wasn't there, did I begin to feel that I still did have some life to live. Soon after that, it dawned on me that I could now at least live it in peace, without any more struggling to please or look after anyone else and with no more worries about earning a living or how the next bill was going to be paid. It started to offer the satisfaction of comfort, which now even the arrival of consultants in my life has not entirely removed. But, of course, even someone of my long experience of people can lose something of her facility in dealing with them when living on her own all the time. This hotel was now so full of people I already know or am shortly about to that it was all bewildering and a little intimidating.

However, it had been a long and, by my standards, hyperactive day, and of course my unfamiliar alcohol intake and the night air took their toll. My head dropped and I snoozed.

I woke, or I was more accurately awoken, by a sound which didn't fit. Even if I hadn't served a long apprenticeship in detecting sounds which don't fit in houses full of children or social gatherings full of eclectic gatherings of people, a retirement village is extra training. It contains some very old and sometimes very sick people, and not noticing noises which don't fit can be a matter of life and death, quite literally. I would hope that, however my illness develops, anyone hearing a pronounced thud on my apartment floor in the middle of the night like someone dropping a sack of potatoes on it from a great height would conclude that such a noise didn't fit. People are not generally in the habit of carrying sacks of potatoes around in the middle of the night, let alone dropping them from great heights.

I was partly hidden on my balcony by a large plant. Beyond describing it as large and green, my horticultural know-how doesn't extend much further, but I think the fact that it was so large had partly kept the night breeze off me and helped my snooze along.

I gazed tentatively through it, and yes, the noise which didn't fit happened again. No more than thirty or forty yards away from the hotel, a bush, partly lit by a hotel security light, was speaking. And whatever language it was speaking in, it wasn't English.

A certain tetchiness added itself to my increasing awareness of getting cold. If I was to have quasi-religious mysterious experiences inflicted on me on an innocent family occasion, they could at least express themselves in my own language.

The bush then uttered again. Almost immediately, I heard a sort of vague scuffling noise and it seemed as if two dark shapes had moved rapidly out of the hotel light's arc.

Two minutes later, to confuse me still further, a much more distinct northern-sounding voice drifted across to me, probably near enough to be no more than a couple of balconies away. I could detect the accent without making out the words too distinctly; I'm not too good with regional accents, which I try to put down to dodgy hearing rather than overt snobbery, though perhaps it has elements of both.

However, by this time I was tired and really getting quite cold, so I exercised an old person's prerogative used ever since first invented by Mr Scrooge himself. I bah-humbugged. Somehow my dodgy hearing had transferred that voice, perhaps when it had been further back from the balcony, from that room to the outside bush, and turned its northern brogue to something vaguely mid-European. In any case, I had managed to consume practically a vat of wine by my usual abstemious standards and it was probably just as well I wasn't seeing large black spiders climbing the room walls.

I went to bed, and it didn't take long for sleep to arrive. But just before it did, the feeling returned to me very powerfully that no, it wasn't all invention or fancy on my part. Something in this place just didn't fit.

Phyllis

By half past seven, my dear husband was still to make an appearance, without enlightening me any further as to when he might eventually do so. Since I did know a few of the assembled company, I thought perhaps a drink and a chat and maybe even gatecrashing Helen and Peter's dinner table might be preferable to room service wine and the view of the car park.

As this was the night before the wedding rather than the wedding itself, I thought it pointless to dress up to the nines and went down looking fairly casual, top and trousers sort of thing. First mistake. After a brief introduction at the bar while I was waiting for a large glass of the house's best vin rouge – on the hotel bill, of course, pick the bones out of that, Colin absentia – with the groom's parents dressed for dinner at the Ritz and the female of the two looking at me with the kind of expression that suggested she had me down as either one of the hotel menials in the bar to give someone a message or a specimen of local yokel who'd somehow stumbled into the wrong room.

'Phyllis is my next-door neighbour,' said Helen, with a certain 'it's not my fault' tone which was a little dismaying, probably visibly, because she followed it up with 'and a good companion'. Vague handshakes from the Harringtons, slightly warmer greetings from Peter's brother Matthew and his wife Mary, and a dismissive little touch on the arm from dear Judi, Helen's whatever the hell she is, before Judi resumed an animated but almost entirely one-sided conversation with Barbara Harrington. Of course, I now knew, as did most of the known world, that someone had done the dirty on the Harringtons and announced their separation to the world, but I had an instinctive feeling that Barbara Harrington never has been the life and soul of anyone's party, even in rather more propitious circumstances.

The Harrington matriarch, Cecilia, I think they said, was regally seated slightly to the left of the group still gathered at the bar. She looked through me, more or less as I was a hologram appearing vaguely on the edge of her eyesight, before resuming her gin and tonic. She didn't look too well, beyond what one or two too many G&Ts might do to her, and I decided not to push my luck with closer communication in case I spent the rest of the evening listening to her symptoms in graphic detail.

Eventually, Helen and I sat down in one of the very plush booths which stretched down either side of the room. I knew Judi was sneaking regular suspicious peeks; Mrs Harrington junior, whom I imagine has never spent a moment of her life being called Babs, had extricated herself from Judi's clutches and was now chatting fairly easily to Mary Densham.

'Am I booked in for dinner, Helen?' I said, one or two tum rumbles already being felt.

'I'm sorry, Phyll, but you didn't seem to know whether Colin was coming, and you know what these places are like for numbers.

65

In any case, I'm not sure you'd find it much fun. It's the sort of obligatory bride and groom's families trying to be nice to each other, though I'm already a bit daunted by Mrs Harrington senior, who has already given me a few details about her son's digestion and internal arrangements which were much, much more than I wanted to know. Is Colin coming?'

'Yes, when he can tear himself away from his labours. If that's what they are.'

'Oh, Phyll.' Helen looked vaguely uneasy, as close as she ever gets to looking worried, at the prospect of once again entering the tortuous and convoluted land that is the Drayton marriage.

Judi, of course, seized her moment. 'Refill, Hel?' she shouted. 'They'll be calling us through in a minute, I rather think?'

How you can go through life with a best friend whose pet name for you corresponds with Satan's realm, I don't know, but Hel seemed to manage.

Her mistress's voice, it seemed. She was up on her feet like someone had bugled the alarm.

She leant over to me. 'Grab a bar meal, or a sandwich or something, Phyll,' she said. When she's not organising her own life, she needs to be organising other people's. 'Please do stay around until we come back from dinner. This is UN negotiation stuff for now; later on, they'll be talking to theirs and we'll be talking to ours, including you, my love. Time to unwind a little, I think.'

Helen has called me 'my love' many times; now it somehow took on a different meaning. Then she swanned off back to the bar and Judi; sure enough, they had been called into dinner. And there I was, marooned on my own in a big posh hotel bar, dressed like a weekend down at the farm, with the word 'hell' recurring in my mind like a mantra.

I took my remaining wine and headed out on to the hotel's terrace, with impressive views of the Devon countryside on all sides. It wasn't a particularly warm evening, but it was still and pleasant, and there weren't many people outside. I sat looking spiritual, and it was quite relaxing there, actually. I wondered whether the Colin story would be the big order arriving late or the duty roster for tomorrow 'fucked again' with unforeseen absences. I might have worried more if he turned up smelling of woman, but he never does; he turns up smelling of that bloody store, with perhaps a particular hint of one of its items of produce.

Twenty minutes later, with another large Malbec, a cheese and ham sandwich 'with crisps and salad garnish' on order and hotel reception tipped off regarding where I was when my husband arrives, in case they thought I was on the game – a fanciful notion, perhaps, at my age, but hell – there it is again – in the evening light, who knows – I was back on the terrace, taking in Devon's quiet beauty, if also its accumulating chilliness.

I had a couple of magazines with me to glance over from time to time, and I was having a glance when an unforeseen phenomenon definitely seemed to be occurring. A besuited male, probably about my age on the most casual of glances, was looking at me. After a few minutes, when I'd reassured myself that I was not having Malbec-induced hallucinations, he suddenly got up and walked over to my table. I had my fingers strategically poised around the stem of my glass, ready to repel if need be, even at hotel wine prices.

'I'm so sorry, I didn't mean to stare,' he said, and there's a faint hint of a Devon accent, like a kind of half-forgotten echo. 'But you're Phyllis, aren't you? Phyllis Damerell?'

I looked up then, very much intrigued to hear my old Devon name, usurped by the nebulous Drayton for the sake of wedlock, and examined his face. That quiet, sexy smile, those mouldering hazel eyes – I placed him almost at the same moment as he introduced himself.

'David Bennett? Clarendon Comp? Good old school? Does it ring any bells? Been a long, long time, I know.'

It took me a few seconds, perhaps befuddled by Malbec, but then I placed him. And the whole thing flooded back, the whole teen mess and mash, exciting, breathless, infuriating, when nothing and everything mattered.

'David! How lovely! Please do join me, if you've got a minute.'

He put his pint down and sat on the other side of the table from me. Then he gave me that smile, and the pleasure/pain of what that smile could do to me also came rushing back. He was still good-looking, even allowing for the spectacles he now wore, but the hair was thinner with little dashes of grey here and there on the temples. David Bennett at sixteen was a phenomenally, ridiculously good-looking creature, with a body to match the face. In the summertime, when the boys were trudging off the athletics track, some of them topless, meaning they had nothing on but small pairs of shorts and trainers, David could temporarily destroy some teachers' lessons, with heads turned to windows and girlish mouths open. The odd boy or two as well, trying not to make it too obvious. His nickname amongst the girls was 'Gordon'.

If he'd played to the gallery, his attraction would probably have diminished, but he didn't; he seemed genuinely unaware of the effect he had on people, especially female people. I was one of a succession of girls to have 'a fling with Dave', because for all his beauty and modesty, he just didn't take anything too seriously, and as soon as anyone tried to lure him into expressions of undying love and affection, they would find themselves 'moved on'.

'Do you live near here?' I said, as more memories, some of them very intimate indeed, started piling up in my mind.

'I do now, for the last eighteenth months or so. But this isn't exactly my local; I couldn't afford it! I'm here for the wedding, on the Densham ticket.'

'Oh, really?' I suppose my face must have somehow formed itself into a question mark. He took a sip at his beer and smiled; oh, God, that smile again.

'I met Peter Densham at Bristol; we were students together. I spent a while abroad and came back to a job in London. But I tired of London, the noise, the smell, the impersonal detachment of the place. I grew up in Devon, of course, and when I heard Peter had a chair, I got in touch. He had several big things in the pipeline which he thought I could help with, and he helped get me appointed. Professor of environmental sciences.'

I smiled and felt a certain sense of gratification that a boy I had fooled around with in our school's equivalent of the bike sheds, an old pavilion which only ever came into use on inter-school matches or sports days, was now a university professor.

'How did you get on with the acting?' he said, and I looked at him with genuine mystification. It can sometimes be demeaning to look back on the grandiose ambitions of your younger years. Now I remembered; two so-so parts in successive school pantomimes and I was suddenly Judi Dench, no doubt during the pavilion adventures period. They didn't allow for huge amounts of conversation if I remember rightly, but we had to talk about something some of the time.

'No, that turned out to be a school dead-end, I'm afraid. I started doing part-time hotel work to earn myself something, and that moved on to receptionist stuff. I turned into a professional receptionist; I work in a health centre now, alongside Helen Densham.'

'Oh, I see.'

Yes, I'm pretty sure you do, I thought. How many of his other old school chums has he met with overblown ambitions which didn't work out? I felt a momentary defensiveness.

'It's more interesting than it sounds. I meet a fascinating cross-section of people, and I think I do genuinely help some of them.'

'I don't doubt it,' he said gallantly. 'When I say, "I see," I mean, "I don't know much about it, so I don't want to ask foolish questions."'

I smiled again. He seemed to be an easy man to smile at.

'Well, let me be brave and venture on a few foolish questions of my own. Is one of the big things in Peter's pipeline this university land sale, and are you allowed to talk about it?'

'Yes and yes. There's not a lot of point in me being secretive about it; the whole thing is in the public domain. The plans are there on the planning authorities' site for all to see.'

'Do you think it will happen?'

'Not if I have anything to do with it, it won't.'

The steel behind the smile. I remembered that too. I watched him play football a few times. I also – yes, I can now, hurtful as it was – remember the expression on his face when I started talking about long engagements. We were both sixteen at the time. I was usurped about a week later, not before he did the whole 'dumping kindly' routine. 'More my fault than yours', 'not ready to commit'; the usual stuff. It occurred to me later than he was pretty adept at it for a boy of sixteen. I cried off and on for five days, swore in front of my mirror never to get involved with any boys ever again, sent him a few caustic messages which he never answered, and then met a lad called Miles, I think it was, not so pretty as David but probably a better laugh, posh name or not.

But it was, of course, all a long time ago. To hell with it. He was looking at me, expecting a question, so let's get back to the here and now.

'What's the problem with it?'

He grimaced and sipped his beer again. 'More problems plural, I'd say. Most of it is rural land, some of it cultivated and the archaeologists think there could have been various settlements on it going back to Roman times. There could be bones, artefacts, coins, just about anything in much of it. It also houses various species of small wildlife who have been living on it, in some cases, for centuries. It's not best suited to residential or leisure housing, whatever they're calling it, and it will take a huge investment of money and resources to change that, with the probable result of environmental destruction on a grand scale.'

I fell back to the here and now with a bump. 'But Peter seems to think quite highly of the idea.'

'Peter is being pressurised, quite heavily so. He's even had to invite the major councillor involved to his daughter's wedding. Peter's is the most prominent voice on the university board apart from the vice-chancellor himself; his daughter is acting for the company aiming to push the plans through. He's badly in need of allies, which I think is where I come in.'

'One councillor doesn't seem particularly threatening.'

This seemed to touch a nerve. He moved closer to me and dropped his voice slightly. 'I haven't been back in Devon for very long, but it doesn't take long to find out that Joe Needham is notorious for pushing through planning applications he is likely to find profitable. He also keeps some very dubious company.'

'Oh, really? Not something I know very much about, I'm afraid.'

He looked at me and spent a few seconds looking as though he was thinking things over. Then he smiled again, that smile, like an ever-giving gift. 'Anyway, we haven't seen each other since school. Catch me up a little. Husband? Kids? Or mind my own business?'

I told the tale of my meeting a man during my days as a hotel receptionist, a man who then travelled around, nationally and internationally, selling things, a man whose experience of the wide world quite intoxicated a twenty-year-old girl who knew nothing much beyond Devon, a man who was now in hock body and soul to a supermarket chain who wanted all of him. The Malbec was making its presence felt. I determined to get on to David's life.

'So leave me there a minute. How about you? Kids? Wives? Mind my own business?'

This time his expression was more a sad kind of rueful grin. 'No, you've told me yours, I'll tell you mine. We did a deal similar to that at school, as I remember, except it was show not tell.'

'Now then, David. Play nicely. And don't play for time.'

Another sip of beer. 'No wives, no kids. Probably something sadly lacking in my constitution, but I don't want kids. I want to live my life, not live it vicariously through offspring; my work demands don't allow time for all that anyway. And I'm afraid to say, I don't want wives either. Partners, sure; I've had several, the last one lasting nearly five years; it broke up six months ago.'

'Oh. I'm sorry.'

'You don't need to be. In the last analysis, we were incompatible. I was fond of her – I still am – but she wanted me body and soul, and I'm not on offer body and soul.'

'Oh, David. You never were, were you? Will you ever be?'

'I doubt it.'

And, of course, it was at this moment, when we were quite close, looking wistfully into each other's eyes and remembering teen angst all over again, that a loud, WTF is going on cough sounded right behind me, and there was Colin, still in his work suit.

'Am I interrupting something here?' he said, in his best Basil Fawlty voice.

'Oh, Colin, hi. I'm glad you could make it. At last,' I said, now with enough Malbec in me to remain undaunted by any situation. Or so I thought at the time.

'Colin, this is David Bennett, professor of environmental sciences, a colleague of the bride's father and, last but certainly not least, an old schoolmate of mine.'

'How do you do?' David said, raising himself slightly in his chair.

'How do I do?' Colin plonked his pint down heavily on the table. 'Oh, just great. I've finished a thirteen-hour working day and dragged myself over here to a wedding where I know nobody except our next-door neighbours to find my wife and a man I've never set eyes on before giving each other lovelorn looks. What could possibly be wrong?'

David rose to his feet, his hand around his glass. 'I dare say you have an old flame or two back in your schooldays. Or maybe not, I don't know. If you ever do unexpectedly run into one of them, I suspect your wife will display rather more grace and understanding than you just have.'

Colin's mouth was still open as David turned to me. 'Hope we might talk again tomorrow, Phyllis. Goodnight, now.'

Shortly after this exchange, I retreated to my room, Colin remaining to have 'at least one more restorative pint'. By the time he returned, having had time for several more restorative pints, I was almost asleep. I had enough consciousness left to say my piece.

'Thanks, Colin. Thanks a lot. Graceless as ever. We know one marriage is ending with this wedding. Perhaps we might even make it two.'

He said something back as he clumps into his bed. Only later, when I woke up in darkness and sobriety, did what he said fully register.

'And maybe not such a bad idea at that, Phyllis. Good night to you.'

Simon

I won't particularise what we'd just done; I always find descriptions of sex acts, love-making, whatever you want to call it, don't even begin to live up to the actuality of the experience and just end up sounding a bit mechanical, I suppose. However, the evening was moving on, darkness had fallen, etc., and even after our fairly energetic indulgence, there Duncan was, on the desk next to the window, on the blasted computer again, sitting there in his knickers staring at the screen, like he does, as if he's expecting a new alien life form to suddenly leap out of it and scurry round the room like a living crackerjack.

It can be galling at times, I'll not deny it. He's a wonderful guy with boundless energy, and don't think I don't appreciate it, but he never seems to be able to completely break free of his work.

Yes, OK, he's very good at it. Duncan is an internet security guy, head of a department which protects one of the biggest corporations in the country, and people who know, which in this case doesn't include me, say he's just about the best in the business, which is why he makes an impressive living out of it. A company which wants to be sure that their secrets are not going to find their way to the bad guys, on the dark web or the shadow web or the bloody totally opaque web, Duncan's your man; if the money's right, of course. If you want to be sure your workforce are not going to log on one day and find themselves looking at a screen telling them where all their stuff has gone and how much you're going to need to pay to get it back, then get Duncan's outfit on your payroll. But if you happen to be one of the bad guys, forget it. He works for money, yes, but he's good enough to be a bit particular about whose money and to be able to tell the difference.

All the same, we were in this place for the wedding of a good friend, it was getting late, and even if it was fresh summer air coming in through the window, it was now getting to be distinctly fresher and I was as naked as the day I was born, as Duncan would be if he wasn't sitting next to the window. Being Northumbrian, the air could be just about as fresh as the bloody Arctic without him needing anything but his knickers. I, however, am used to gentler climes.

'Dunc, sweetheart,' I said, even as I took in that torso and wondered if either of us still had anything left in the tank, 'isn't it getting just a little bit nippy for wide open windows?'

He's so easy going a lot of the time that he didn't bother to argue. He stood up and leant towards the window, then something seemed to disturb him, and he froze, looking for a moment or two like a classic Greek statue with a pair of pants on and a bit more chest hair. Sort of butch David. Then he closed the window and resumed his seat, not bothering himself with informing me about what froze him. He can be just a bit too laid-back at times.

'Something out there? Bride and groom jumping the gun in the night air?'

'Jumping the gun? You think those two have waited until they're wed? I doubt it, Si. He practically drools when he looks at her, and she looks at him like she wants to eat him.'

'True.' Laid-back, yes, computer-obsessed, yes, but he doesn't miss much. I was about to press him again on what he saw, but then he volunteered it.

'Some guy scampering about in the night, by the look of it. Probably pissed. Just because your friend Robert is a sensible groom, it doesn't mean all his friends are likewise.'

'Can you not wrap up work now and come to bed, or whatever else you might have in mind?' I said, wondering what I might be letting myself in for with such boldness.

'You are a bad lad and a naughty boy,' he said, moving over to sit on the bed. Even at this stage of the day, his words and the proximity of him were stirring me again.

'Tomorrow I'm going to deal thoroughly with you, young Simon.'

'Oh, God, are you? Do you think we'll get away with the noise?'

'All the rooms are sound-proofed. I read it in the hotel notes. The happy couple could be doing the Kamasutra from back to front and nobody would know any different.'

I was blushing, I was actually blushing, when his damn computer made a weird noise, one of its unbelievable range of weird noises, and there he was transfixed in front of it again.

'Dunc, give it a rest, can't you?'

'Not at the moment, dear boy. Some weird and wonderful things are happening here. I'm intercepting a message from abroad directed towards someone staying in this hotel. It's in code, but I know that code, and I think I know the outfit who are sending it. Based in East Europe, but they move their transmissions around a bit.'

'Bad guys?' I was intrigued in spite of myself.

'Yes, very much so, I'm afraid. They're into all sorts of stuff – drugs, human trafficking, prostitution, you name it. They try and latch themselves on to legitimate companies and make it look as though they're acting in their name. They've tried it with mine, but I completely jammed them.'

'So who are they trying to talk to?'

'Joe Needham. Councillor Joe Needham, Suite 27.'

Another rustle in the night air outside. This was turning into a very strange wedding.

SATURDAY MORNING,
June 15th

Matthew

As usual when I sleep away from home – it doesn't happen very often now, thankfully – I slept fitfully and woke early. There was a sliding doors arrangement going out on to the balcony, and enough light was coming through the blinds covering them to suggest that dawn happened some time ago.

I checked my watch; it was just gone half past six. The hotel provided a couple of dressing gowns, which looked and smelt clean; they hadn't got pom-poms on or flowery patterns all over them, they were just dressing gowns. I saw them draped over the back of an armchair. I didn't want to wake Mary if I can avoid it; this was going to be a long and demanding day, and she tires easily these days. I supposed it would be just as well for me to doze on, but I've always tended to be awake when I'm awake, and in any case, there were things on my mind.

Although my paper is only a local one, we do have long-standing connections with one of the nationals which will enable them to pick up a story we've started, part of the deal being they'll go with the original editor and writer, i.e. me and mine. I've had a few opportunities to join one of the nationals, but I'm a Devon lad and living anywhere else, particularly now I am, let's face it, middle-aged, doesn't appeal. In spite of its holiday honeypot and cream tea image, there's a lot going on in Devon, some good, some bad. There are traffickers and drug dealers who regard the southwest coast as a big, yawning gateway to get people and goods in, though, being land lubbers, they don't usually take into account the many dangers of the south coast, and not just in winter. Devon also has problems which could relieve it of much of its younger population if there simply aren't the jobs for them, and of course, it's seen as tailor-made for property developers putting together pricey leisure/retirement housing, some legitimate, some not, some genuinely wanting to invest in the region and benefit from it, which is fair enough, and some wanting to launder money gathered from much less reputable business, which isn't.

I rose quietly, put a dressing gown on and pulled a blind back enough to let me move on to the balcony. Mary was breathing regularly enough to suggest she was still fast asleep. I pulled the door closed behind me, because it was a pleasant but fresh morning, shaping up to be one of those glorious Devon days with the kind of light artists love and plenty of sunshine, even if a nippy little breeze was still playing about.

However, the dressing gown was adequate enough, and the Devon countryside stretching out below, full of what I suppose you could call the pastoral peace of morning, was enough to occupy my mind for a while.

But eventually, my thoughts always inevitably turned to whatever was happening with and to the people around me. My brother found himself in a difficult situation, but it's far from being the first time with that, and in spite of all its ramifications and mysteries, my mind turned away from it and towards my wife.

Mary and I married in our thirties – she was thirty-one, I was thirty-three. We had both had previous relationships, neither of them particularly successful, and we both had to persuade each other into re-marrying. Her first husband was adamant that he didn't want children, though he hadn't said that before they married, and she'd been rather indifferent herself. When we got together, we decided to try for a child before we got into our late thirties and found ourselves with the prospect of bringing up teenage kids in our fifties. Mary got pregnant, but miscarried after five months, in the second trimester of pregnancy, the cause being, it seemed, the longer-term condition of an overactive thyroid gland.

The treatment consisted of taking drugs called thionamides. These produced such a battery of side effects – nausea, heartburn, joint aches, headaches – that it made doing her job more difficult than it had ever been. She was constantly told that the side effects would go away, but they didn't, and we both realised eventually that another pregnancy could well be even more difficult than the first and might have the same outcome. She gradually withdrew from the treatment, feeling progressively better, and we both accepted that children weren't going to happen, having rejected adoption as too hit and miss to warrant such a lot of hope and emotional involvement. We concentrated on the positives – our careers, holidays abroad, money to spend on ourselves. Not long after that, Mary secured a head of English job and I became editor of my paper.

But even pleasure at what has been can be accompanied by a residual sadness at what might have been, and I think Mary, surrounded by children day in and day out, finds it difficult not to reflect on what her own children might have amounted to and is increasingly susceptible to adolescent noise and boisterousness. My earnings and our savings and investments mean that she does not have to continue in teaching at all if she decides not to; she certainly doesn't have to carry on as a head of department.

I was reflecting that I might have been getting my priorities confused when the blinds behind the French doors were opened completely, and Mary, also clad in a dressing gown, emerged on to the balcony. For all she needs her sleep, she also doesn't take to unfamiliar places, and her pallor and bleary eyes suggested she hadn't had the most peaceful of nights either.

I glanced at my watch. It was five past seven.

'Morning, my love. How was your night?' I said.

'Morning, darling. Fitful as regards sleep, even allowing for the wine with dinner. And after dinner, for that matter. But I have at least made a decision. Sometimes it takes a change of surroundings to make things clearer in my mind, and I suppose occasions like weddings do trigger a certain amount of life review, taking stock of what you're doing.'

'So what's the decision?'

She turned her chair directly to me and looked me in the eyes. 'I'm going to resign, Matt. I'm not sure how the timings will work out, and I may have to do the first half of next term, but I'll have left not later than the end of October.'

I have coveted this, wished in my heart for it, sometimes so strongly that I've even been tempted to lean on her or coerce her in some way. Her job is eating her up, and she deserves a proper retirement, or perhaps even a go at something else.

It was a moment for actions, not words. I went across and put an arm round her shoulders and a kiss on her cheek. She smiled, the eyes already showing more animation, as I sat back down.

'I've been through the alternatives about a thousand times now. Yes, they would probably let me revert to being just a member of the department, or even let me go part-time, but it wouldn't work. Every time anyone was annoyed or aggrieved by the new head of department, I'd get the brunt of it from the moaners and tale-tellers, and there are too many of them in teaching. They might even think about booting me upstairs; Roy Miles has been hinting at early retirement from deputy head for a while, and Sheila would probably prefer me to be her dogsbody than Roy, but I don't want to be Sheila's dogsbody. Out of the frying pan, etc. I'm going to take a few months off and think things over. It won't be full retirement, not at fifty-two, but something different; educational research, perhaps, admin, maybe in a university, a postgraduate degree if I can get funding. I'll think things through, Matt, talk to people.'

'Well, for what it's worth, I think you're absolutely right. Give yourself room to breathe.'

'And what about you?' she said, the eyes very much awake now.

'What about me?'

'Come on, Matt. This place, this weekend, is getting to be like a who-dun-it. Someone leaks the Harringtons' divorce proceedings the day before their son is due to get married. Councillor Joe Needham turns up at the family wedding, a man I've heard Peter fulminate about more than once. Kate and her fiancé seem to be working with the same company who are trying to secure a huge land deal with Peter's university. You talking to your guys at the paper almost as soon as we got here. I may be a simple school marm, but I've not daft. Or blind.'

'No, I know. But you have been tired. I was hoping, in my naivete, that this weekend in a nice hotel might be a relaxing break. Fat chance—'

My phone went. It appeared to be Kate, the bride, on the morning of her wedding. Further alarm bells rang. I looked at my watch. It was just coming up to twenty-five past seven.

'Kate? Is everything alright?'

'Morning, Uncle Matt. Are you and Aunt Mary up and about?'

I knew immediately something formal and professional was in the offing; those are the only occasions now when we still get 'uncled and aunted'.

'Sort of. We're sitting on the balcony in our dressing gowns.'

'Can I come and talk?'

'Of course you can, Kate. But it's your wedding morning, love. Aren't there things—'

'Yes, lots, but maybe not what you might expect. Robert's locked in conversation with the office in London, I gather my father is likewise embroiled with his university, and while none of us wanted to lug you into it, it seems you might soon be anyway. I'm only just down the corridor. Be with you in a minute.'

Mary and I hadn't had time to do anything except place a third chair on the balcony and exchange very puzzled glances when the knock came on the door. In she come, and even at this time of the morning, and even with a clear anxiety showing on her face, she was a lovely girl. Her hair was just a little bit dishevelled and there was still a bit of sleep in her eyes; she was dressed in a loose light blue top and jeans. Not unusually with Kate, there were no social nicety preliminaries. She sat herself down on the other side of the balcony table from us and started straight in.

'You're right, Uncle Matt, I've got things to do. Have I ever. But this is shaping up to be one very strange wedding. There's limited time available for questions and answers, so please just let me rattle on for a few minutes at least before we get to them, as we will.'

She took a breath and organised her thoughts. We waited dutifully.

'Dad got involved in setting up a land deal, and I mean a big land deal, for the university. The university made it known in relevant circles that it intended to sell a pretty huge chunk of land, some of which it's owned since Georgian times, but it wasn't going to just sell it to anyone; it took its environmental and development responsibilities seriously, and it would only sell to companies whose plans were approved by the local planning authorities. Companies were invited to submit their plans, and one very grand scheme was submitted by a large corporation, based mostly in Bulgaria and Turkey. Councillor Needham got in touch with the university to say that the company had also contacted him, and "on balance, I think it may have legs, though it will need a tweak or two", which is Needhamese for "I've done the deal, it'll get through planning, and there could be drinks in it for us all". The vice-chancellor, who sees my dad, with his political and economic expertise, as his sort of link to the real world, asked Dad to check things out with Needham. Dad knows him, and pretends to get on with him as well as he can, for the sake of keeping the university right with the local political set-up. But Dad was trying to be Machiavelli, like he does.'

'Tell me about it,' I said.

She shot a sharp glance at me, then smiled ruefully. 'Yes, Uncle Matt, you would know, wouldn't you? I was already an item, as I suppose you'd call it, with Robert, and Dad knew we were part of the land law operation of our legal company, of which Robert's dad is a director. Dad got in touch with me to ask me how I felt about it before he told Needham he'd back the deal if my company handled the investing company's interests in this company. He said it would be the perfect opportunity to see at close quarters how Needham worked, and maybe even get something on him which would finally take him out.'

I found myself unable to keep quiet at that. 'Didn't he know he would be putting you and your company at great risk? This isn't the Salvation Army we're dealing with here.'

She suddenly leant towards me. 'Uncle Matt, you know as well as we do what Needham does. Overpriced houses which start falling apart as soon as people move in; community facilities, even youth and children's, with dangerous, cheap equipment; tower blocks arguably even more dangerous than Grenfell. And that's not to mention some of the other activities these companies are going in for, to then launder their money through the safe British housing market.'

I leant right back. The only way, with Kate. 'I know all that well enough, Kate. I also know that my paper has been keeping tabs on Councillor Needham for years, and the kind of threats which come our way are not subtle. This is dangerous stuff, which needs to be handled very, very carefully.'

'May I just say something?' Mary said, and we both turned in her direction. I thought Kate noticed, perhaps for the first time, that Mary was not in the prime of health.

'This is a wedding day. A special day, the sort of day people are supposed to enjoy, the sort of day which remains in the treasured memories of people for years. Is this a day to be worrying about all of this? Wouldn't tomorrow do just as well? Or, even better, next week?'

Kate moved her chair closer and took Mary's hands in hers. I was going to be a spectator for a little while. But I was listening. Never underestimate what you can learn from listening to women. Or what you might incur by not.

'You are absolutely right, dear Aunt Mary, but you're talking about civilised people. Rob and I know enough about Needham now to know he sees occasions like this as the real meat behind deals, when you can check out the opposition right in their own backyard and start bringing them to heel. Needham, or the company he's working for, tried to intimidate Rob's father to make sure his son was a good boy and helped the deal go through with no problem; it seems they already suspect that Rob and I might be playing a double game. Rob's dad told them no deal, as he always would. Then, the day before the wedding, the Harrington divorce is suddenly in the public domain. None of the media, of course, will say where they got the information from.'

Her head dropped. Mary's hands returned her caress.

'Come on, love. And? I'm listening.'

Kate's voice seemed to change slightly, as if late girlhood was returning. 'Now they are leaning on my father. Via Needham, of course. All most regretfully expressed by Joe, posing as Dad's "best pal", one of the "most valuable type of friends, the tough love ones". My dad is known to be a "serial adulterer", mostly because my mother is, and has been for years, in love with Judi Curzon. This is now very likely to emerge on my wedding day, unless my dad agrees to lend his personal support to the company's proposals, which will pretty much ensure that it goes forward, the vice-chancellor not wanting to bother himself with the "small print", as he calls it. If that happens, I don't think Robert and I will be able to stop it, even though we are discovering some interesting stuff about the bidding company day by day.'

For the moment, aunt and niece continued with their hands together. Kate had reddened slightly, and she was clearly not far from tears. I think the last time I saw Kate cry, she would have been about nine years old.

I wasn't sure what to do at this juncture, but not for the first time, Mary did. She stood up and went behind Kate, to put her arms around her. For a moment or two, they rocked quietly together. Perhaps Kate is the daughter Mary never had, but she has always been very careful not to even attempt to supersede Helen, though I would not find it hard to believe that Helen can be a difficult woman to love.

Mary sat back down again. 'Does Tom know about this?' she said.

'Oh, yes. He's here. Has been since late last night.' A different kind of expression, almost a smile, came over her face.

'Have you seen much of Tom lately?' Mary looked across at me. Signal to rejoin.

'We've both been very busy. Must be six months at least.'

'Well, you'll probably be a bit taken aback when you do. He drinks next to nothing these days, he's lost weight and got fit. He applied for a job as an assistant manager of a large private gym a few weeks ago and got it.'

'Good for Tom,' I said. 'Would there be a woman involved at all?'

'Man of the world as ever, Uncle Matt. Yes, there would. A French girl called Claudette Comtois, from Normandy. She initially came over on an exchange scheme and worked as a swimming tutor at the leisure centre where Tom was working at the time. To be fair, Tom had already started sorting himself out; the rugby lads were starting to grow up, marry and move on, and Tom started finding the boys coming into the team a bit wearing. It wasn't exactly love at first sight, but it wasn't far off. Then, to the delight of both of them, the leisure centre were so impressed with Claudette that they offered her a permanent appointment. She will probably be my sister-in-law before much longer, and I'm happy with that. The effect she's had on Tom is incredible.'

Mary smiled as she got to her feet. 'I'll look forward to seeing my rejuvenated nephew. But logic says to me that you didn't just come in here to unburden yourself to us, Kate, my love. For it to be this urgent, you want us to do something, and that means you want Matt to do something, because I can't see how my teaching would get into this, while I can see very clearly how Matt's editorship would. I'm going to have a morning bath. It's now nearly eight o'clock, and we will need to get some sort of breakfast inside us on a day like this. Talk to Matt, and if he can do what you would like him to do, I don't doubt he will.'

Mary left us. The sun was out on the balcony now; as usual, it and Kate made a striking mix, though the troubled look on her face remained clear enough.

'OK then, Kate. What would you have me do, love?'

She seemed now to be awakening and turning to face the situation head on.

'You wouldn't think, on the basis of who's in this hotel, that our side would be outnumbered. But it's become apparent that some of the people booked in today and tonight who are not with the wedding are connected with Needham; my dad says he has recognised at least three or four who are known associates of

Needham, and Robert and I think a few others may be associated with the bidding company. We've also had a tip-off that the hotel may be under surveillance, and not by the police. They probably don't have many rooms left, but it's a sizeable hotel, and they have an arrangement with a kind of sister place a couple of miles away that mutual facilities can be used. Could you book a couple of your guys in, Matt, or at least arrange for them to come here for some occasion, invented or otherwise, a birthday or something?'

'I could, yes, though Needham would probably recognise them.'

'Yes, well that's what we want.' She was suddenly animated again. 'We want them to know that we have a side too, that what they sneak into the public domain may not be treated as sympathetically as they might hope, and any dirty tricks are going to have to be done in the local public gaze. Maybe you could even tip off that national you're linked with?'

'Yes, I could do that.'

'The easiest way to do this would be to frighten that bidding company off. Dad knows of a rival bid waiting in the wings from a more reputable outfit.'

'Of course, Kate. I will do anything I can. But there are two things I want you to do for me.'

A look of mock suspicion spread across her face, near enough to a smile to hearten me.

'Firstly, I don't know whether you know that the partner of Robert's gay ex-school friend is reputedly one of the best IT security men in the country. I met both of them last night. Neither of them told me that, but one or two others did, people with their own connections to security. He's reputedly a bit of a workaholic who takes equipment with him wherever he goes. If this hotel is under surveillance or sending in messages to people, he might well know something about it.'

'Yes, of course,' she said. 'I've met Simon; he's a poppet, and he works in the hotel business himself. I wouldn't exactly describe his partner as a poppet, but he does look like the kind of guy who knows what he's doing. And what was number two?'

'When all this is over, Kate, this thing which has got its fingers all over your wedding, maybe we could have another, smaller do, family only. Not another wedding, just an easy-going get-together. I think we might find, when all the family dirty linen has been washed in public, we might all have actually come closer together as a result. What do you think?'

'I think you're spot on, Uncle Matt. I would like that, and I'm sure Robert would. Thank you.'

I got to my feet. 'And now, beat it, young Kate. Your uncle needs to shower himself and put on his best bib and tucker for a very special wedding. Yours. And try not to worry. It's your day, Kate, yours and Robert's. Don't let anyone take it away from you.'

She planted a kiss on my cheek and went, hopefully in a better state of mind than when she came in. I needed to make a phone call or two, and while Mary was still in the bath, that was what I'd do.

The game was afoot. Cry Harry, and let slip the dogs of war. But let my niece have something resembling a wedding along the way.

Celia

A little to my surprise, I slept quite well, but then again, one could as well describe the state as drunken stupor as much as sleep. By my standards, last night was extravagantly indulgent. There was a time when impossible amounts of booze could be managed by the strategic use of a nearby plant pot, even allowing for the probable demise of someone's blamelessly innocent money plant or aspidistra. The option is no longer really available these days, with these cameras all over the place no doubt recording in detail alcoholic assaults on the hotel's carefully tended flora. In any case, for someone like me, who arrived at a life of plenty fairly late in it, paying the sort of prices demanded of hotel wine only to furtively disappear it amounts to something like criminal waste. But wine and conversation do go so very much hand in hand, and one can hardly go about saying to people, 'Don't speak to me until I've spent at least half an hour drinking this glass of wine.'

However, having spent 6.30 to 7.15am suspecting I might mark my dear grandson's wedding by snuffing it on the same day, I began to feel human enough to venture on a bath. Proper baths are an essential now as and when I stay in a hotel, which isn't very often these days. Standing naked under a positive torrent of water – there is no such thing as a gentle shower any more – and unable to see or hear anything other than water or steam while groping desperately around for somewhere to pick up or put down soap, shampoo, etc., is far from the ideal way to start any day, in my book. This is to assume that one is sufficiently au fait with the various bizarre combinations of knobs, handles and hooks associated with getting the shower to function in the first place.

A bath is an altogether more relaxing proposition, though even there, whether it will be a case of hot water coming out of one tap and cold water out of the other is far from assured, and alternately burnt and frozen fingers might be needed until a suitable combination is discovered, usually by trial and error.

But I was in one of the best suites in a four-star hotel, where the establishment has a vested interest in not having guests screaming at them in the morning about having a bathroom more difficult to operate than an average spaceship, and everything is logical and pleasant enough. By 7.45 I was suitably cleaned and relaxed and sitting in my comfortable dressing gown with my French windows open gazing out over Devon. It was not quite warm enough for the balcony, unfortunately, though I suspected it would be later on; Robert and his bride-to-be seemed to have a reasonable chance of being successful with the climate on their big day, however dodgy other things might be. Some of last night's peculiarities in the hotel grounds, etc. came back to me, and I knew again that simply dismissing them because of the wine wasn't the full story. I had had quite a lot by my standards, but little in comparison with the amounts being tanked down by my fellow diners, and I retired, I suspect, a good while before any of them did.

I was in the usual quandary of the single person in these situations. I've never quite got used to it, having spent so much time with Derek. Do I go to breakfast alone, gamely trying to work out coffee machines, toasters and the inevitable buffet arrangements and probably finishing up spreading both solids and liquids all over me, the floor, or both, or do I try room service? If I wanted breakfast in my room, I probably should have ordered it last night, and even if I had, I am going to have to eat it either on a bureau-looking desk thing or a coffee table so low slung I will get a crick in the back in the attempt to get the food from my plate to my mouth. Or I could forgo breakfast altogether, with the probable consequence of sitting in the wedding service with my stomach rumbling like a steam train leaving the station. Such are life's dilemmas.

But it is all to reckon without my dear son Malcolm. I was still gazing out over Devon, trying to resolve life's dilemmas or persuade them to sod off for a while, when my room phone sounded, with a peculiar click/quack like an asthmatic duck.

I picked it up with grave suspicions, but it was Malcolm's voice on the other end. 'Mum, I wondered if you might like to join me for breakfast?'

'I would love to, dear, but there is a bit of a snag, isn't there? You have a wife?'

'Barbara and I ordered a breakfast to be delivered to the room last night; there are various media people in and around the hotel, and we could not have been sure of being allowed to have breakfast in peace downstairs on the occasion of our son's wedding. However,

Barbara finds the atmosphere of the hotel oppressive; there are still media people popping up at us from time to time. She's decided to leave the hotel until it's time to dress for the wedding. There is a pleasant little town only a few miles away, and of course we have Ron at our disposal. So I have rather more breakfast than I can do on my own, and I'm guessing you are perhaps a little daunted at the prospect of managing breakfast downstairs?'

Having a dutiful son is a joy; having a dutiful son who is also intelligent is a positive delight. Sitting in for Barbara is not my favourite role, but at least Malcolm and I could have a civilised conversation without her oppressive sour prune silence all around us.

'How very thoughtful of you, darling. Yes, I've always regarded hotel breakfast rooms as assault courses, essentially, and as in so many areas of life, I miss your father's easy competence with these things. I would love to join you; I will put on something respectable and come over to you now.'

There has always been an element of this with Malcolm; for all his brashness and assertion, a constant streak of thoughtfulness and consideration towards his nearest and dearest has been characteristic of him since childhood. And I know well enough that he would be hurting inside now, not just because of the break-up of his marriage but because of the public nature of it, which I remained unconvinced was an accident. Lawyers can be targets of people's vengeance when they work in contentious areas, which almost all of them do; in Malcolm's case, more so than most. There can be few more bitter areas of human conflict than divorces, and whenever Malcolm has represented one half of the parties concerned, he will either be championing the winner or the loser, meaning one party or the other is likely to be aggrieved, possibly permanently. Nevertheless, I hoped the culprit would be tracked down; it was a mean-spirited and petty-minded thing to do, to announce a couple's separation against their wishes and on the day of their son's wedding. Derek would probably and inelegantly, I know, refer to such a deed as a 'shit trick', and, scatological as the phrase may be, it can sometimes be the most accurate description.

Malcolm had yet to don a tie and suit jacket, but he was otherwise dressed for the day. Wedding attire, such a problematic and convoluted area for women, is a breeze for men, and I don't think most of them are all that sorry about it.

His breakfast abundance had already been delivered by the time I arrived, and I knew I had to be careful not to sabotage my lunch appetite, but in my experience, wedding lunches never ever start on time and because of the tension crackling around the dinner table, I didn't do myself particular justice with the food last night, even if I managed it with the wine. There was a startlingly good marmalade, by hotel standards, and some very tasty local cheese and ham. The Full English is a bit too much for me these days, especially on summer mornings, and I did myself quite well by browsing and picking. Malcolm also tucked in; I suspected he also found last night's dinner table rather difficult.

For a while, we contented ourselves with inconsequential remarks concerning the food and the suite, which was bigger than mine, of course, and exceptionally well appointed. Afterwards, we took the remains of the coffee pot out on to the balcony; fully dressed, I could cope with the morning air and Malcolm was quite comfortable in his shirt. He's always had a curious indifference to temperatures, in either direction. I suspect that when boys go to the kind of school Malcolm attended, their extremes of cold showers and long runs on warm summer days develops this sort of physical toughness. Once upon a time, which included Derek's schooldays, the regime would also have included uncompromising beatings on regular occasions, but fortunately a certain enlightenment had dawned by the time of Malcolm's education. In my case, discipline could probably best be described as mean, with 'gatings', 'groundings', detentions and the like. Even occasionally, fines, particularly resented by girls whose parental allowances were not too generous.

We turned to the issues of the day quite rapidly. My son, who has always enjoyed the rudest of rude good health, was looking pale, by his standards, and there was an unaccustomed downcast tone to him this morning, on which should have been a happy occasion.

'Have you tracked down the culprit yet, Malcolm?'

'Culprit, Mum?'

'Yes, culprit. I simply refuse to believe that news emerging of a divorce lawyer's divorce on the day of his son's wedding is just bad luck or media carelessness.'

'Oh, I know who did it.'

'Really? Are you going to sue or something? And how on earth did they know?'

I could see him hesitating, wondering whether he could trust the old lady in such matters, even allowing for the fact that the old lady in question is his mother, who has been round life's houses so many times that nothing, but nothing, could come as a surprise. It was suddenly very exasperating.

I put my coffee down. If one has determined on expostulating in a vaguely indignant manner, it does rather take away the effect of it if one also precipitates coffee over one's person, even if one isn't yet in one's wedding finery.

'For goodness' sake, Malcolm. I do try not to whinge on about the penalties of age, because I get enough of it in the village. They will buttonhole one and then go into their ailments in great and occasionally stomach-churning detail, usually followed by lists of what they consequently can and can't do, which can also curl the toes at times. But that's all par for the course, as Derek would have said. What really niggles is being parked permanently on the sidelines because people think you can't cope with reality anymore. I was a professional wife, essentially, which perhaps is no longer very fashionable, but Derek moved very much in the business world, where dirty tricks and dubious practices abound. I grew up in a family business atmosphere myself, as you know, and once Derek realised, as he did early on, that I was neither naïve nor stupid, we discussed everything together, and yes, I'm afraid we could pull a dirty trick or two ourselves if it really needed to happen. Why isn't it obvious that it's usually only people who can cope with reality who get to be old in the first place? Ever since we gathered in this hotel, it's been obvious to me that something is going on; the divorce news being so gracelessly released, people apparently keeping this hotel under surveillance, the presence in the assembly of Councillor something or other, a local villain from way back, some say, regardless of whether he's a friend of Peter Densham. I could go on. What is going on?'

He looked at me rather ruefully, that look I can remember from his early days when I had tumbled to something he didn't think I was clever enough to tumble to. 'It's a long story, Mum.'

I looked at my watch. 'It's now nine o'clock. The wedding ceremony is at eleven thirty. If Barbara doesn't like the hotel atmosphere, and she can hardly be blamed for that, I doubt very much whether she'll be back before ten thirty. We have at least an hour, Malcolm. If Barbara does come back earlier, of course I'll leave.'

He is my own child, but even now I struggle to read him. He was obviously wrestling with himself. He sipped at a coffee which was probably stone cold and looked across at me several times. I don't think he ever fully understood that when he started having business conversations with Derek, the gist of them would be relayed to me later by Derek, who rarely did anything important without consulting me. I knew well enough leaving the boys to their games made it much less likely that they would play nicely.

He took a deep breath, and then the decision was made. I know him quite well enough to recognise that happening.

'OK, Mum, I'll tell you the story as I understand it now, having discussed it with the various principals. It will make a pleasant change to confide in a woman I actually love.'

My heart wrenched. 'Oh, Malcolm. Is the marriage as bad as that?'

'Pretty much. However I would characterise what happens between Barbara and me, it's been a long time, if ever, since it could realistically be described as "love". But that to one side. We will have time enough to dissect what went wrong with Barbara and me, and it would be less than honest of me to describe it as all her fault. Far from it. For another time, Mum. As for this case, the initial approach was to Kate Densham, who works in the same chambers as Robert. As you know, Robert decided not to work in the same chambers as me, because he was afraid of walking in my shadow.'

'Or he wanted to specialise in a different area of law, Malcolm.'

'Yes, possibly. But I think I was the main reason.'

You would, I said, but to myself. Mummy knows when to keep schtum.

'Robert had been with his chambers for not much over a year when Kate arrived. I don't know about love at first sight, but there was certainly a strong attraction from the start; Kate is smart, in both senses of the term.'

'As is Robert.'

'Well, yes, I would say so, but I'm his father. However, Kate was approached by Councillor Needham, who she knew through her father mentioning him. He told her he was a friend of both her father and her uncle. Friend is and was pushing it a bit; Peter and his brother Matthew know him, certainly, and it is in their interests to keep him on board, as it were. Peter has the university's interests at heart, and Matthew is editor of the leading local newspaper; they both have a vested interest in local politicians, though I gather they both privately regard the man as odious.

'Kate was asked to act for a company which was making a planning proposal to buy a substantial plot of land, much of which is presently owned by the university, for what they described as a "leisure housing development", including several on site restaurants and shops, a sports centre, etc., and houses and apartments which would be clearly be sold as holiday or second homes. Kate was approached because, even allowing for her relative youth, she was London-based, she knew a lot about the local area where the development was to be set, and her father was a prominent figure at the university.

'Needham said he had no personal investment in the proposal and it would be considered by the planning committee in the usual way, but he added that he thought it was a sound idea; the development was promised to be upmarket and very generously budgeted. The university would make a great deal of money, with which they could do constructive educational projects, and the local area would be provided with a considerable amount of employment, with the prospect of a lot of new money coming into the area as well.

'Kate consulted Robert, who said he had already come across the company making the proposal, and rumours constantly linked them with dubious activities including trafficking, prostitution and modern slavery. Rumours were all they were, and attempts to find more concrete proof had sometimes resulted in investigators having sudden accidents or even disappearing completely.'

'Oh, my God.'

'Quite. It gets worse, I'm afraid. Robert and Kate then made a decision which, in my book, can kindly be described as reckless, and perhaps not so kindly as stupidly foolhardy, with all the blithe confidence of youth. Kate knew Needham and Robert knew the company. They thought that if they took the case on, they could play a double game, and perhaps gather the necessary evidence to take the company out of business. Kate also felt strongly that what the area needed was affordable housing for the local people, not yet more expensive holiday and leisure homes. She told Robert that one of the reasons why she applied to a London chambers was because working on London levels of salary would make it easier for her to get together enough money to at least buy a house in Devon for her and her future husband, whoever he may be, even if London itself might still be beyond their means. She also still loved Devon, and she believed the two main reasons why so many young people left Devon were the lack of varied employment and the abundance of leisure housing and second homes crowding out the locals.'

'The more I hear of this girl, the more I like her, reckless or not,' I said.

'Oh, I suspect the recklessness was largely Robert. He has always had the tendency, from time to time, to plunge in feet first without thinking the thing through properly.'

'So speaks the father anxious not to let the boy get above himself. Derek used to say the same thing about you at times. Well, so did I.'

'Thank you, Mother. Nice to know you both had such faith in me.'

'Oh, we had faith enough in you, darling. We just didn't have any illusions. Charging off to a then obscure London law firm with the intention of specialising in divorce issues when you were twenty-two, had yet to have a serious relationship, let alone a divorce, and hardly had two pennies to your name, some would say that was just a bit reckless. But that's water under the bridge. This isn't. Please go on.'

He sighed, and shook his head, gazing with sudden fascination at the coffee pot. 'Well, whoever the main driving force was, Kate and Robert agreed to take the case on, and that's when the trouble started. They initially tried to say the case should be relatively straightforward if the chairman of the planning committee had already decided it was a good idea, but they needed evidence of the company's probity and bona fides, which meant seeing the company's books and establishing whether they had any dubious connections. The company began to suspect their motives.'

'Why didn't it just sack them?'

'Well, firstly because a pretty watertight contract had been signed, and secondly because they needed lawyers either in Devon or London; a company being represented by foreign lawyers who might or might not know the intricacies of UK land and property law would be unlikely to be able to push through such a substantial development as this. Devon lawyers would know the local terrain, but many of them have become wary of developments like this, which are not popular locally. Many London lawyers are aware of this company's murky reputation and their rough dealings, and in any case, the first thing they'd do is contact Robert and Kate's chambers to get more information. Robert and Kate's chambers would also sue them for a lot of money, and being in the UK, they'd probably win.'

'So they decided to intimidate people into getting their way?'

He looked at me as if the scales about Mummy were falling from his eyes.

'Just so. They let Robert and Kate have a certain amount of information, but they accompanied that by remarks along the lines of "inadequate representation could have wider consequences; sadly, others can get dragged in to these matters". Robert and Kate stuck to their guns about the extent and type of information they needed, and some interesting links started to be uncovered. Robert also got in touch with his ex-university friend, Giles Cavendish, who he knew had become what in common parlance has become known as a "spook", as in working for a secretive government organisation. He told Giles about the case and sought his advice, without mentioning any involvement with Giles's department; Giles is simply classified as a civil servant. Without committing himself to anything, Giles said he did know the organisation concerned, or the organisation behind the organisation, and he thought it would make sense for him to have a personal interest in Robert's wedding. For them to work together without suspicions being aroused, Giles suggested he should be given a function in the wedding, and the one which would create least suspicion would be for him to be Robert's best man. The organisation would know, or they would find out, what Giles did for a living, but the university connection was still there. Personal occasions like weddings were known to be typical of the many ways the organisation would use to find to put pressure on the principals involved. When the organisation realised Giles was best man, their suspicions grew, in spite of the university connection, and that's when they decided to begin turning a few screws. Robert was told the "circumstances of the wedding could become more difficult" if the planning proposal was not well on the way to completion by the wedding. They'd found out that Barbara and I were divorcing on the grounds of adultery—'

'What? Oh, Malcolm, no.'

His face suddenly had the gleam of boyhood 'I'm found out' in the eyes.

'Yes. Well, affairs-wise, it's actually two-one to me. I had the first, not long after Barbara had cut short conjugal relations altogether, on the grounds that a further pregnancy would be very difficult for her after the trouble she had with Robert, and her taste for love-making just for the hell of it had somewhat ebbed away. A friend of a friend, going back to before I'd met Barbara. Whether to pay me back or whether her taste for love-making just no longer included me, she then had a fling with some guy she'd called in to make our internal décor more to her taste. So when, not long after that, a young – well, younger than me – lawyer in another chambers near us gave me the come-on, I didn't see too many reasons for refusing. In fact, I suppose I was quite flattered.'

For several seconds, I simply didn't know what to say. I never have seen Malcolm as any kind of Lothario, but of course, he's my son, and guessing the sexual attraction of one's own offspring is pretty much beyond most parents, I suspect.

Malcolm misunderstood my silence. 'None of it was meant to happen, Mum,' he said quietly.

'What? Oh, no, Malcolm. I'm not in the business of being censorious in these things. Derek was never, to my knowledge, unfaithful to me, and I had quite a sophisticated network, I can tell you. He was an attractive and quite well-heeled man, and I didn't want to lose him. I've had one or two chances myself, of course, but I really couldn't see the point of making life so complicated.'

'It is certainly that, yes. In any event, we were threatened with that, and of course, Robert consulted me, offering to withdraw from representing the company. I said I suspected that they would probably be annoyed with that as well, and that the divorce petition would probably soon come out anyway. Barbara felt the same. Barbara is divorcing me on the grounds of adultery, and while I should perhaps contest it, since she has herself also been adulterous, I don't want us finishing up having our lives dragged through the mire in court – Barbara's frigidity, my double betrayal, her betrayal of me—'

He stopped, as near to tears as I have seen him since he was ten years old. As near as I was myself. Any parent tries to prepare their sons and daughters to go off in the world and be successful without getting hurt. Perhaps Derek and I concentrated too much on the successful and not enough on the getting hurt. Boys are much more delicate creatures that they would want you to think they are, and keeping track of how they're feeling can be very difficult once all the male barriers are up.

At this point, someone knocked and asked to come in to take the breakfast stuff away. I couldn't help wondering how everything connected with this wedding was coming across to them. Awkward silences and tense situations must have puzzled them. On the other hand, perhaps not. Weddings are about people, some of whom have never met each other, getting together and at least making a show of having a good time. It's sometimes difficult enough even within families, let alone having a totally unfamiliar family to deal with.

But the silence at least allowed Malcolm to recover himself. He continued.

'So Robert and Kate know they really are in a fight, and possibly a dangerous one. We know people have been seen apparently watching the hotel, probably with someone on the inside filtering out information to them on what's going on. They don't seem like the kind of people who will hold back on doing what they think they need to. I think they also have something on Peter Densham, possibly to do with the relationship between his wife and her old school friend. If Robert and Kate don't do as they're told, which means at least giving the nod to Needham that their investigations have concluded and the company are a fit and proper organisation to take this project through, then their wedding will be pretty much wrecked, and that will just be the start of it. But Robert and Kate are very young, and very tough – amazingly so, given their years – and they are getting nods themselves, from Giles Cavendish, from Kate's uncle Matthew Densham, whose paper has a whole dossier on Needham, and from the fruits of their own investigations. They could soon have enough to prove this company's involvement in various very dubious areas and bring their whole operation crashing down around their ears.'

I found myself looking at the carpet, looking but not seeing. Once again, Malcolm put his own take on my silence. Perhaps it's a lawyer's habit.

'So there you are, Mum. Now you know. Yes, you're right in the situation now, and I should think it's completely ruined the entire wedding for you and made you acutely anxious about your grandson and his bride—'

I raised my head. 'No, Malcolm, I'm not daunted to that extent. Your father and I had one or two hairy situations to deal with; when you qualified as a lawyer, your advice at times eased that burden. I'm proud of you all for standing up for what you believe in against these guttersnipe people, and I'm especially proud of the guts and integrity of my son and grandson. And I have a suggestion to make.'

'Make it, please. The more ideas we have, the better it will be.'

'It isn't a particularly revolutionary or sensational an idea, but I think you should inform the police. Or more specifically, I think Giles Cavendish, who will clearly have a good deal of clout in matters like this, should inform the police. These people are breaking the law in several ways. They are keeping the hotel under surveillance, which they're not entitled to do; only properly authorised people like the police can do that. They are also practising blackmail, and that's illegal too. And the very fact that people acting on behalf of this company are breaking the law should be enough to disqualify it from being allowed to go ahead with a property investment project in this country. On more than one occasion, Derek and I had to deal with concerns who were all too willing to invest in our business. These things have to be checked, or you can find yourself inadvertently mixed up with some very dodgy organisations.'

'They will deny any involvement, of course,' Malcolm said, looking a little shell-shocked, his eyes as wide as if his pet monkey had just uttered the big speech from *Hamlet*.

'Check Needham's phone,' I said. 'Arrest those men lurking outside and check their phones. Look at who's been talking to whom. People can't be allowed to invest in UK property if they have broken UK law in a number of serious ways.'

For fully two minutes, Malcolm sat there, half staring at me and half working his little grey cells. Then he spoke again, with a slightly different, more measured tone. 'Yes, there's a lot in that.

This could all be rather simpler than we thought. Perhaps we've all been so buried in the woods we haven't been able to see the trees. Maybe it doesn't need to be weeks and weeks dragging through the courts—'

We heard the clunk of lift doors opening at the end of our corridor, followed by a cough, followed by footsteps coming towards the room. Both the cough and the walk were unmistakably Barbara. When you've known someone for as long as Malcolm and I have known Barbara, you know the coughs and the walks well enough. We'd probably have known her by a sniff.

'Oh, God,' said Malcolm, and I didn't blame him. An upper and downer with Barbara was about the last thing he wanted on the morning of what was supposed to be the joyous occasion of his only child's marriage, but it looked like that was what he was going to get when she discovered hubby had been having a heart-to-heart with his mum.

Enter Barbara, and although I was expecting her speciality 'what drain did you crawl out of' look, it isn't what I got. Her expression was almost neutral, and around her lips an expression vaguely resembling a smile lingered, though I'm no expert on what Barbara's smiles looked like.

'Celia. Hello. Is there a problem?'

I got up. Malcolm found his voice. 'Mum had forgotten to order breakfast and didn't want to brave the breakfast room. So I offered her part of ours, since you clearly didn't want it.'

'Absolutely,' she said, somewhat to my surprise. 'I find it difficult, especially with all the food which will be facing us later. Hope you enjoyed it, Celia.'

'Very much so,' I said. 'But now, if you'll excuse me, I've got to go and get dressed for the occasion. Big day for Grannie; effort to be made.'

Barbara looked at her watch. 'Twenty to ten. We should be wandering down not long after eleven. I'd appreciate it if you could give me five more minutes, Celia. What I have to say does concern you as well.'

Mystified and intrigued, I sat back down again. Barbara took a chair for herself and sat to Malcolm's left and my right. Yes, that thing like a smile happened again. 'I needed time to think. Ron drove me to a peaceful spot where I could walk and think undisturbed, which I certainly can't in this hotel.'

I nodded; I could understand that. Malcolm kept on staring at the floor.

'I want to drop the divorce proceedings.'

That brought Malcolm's head up and my jaw down.

'I resent these people who are making mischief and will enjoy making them look silly. But that's not the main reason. Now that this business is in the public domain, we will have the media's noses in it even if we try to do it as smoothly as possible. Once they have sniffed out the word adultery, which I don't think they have yet, or we would have heard about it, they will start dragging other people into it. Even if not in court, it will still mean gross intrusions into our private lives. I know from your own cases just how much it does cost people, and I don't mean just financially.'

She paused, perhaps to see the impact of her words. Malcolm and I remained speechless.

'I think we should agree to nothing more than separation for a while. I would prefer to live in the house for the time being; you already have a flat in London, Malcolm, when cases are on. You could easily rent something grander for a few years if you wished. Perhaps two or three years. If, by that time, either or both of us have met someone else, we can part amicably with an uncontested action. In the meantime, Malcolm, I won't make any claims on your salary. The house is paid for, and as you know, I've always had my own money.'

I've always suspected her of 'coming from money' because of her family background and her indifference to finding jobs. And now, all those Selfridges, etc. trips came into a new perspective. So she'd been a woman of independent means all this time, and never thought to tell me. Yes, it was her business, but she could so clearly have made me think better of her, and she simply hadn't been concerned enough to do so. I felt both glad and sorry.

This was the obvious point where Malcolm needed to say something, but for a little while, he didn't. He seemed to be sizing up the pair of us, the two prominent women in his life. Just when the silence was starting to stretch to uncomfortable lengths, he spoke, and I saw that mind-made-up look again.

'I think what you're suggesting is eminently fair, Barbara, and I'm happy to go along with it in every particular. The London flat is comfortable enough and I suppose I tend to spend more time in it than I do at the house anyway; perhaps that's been part of the trouble. I'm sorry it hasn't ultimately worked for us, but as you say, having our private lives paraded through courtrooms makes no sense at all. There's one more thing. I know the father of the groom doesn't traditionally say much at weddings, but it would please me, and I think probably you as well, to make a public denial of our supposed separation, firstly, to rescue Robert's day as much as we can, and secondly, to demonstrate to these people who are trying to intimate us that they can't and won't.'

Now it was Barbara's turn to think things over, but the atmosphere of entente cordiale had got in amongst the two of them to such an extent that it was rather like a battlefield after the battle; no-one had the energy left to do anything else but sit round the campfire. It is exhausting and demoralising to be constantly at loggerheads with someone you see or talk to practically every day of your life. Derek and I had various crises to get through, but none of them was about our relationship; we had occasional set-tos, but nothing dragging on for months and years, as it had been doing for Malcolm and Barbara. Like bashing your head against a brick wall, it's most fun when it stops.

'Yes,' said Barbara, in a tone of voice I've rarely heard from her. 'Yes, Malcolm, I think I would like that, though you would do well to ask Peter Densham first.'

'Oh, of course. And I think we should both have a word with Robert, when we get the chance. I think it would boost his morale on what could be a difficult day.'

'I'll make the chance.'

I got up again, and both of them did too. It is refreshing to see old-fashioned good manners now and then.

'Now I must go and make myself look presentable. One gets to the age where this can mean a rather more laborious effort than it used to, and a certain amount of time and effort becomes necessary. Looking windswept and unkempt when young can come across as spontaneous; when old, it comes across as drunk.'

They both smiled simultaneously, and it had been so long since I'd seen that happen that I was genuinely touched. To Barbara's initial alarm and then at least convincing-looking pleasure – whatever else she is, the woman is well-bred, out of that old country gentry family of hers – I took her hand and planted a kiss on her cheek.

'When all the formalities are over, Barbara,' I said, 'and we are both having a well-deserved restorative or two, perhaps we can talk. Properly.'

'Yes, Celia, I would like that,' she said, and to my surprise, the kiss was returned. I moved across to Malcolm.

'We're so glad you're here for this day, Mum.'

'Yes, darling, so am I.'

A final cheek kiss, and I made my exit. I'm good on exit moments.

I made my way back to my own suite, and just as I reached my door, I saw Robert, bare-torsoed and in his jeans, apparently concluding a conspiratorial-sounding sotto voce conversation with Giles Cavendish, who was, of course, already in his finery. As Robert made to shut the door, I called down to him.

A sotto voce remark emerged from Kate in the room behind him, and he was momentarily torn between his fiancée and his grandmother, but he said, 'It's Gran, give me a minute, Kate,' which was encouraging; however clever and attractive the girl might be, I don't care for my grandson turning into a doormat. Many traditional wedding devotees would be shocked to the core at the bride and groom being in the same room together on their wedding morning, but young people today seem to make up their own rules as they go along.

He left the door slightly ajar and headed up towards me, with the habitual Robert smile.

I didn't want to be the cause of a row on their wedding day, so I grimaced at him. 'Does Kate need you for something, darling?'

'Kate has me for the rest of my life, Gran. I think I can spare you a minute or two.'

I looked at the boy's handsome face, open smile and torso like a classical statue and thought, well, girl, you haven't done so badly for yourself. Don't be greedy.

'Is everything alright?' I said – fishing, I suppose, if I'm being honest.

'Oh, yes. There are so many consultations, conversations and information flying about that it may well be like no other wedding you've ever been to before, and I dare say you've been to a few.'

I lowered my voice. 'Your father has told me the gist of what's going on. Those people watching the hotel are acting illegally, both with that and with trying to intimidate people. You might be best advised to call the police. Your grandfather and I were not unfamiliar with such situations.'

His face showed almost exactly the same monkey-reciting-*Hamlet* expression as his father's. 'Nothing much gets past you,

Gran, does it? After the conversation I've just had with Giles, something even grander than the police may be on their way. But hush-hush for the moment. We think we've just about got enough on them, and we're organising it.'

His voice and manner were so convincing, half-naked and bare-footed as he was, that the fact of him being a young lawyer heading for the top was becoming very credible indeed. It is difficult for the old sometimes, for whom time tends to race by; the days when he was an eager little boy with a ready smile and a tendency to ask endless and sometimes unanswerable questions seems not much more than yesterday.

'Busy as you are, Robert, I wouldn't waste much more time before you talk to your parents. I think they have something they want to tell you. Something good, that is.'

I nodded and smiled as I turned into my suite, thinking how much more fun it was being where the living is going on than out in old-lady wilderness.

Only when I was donning my gladrags did it dawn on me that this might be the last big occasion where I could be where the living is.

Well, I made myself think, all the more reason to make the best of it.

Phyllis

I was drifting between asleep and awake from dawn onwards. Even after I heard movement, there was a reluctance in me to leave my sleep, partly to do with the wine intake, no doubt, but also because of a peculiarly vivid if rather confused dream which seemed to cling around me and demand it got the chance to live its natural span, whatever that might be. I suppose I do usually dream – most people do, it seems – but I rarely remember them, and even when I do, they're usually better forgotten.

I was cavorting around with David Bennett behind some miscellaneous building. We were both stark naked, and too interested in looking, examining and fiddling about to get round to 'going all the way', as they used to say then. We did fool about a few times; I think this one was some kind of a dare, to have totally naked sex somewhere on the school premises. Dares he could do, and even when his body was being as desperately unsubtle as boys' bodies can be, making my eyes stand out from my head, he just saw it as fun time; he didn't seem to have a modicum of embarrassment about it. I was almost dying with embarrassment, trying not to look at my inadequate little breasts and wondering how tits that size could possibly be on the same body as my enormous bum – again, as I saw it at the time. He didn't see it like that; he was quite fascinated with both, which pleased me and scared me witless at the same time. It became obvious that the way things were going, that huge boner of his could well be right in me quite soon, and the really dangerous thing was that seemed to be what I urgently wanted to happen.

I got hold of it, and it has to be said that my idea was to direct it to where I wanted it to go, but he, to his eternal credit, I suppose, stopped the direction of my hand even though he had no problem with it staying where it was.

'Why don't you just watch what it can do before you decide you want that happening inside you?' he whispered.

I'd been around long enough to know what he meant. He wasn't my first hand job. I don't think I was a particularly tarty girl, I just reckoned that if the deal was that they stuck those things in you, I could at least get to know a bit more about them; there was no way that I intended to be one of these girls who wakes up one day to find herself pregnant and wonders what the hell happened and when. They did the theory at school, sort of, but a girl needs the practical as well as the theoretical and my parents were the kind of people who would react to anyone saying the words 'vagina' or 'penis' in front of them by looking at them as if they'd just shat on the floor.

So I went at it, and it didn't take long; once again, what it did to the boy startled the hell out of me, and the spectacular consequences did make his point for him; he was young, and let's say productive, and all that cascading inside me would have had every chance in the world of turning me into a single mum at the age of sixteen, which wasn't the life pattern I'd mapped out for myself.

So we did that stuff, and it wasn't all one-way traffic by any means; he actually knew how to bring a girl to orgasm without the cock being involved at the crucial time, and that impressed me, even though it made me wonder just how long and with how many people he'd been doing this. Yes, there was always a respectable eye on the girl's interests, but his were well represented too. He was dare, not daredevil.

Anyway, back to the dream, and it was at that moment of David's climax, accompanied by a noise from him which I was sure would summon every teacher on patrol to us within seconds, that I looked to my right and saw, not a manky old disused sports pavilion, but the large French windows of a hotel, with various people, including the Harringtons and the Denshams and Judi bloody Curzon, gazing down at the naked adolescent David Bennett and Phyllis Damerell. And right at the front of the assembled multitude was my husband Colin, looking like he wanted to murder someone. David, or David as he was, waved cheerily and pointed his bottom towards them. Colin crashed the door open and came through it.

At this moment, I half woke up. Very Freudian, I was thinking drowsily to myself, but quite fun all the same and probably more fun than pre-breakfast chat with Colin.

Then I heard the shower going and realised he was getting up. Then I dropped back off again, though the dream had gone, which is maybe, I think, the story of my life. When I woke again, and this time fully at last, even allowing for a slight headache, I realised I was on my own. For a moment, I thought he had left the hotel, but no, his clothes were still in the wardrobe, including his wedding-attending suit.

Since this room didn't have a balcony and I tired of the view of the car park about three minutes after first seeing it, I plunged recklessly into the shower, after which I put on a few basic garments and made myself a coffee from the tray generously provided. I was sipping gingerly at this when the spouse returned. He was dressed in suit trousers and an open-necked white shirt; like many men, he doesn't actually like wearing ties much and only wears them for whatever length of time he has to.

I was more relaxed now and recovering from the night before, but when he was being as graceless as he was at the moment, I did feel inclined to point out that I don't like it.

'You might have waited until you knew that I didn't want to go to breakfast.'

'Might I,' he said, but it wasn't a question, it was a statement. I wasn't quite sure where this was leading to now; another row on top of last night's exchanges wasn't going to make for a good day. But Colin hadn't finished.

'We've been in hotels many times before, Phyllis, both in this country and abroad. You don't like breakfast rooms, a fact which you make very obvious whenever you go down to one by moaning about everything; the food, the seating, the strange coffee machine or toaster. You often decide you don't want to go down to breakfast at all, and usually by the time you make your mind up, breakfast is just about finished, as it is now. So I went to breakfast while I had the chance. So sue me.'

This was so loaded and pointed that I was momentarily knocked out of my stride. But it wasn't a tirade I could let go.

'That all may or may not be true. I still think you could have asked me—'

Suddenly, he was next to me, sitting on the bed and leaning forward. And there were, there really were, tears in his eyes.

'Is there any point to this, Phyllis? Is this what we want to be doing for the rest of our lives, niggling and biting at each other like two ferrets in a sack? I'm tired, I'm working all the hours God sends, I want relaxation, peace and harmony on the rare occasions when I get a bit of time off, and I'm not getting it. I got to the hotel last night as soon as I could, and even then I had to rely on a fairly junior assistant manager to close and lock the place, which could rebound on me big time if he'd made a pig's ear of it, which fortunately he didn't. I get here and find you making goo-goo eyes with some guy I've never met—'

'You've got someone else, haven't you, Colin?'

He looked at me as if I'd just spoken Greek. 'Someone else? When the hell do you think I would get time to have an affair, Phyllis? I'm at that store twelve hours a day, and that's before travel time. Even if I ever did get time for the occasional knee-trembler in a back storeroom or something, I'd be too knackered to raise a cheer.'

His eyes were still moist. I reached over and touched his arm, feeling the hard muscle there and remembering how that used to turn me on.

'Isn't it time you thought about doing something else, Colin?'

'Such as what? I'm not exactly top of the heap, Phyllis. I've got no fancy degrees, no posh connections or inherited money. I'm nearer fifty than forty. What else would I do, and what's the odds I'd be any better off?'

A pause. This was more immediate connection than we'd managed for some time, and we were both taken aback with the force of it.

'You won't be any better off if you're dead, Colin,' I said, wondering at my own words, emerging with such quiet certainty.

For a moment, he daggered me with his eyes, then a look like a just-punished boy. 'That's below the belt, Phyllis.'

'Below the belt? God, Colin, I'm your wife, if anyone in the world should be telling you that you are slowly killing yourself, I should.'

He sat there, nodding slowly to himself. 'So what if I resigned? Could you face that uncertainty, that anxiety, about whether I'd ever get another job? Could you stand me being at home all day?'

Now, I thought, we were finally talking. For so long now, this guy, who was once the greatest presence in my life, had been a tetchy and exhausted occasional visitor to it. I didn't know if we've got past the stage of being able to rescue it, but suddenly we were in discussions. In twenty minutes, as the clock edged on and I knew more and more that we should be doing something about getting dressed and ready, we took a good look at what might be possible. It seemed the company have a voluntary redundancy scheme, though senior management were not usually counted as eligible. It seemed he could take a lump sum and a pension, though it would be way down on what he would have got if he served his full term. It seemed there might be a possibility of ill-health retirement, if the GP supported him. I should have known all this. If I hadn't been so fond of being Dolly Daydream living vicariously in the lives of the posh neighbours rather than attempting to put my own house in order, this could have been sorted by now. Then he dropped a real humdinger into the conversation.

'They owe me about twelve weeks' leave by now, because of hours worked.'

'What? Well, why don't you take a bit of it?'

'Well, it's generally the way that they prefer you to take it when it suits them.'

'Which it never will. As far as I'm understanding it, all these entitlements you're telling me about are contractual agreements, which they're legally obliged to honour?'

'Yes, I dare say. But there's always the small print, isn't there?'

'You're in a professional association, aren't you? I know they don't like calling themselves a union, the management guys.'

'Yes, I am. Charlie Temple, I think it is, in our region.'

'Well, why don't you talk to him to prepare the ground? Then go see the GP, Pam Brooks; she's good, you know that. I think you wouldn't need to have much of a medical, Colin, to show that you're stressed out. Then tell them you're taking three weeks of the leave you're entitled to, with the backing of your doctor. We'll go on holiday somewhere nice, spend some of the money you've been making working yourself into the ground and talk things over, really talk things over, work out what we can do. No job's worth your life, Colin.'

And suddenly, that grin again, the very sexy one he used to have as a young man, the one that said wicked intent with a laugh attached. 'You're a little firebrand when you get going, Phyll, aren't you?'

I couldn't remember the last time he called me that. Now we were grinning at each other like a couple of kids in a cake shop.

I looked at my watch. 'Oh, bloody hell. If we're going to manage two baths—'

'Well, if we can't do two, why don't we just have one?' he said, and the grin was there again.

'You mean—'

'I do mean, you siren, you temptress, luring me into your boudoir.'

Ten minutes later, I was in the bath. Twelve minutes later, naked Colin was in it with me. I was trying to remember the last time I saw him naked; it must have been a good while, and perhaps even longer since I'd seen him as visibly excited as he was then. He has a good body; he works too hard to put flab on, and a proportion of his work is quite hard physical stuff. The days when the store manager sat in his office and let everyone else run around are long gone, if they ever existed in the first place.

The next twenty minutes came with an X certificate; it's enough to say that we managed an unusual degree of athleticism and enthusiasm compared with the recent past. Orgasms are every bit as good to receive as they are to give, and I didn't need to fake a single screech of mine. He seemed quite pleased too. I reflected that once upon a time, he could and did do that to me on a regular basis. It was as if we need to look back on the road we'd travelled and try to identify how and when we took such a wrong turning.

By the time we were both out of the bath, it was pretty much panic stations, but we'd got such finery as we had already prepared and we were both perhaps less bothered about the whole business now. Weddings tend to be dominated by the two families involved, and everyone else cannot be much more than peripheral, outsiders peering in.

By the time we were pointed in the direction of the room where the wedding ceremony was to take place, not necessarily immediately obvious in a hotel, we were sneaking in at the back, grinning conspiratorially at each other like a couple of kids.

I don't know what it was – a change of scenery, a lung full of country air, actually having the time to talk to each other – but something very important to both of us had just happened and I wanted to hold it to me, to try and ensure it didn't get away again.

Simon

I found out what happens to naughty boys – again – before breakfast. It's what happens to naughty boys which keeps me being a naughty boy; as a deterrent, it's a bit of a wash-out, but there again, we were both having such a giggle that it doesn't much matter.

Duncan has always had more enthusiasm than I have for sex first thing in the morning. With anyone else but him, I'd probably knock it firmly on the head, but like everything else he does, he's so good at it that it somehow works. And we did shower first, of course; I was a bit dubious as to whether there was enough room in the shower for both of us, but we managed somehow. Where there's a will.

One drawback of finding out what happens to naughty boys before breakfast, of course, is sitting in the breakfast room dealing with one's cornflakes and croissants with a bum that feels like it's been toasted. Eating standing up in a hotel breakfast room tends to excite remark, or at least people goggling at you.

For once, the whole buffet procedure was relatively straightforward, though even if it wasn't, I could probably have worked it out. Hotels are what I do, after all. They're not what I've always done, but they are what I've been doing for the last eight years now, since the tender age of nineteen and the end of a frustrating university experience. Call me shallow, but living on fresh air and the goodwill of fellow students while still running up an overdraft which will leave me owing thousands of pounds when I leave the place doesn't strike me as a good deal. Leisure and hospitality has always been the kind of area for me, but it became very clear very quickly that learning on the job was my way, and given the gay population of the hotel industry, learning on the job is a particularly appropriate way of putting it. But all that stopped when Duncan came along.

One of the hotel staff serving in the breakfast room, serving amounting to replenishing the buffet stands or delivering pots of tea and coffee to people – good policy on the hotel's part, because queueing up to use those infernal machines does not endear the place to guests – was so obviously a Friend of Dorothy that we got chatting a little. We first established that I was in the business myself when he was lobbing rashers of bacon on the relevant tray, then he was the one who brought us our coffee.

'Well, how are we measuring up?' he said, as camp as a boatload of kittens. Duncan, who hadn't registered my previous conversation with the lad, gave him a WTF-are-you-talking-about look, but I responded happily enough; it took my mind off my bum.

'Very good. I think you've got the right idea with the tea and coffee. When you've got one of those machines, it just takes a bemused geriatric or two to gridlock the whole breakfast operation. Hope the coffee matches up to the delivery.'

I beamed a smile at him and he actually blushed. Bless. As he sashayed off, my breakfast companion gave me one of his looks.

'Maybe the naughty-boy lesson didn't get through to someone,' he muttered. 'You'd think you could give over flirting for long enough to eat a bit of breakfast.'

'He's just a happy little twink, Duncan, and you know that's not where I'm at, or what would I be doing with you? In any case, we've got a wedding to go to, and I'm not bobbing up and down on pews or whatever the hotel equivalent is here trying to repress a yell every time my arse touches the seat. Maybe even failing at some crucial moment when someone's plighting their troth or something—'

I stopped in my tracks. A presence was hovering over our table, a presence not necessarily welcome in our territory, which this table had temporarily become. I knew it was Giles Cavendish, having established that in the bar last night, and while Robert's explanation made me feel a little better about things, it didn't mean I wanted the guy who had supplanted me as best man strolling up for chit-chat at breakfast.

And he was just too cool; he was wearing a casual light blue top and jeans, presumably waiting until breakfast is over, as I was, before donning the finery, in case one finished up going into the ceremony with congealing poached egg decorating the made to measure. He filled both top and jeans too damn well, but there was just something too serious about him, too mature and sensible, like he'd got at home an invaluable collection of vinyl originals carefully arranged in anally retentive alphabetical order.

'Hi, Simon,' he said. 'I'm Giles, the best man.'

'Yes, I know,' I said, pretty much through my teeth. 'We exchanged a few words last night, if you remember.'

He was supposed to be something important, governmental even; it doesn't sound good if he was so pissed last night he can't remember who he spoke to.

'Yes, I do, but it was a bit en passant, as I recall. I thought, if anyone's entitled to a personal introduction away from a noisy hotel bar, it's you, the guy who should have been best man.'

Now he was flustering me; I was all set up to loathe the guy with a gratifying passion, and here he was being nice.

'No, not at all,' I said. Noblesse oblige, and all that. 'It's Robert's choice, and he made it. I'm sure you'll be fine.'

'Thanks, Simon.' And he held out his hand. And instead of reaching across, gripping his testicles and shaking him up and down until his breakfast returns, I took it. Cool again. Cool and firm.

Then, a little unexpectedly, he turned to Duncan. 'And you, sir, unless I'm very much mistaken, are Duncan Allen. I know your work.'

'Oh, yes?' Duncan said, with a decidedly dour tone. One of Duncan's maxims is 'the smoother the southerner, the more careful you need to be', and this southerner was as smooth as a horse's earhole.

'I think you know a colleague of mine,' said Cavendish, and then he mentioned the name, but so softly that I don't get it. But it seemed to have a galvanising effect on Duncan. To my astonishment, he rose almost halfway out of his chair and grasped the guy's hand.

'Yes, I know him right enough.' Now Duncan lowered his own voice. 'And I also know that some very interesting messages were coming in last night for a certain local worthy.'

'Really?' Cavendish was now agog himself. I felt like the last gooseberry in the bush now.

Next they were exchanging phone numbers. The breakfast boy went past, looking at them, then at me, then rolling his eyes. If my buttered bun was of a lesser quality, I wouldn't have hesitated to throw it at him.

Cavendish then came out with a remark which interested me on a number of levels, again delivered distinctly sotto voce. 'We have a kind of Densham-Harrington alliance established, above and beyond the one about to take place in the wedding room. But we don't want to be seen conversing in public, for obvious reasons. I'll phone when you get back to your room. Ten minutes?'

Duncan nodded immediately, almost humbly, apparently under the Cavendish spell in a matter of minutes. Then off went Giles, blast him, his pert little bottom swinging from side to side.

'Well,' I said, and I thought Duncan knew which kind of well this is. 'Maybe someone else should be finding out what happens to naughty boys. Why didn't you just roll on the floor and let him tickle your tummy?'

He grinned his inscrutable Northumbrian grin. 'Beware the green-eyed monster, dear boy,' he said. 'I'll tell you all when we get back to the room. Or as much as I know, which isn't a lot.'

Back in our suite, I sat on our sofa while he started getting the suits out and checking them.

'Well, what's the score? Who is the guy anyway?'

He placed a jacket on the bed and then sat beside me. 'You know what a spook is, Si?'

'Of course I do. I work in a hotel in London, Duncan, with guests coming in from all over the place. Having a spook taking an interest in one of our guests is not that unusual.'

'Well, that's what he is. And knowing the department where he works, I'd say he's a fair way up the greasy spook pole, young as he is.'

'Good degree. Whiz kid, I suppose.'

He looked at me oddly, as if I'd disappointed him, and it was just beginning to look as if my friend's wedding day was going to feature something like a row between me and my partner, though rowing is difficult with Duncan, because he comes over all northern and dour and clams up.

But at this moment, his phone went off with those northern bagpipes again, which gave me time to retreat to the balcony, where I pulled the door almost shut behind me, not wishing to listen to my partner getting cosy with the guy who'd usurped my legitimate bestman-ship.

It was slowly turning into a beautiful day, as it was always going to do. Robert Harrington tends to be associated with good fortune; he's the kind of guy who could walk under the most careless building site in the world, when bricks and mortar, wood and glass, were cascading down from the inebriated workforce above, and none of them would as much as scratch him. That he should get married on such a day has a kind of inevitability about it.

Such weather improved my mood. I knew I was being a pain and just a bit childish. I asked myself if I want jam on it; Rob himself had said he would have asked me if he could, even if I found the whole thing rather mysterious and puzzling. Cavendish – oh, call him Giles, you sad git – Giles had even acknowledged that I should have been best man, though I knew well enough that it didn't really work like that.

Only when I'd been sitting for several minutes, watching Devon waking up to its gentle morning business, did the real reason why I was miffed dawn on me.

Rob Harrington has for some time occupied the exalted position of my Hetero Best Friend. My social circle consists largely of gay men and not necessarily gay women, plus various members of my family and Duncan's family, ranging from my sister Jen and her husband Alec, both perfect gems, to one of Duncan's aunts called Muriel for whom we are both the spawn of the devil who will finish up in Hell being poked with red hot toasting forks or something. The first time I ever attended an Allen family do, someone's wedding, I was treated with general if slightly distant good nature, Duncan having made abundantly clear to all and sundry how he would take it if I wasn't, but Aunt Muriel took every available opportunity to glower at us, tut loudly occasionally, and make remarks to whoever was unfortunate enough to be in her vicinity. Eventually, Duncan, who is not a guy who sits and takes it, went across and had a few uncompromising words with her, featuring a few Northumbrian expressions I didn't understand then but I do now. The woman then stopped staring at us, but I got the distinct impression that she wouldn't be linking arms with me in any forthcoming renderings of 'Auld Lang Syne'.

Be that as it may, Rob is a very decent guy who is always there to remind me that Heteros are People Too, whatever evidence there may sometimes be to the contrary. And I had a very distinct feeling in my bones that he was, in some specified way, in danger. I ran over our meeting in the hotel grounds, as I have a few times before, and while he was obviously worried about his parents, something else was happening, something connected to whatever it was putting him under threat. You can't work in the hotel business for very long without becoming aware of the complexity of the law and the way it gets itself into so many facets of everything, and I know how easy it is to fall foul of it without even knowing. We've had situations relating to food, accommodation, parking, booking, hygiene, weather and all sorts of areas where the management can find itself under pressure from factors beyond their control. I could quote examples, but we'd be here for hours. Rob works in a particularly contentious area of the law; his father's is contentious enough, of course, but that's on a personal level; Rob's is about big companies, huge corporations and mind-boggling amounts of money, and there are few more dangerous subjects than money.

I knew that, had I been best man, I would almost certainly know by now the details of what was happening in Rob's life, and that's what was getting to me. Speech making and dressing up in penguin suits, drunken stag nights and risqué stories at the groom's expense – though I've got one or two of those – didn't do a great deal for me. My pal was in some kind of danger and I didn't even know what it was, meaning I had no way of helping him with it.

By the time Duncan came out to join me on the balcony, I had smoothed out the dents in my self-respect and restored my sunny wedding-day disposition. Ish.

He was smiling his 'I know something you don't know' smile, but I know the usual result of that is him telling me what it is.

'Well, first of all, he particularly asked me to tell you something.'

'What? Sod off, loser?'

'No. He said the reason why Robert wasn't in a position to explain his choice of best man to you was because he, as in Giles, had asked Robert not to. Robert chose Giles as his best man to allay the suspicions of the people both of them are trying to bring down. Giles thinks the people in question might well know who he works for; if he'd simply suddenly appeared as a guest, they would immediately have been suspicious. However, as he and Robert have been to university together, the choice wouldn't be as odd as all that. And Giles knew he was going to have to work closely with Robert to achieve what they're trying to achieve. He advised Robert to choose him as his best man, and Robert, after initial reluctance, did. They've worked closely together since, on the particular achievement Robert and Kate wanted to mark their wedding.'

I was experiencing an actual physical glow about the heart at that moment, but this still struck me as an odd aim for a wedding.

'For most people, it's a honeymoon. Or a home. Or, and admittedly we're not talking about many these days, first experience of – hem, hem – full-blown sexual intercourse.'

I reflected that, on the night of our civil partnership, 'full-blown' was quite a technically accurate term, but of course, there had been previous occasions.

'Well, as for a honeymoon, I suspect they've been away together quite a few times. And it seems they've been living together for three years in a decent-sized flat which Robert's parents helped him to buy. So they decided that, since their decision to marry had a lot to do with family pressures and legal matters, they'd try to mark it with a resounding professional achievement, in this case putting a particularly nasty organisation permanently out of business, and when Kate found out from her father about this land deal and the invitation to her to handle it from the Devon angle, it seemed to present them with the perfect opportunity.'

'You seem to have found out a hell of a lot about it.'

'Yes, mostly because of Giles, who is one of those southerners, nowhere near as common as I would like them to be, who can impart a lot of information without taking an age over it. No side-tracks, irrelevancies, repetitions. And I can tell you this, dear boy. This is going to be a wedding the like of which you have never experienced before and you will certainly never experience again. And you are going to play a much more significant part in it than you might have thought.'

'Oh, yes? Tell me more. But you'd better be as succinct as the wonderful Giles, because we will need to get booted and suited soon.'

Tell me more he did, and as I listened – I'm a hotel assistant manager, listening is part of the job – my eyes and my grin grew gradually wider. I knew an Irish lad at school – he was a good mate for a while, if lamentably and resolutely hetero, and he used to talk about doing something 'just for the crack'. It's one of those words which only situations and enterprises can define. This was one of them. Yes, there were serious issues and risks involved in what was planned; we had no illusions about the people we were dealing with. But all the same, it was eminently worth it just for the crack.

THE WEDDING, SATURDAY, June 15th

Matthew

After my conversation with Kate, I phoned Tony Fenwick and asked him to come to the hotel with Ben Sanderson, probably the best of our photographers, and bring everything we had on Councillor Needham. We could justify the coverage on the basis that Councillor Needham was here, and one or two other local worthies, known to be cronies of Needham, had also been seen around the hotel. This would have the effect of leaving Ken Slater in charge at very short notice, which was a risk but a justifiable one; it said to Slater that I am prepared to put him in charge occasionally if Fenwick and I are needed elsewhere, but I want to know that he is competent to do it.

I also asked Tony to bring a 'runner', as in one of the junior reporters; I was going to be directly involved in the ceremony, and perpetually having my phone going was certainly not going to make me any friends, so a runner would let me communicate with Tony and Ben. Boys are better suited to the role; they excite less remark than girls, and as it happened we had a work experience lad with us at this time, Russell Michelson alias Russ, a bright lad who might well notice one or two things we didn't.

But if I thought, when I put my phone down, that the morning would cease being so hectic and let me attend to showering and suiting, I had another think coming. Kate left us at ten past ten, and we absolutely had to be downstairs by half eleven, with the wedding due to start at twelve. At just before 10.25, Giles Cavendish, the best man, amongst other things, phoned me and explained what they had in mind for the wedding speeches after the lunch. It seemed that Needham had collared Peter Densham during breakfast. Helen had only the most cursory of meals before going to Judi Curzon's room to dress for the wedding, leaving Peter on his own with the full breakfast he felt he needed on such an occasion. Needham actually made the outrageous suggestion that he be the first to speak when the time for speechifying came along. As usual with Needham's outlines of what he wanted to happen, it came with a thinly veiled threat with references to Helen which made it clear enough, without being explicit, that Peter's marital situation would be blathered all over the place for all the rest of the event after the wedding lunch, and an evening do was planned. There was also an implied threat of action against the university if the planning proposals were not approved, on the basis of breaches of contract; even though no contract had actually been signed, verbal undertakings had been given and were on tape. This Peter doubted, but bluffing was well known as a regular shotgun in Needham's armoury.

Peter was at first going to slap the idea down, knowing the impact it would have on the guests generally, but then he thought it might just suit the purposes of 'the opposition' to let Needham do what he was suggesting, so he agreed. He then immediately informed Robert, Kate and Giles, who agreed that it could be the perfect set-up. He then outlined the order of speeches to follow Needham and the person who was to introduce them and connect them together. It seemed that I had a role in it, and when he described what my role was going to be, I found myself grinning at the phone like an idiot.

Mary had emerged from the bathroom during this conversation; when I put the phone down, it was quarter to eleven. I showered for ten minutes, and I was still dripping wet from the shower when my phone went again, and this time it was Robert, giving me the finalised plans. By five past eleven, I was booted and suited, Mary was ready to go, and Tony Fenwick phoned, saying he was fifteen minutes from the hotel, he had the stuff on Needham and how did he want me to play it? I gave him Giles Cavendish's number and said to say I'd referred him for liaison purposes; Cavendish would know what I meant.

At quarter past eleven, with Mary starting to look pale and harassed, we walked downstairs. We'd been told the actual ceremony was going to take place in what they called the Coleridge Suite, very literary in conception but more often than not used for conferencing or meetings involving substantial numbers of people. We made our way there, and I suppose the best way to describe it would be as a very large and rather more comfortable registry office. Neither Kate nor Robert have any religious affiliations, and where the altar table would be in the church was a large table decorated tastefully with flowers, a colourful and cheering display. There was also, on the left, what is probably best described as a 'Robert' display, with pictures from his school and university days, including his graduation, posing proudly with his parents. Included in the presentation was a curious flag, a large and apparently chained swan on a red and black background, which I subsequently discovered was the flag of Buckinghamshire, representing the swans they used to breed for royalty. Robert grew up in Aylesbury, not far from his mother's birthplace in High Wycombe.

On the right was a similar display for Kate, with one or two pictures from her rather gawky schoolgirl days which she'd probably hoped her parents had thrown away, but which brought back fond memories for me. It had been obvious to me from her early years that here was a very clever girl, whatever she might look like at various stages of the often cruel business of growing up, and when she started to turn into the beauty she now is, round about the age of seventeen to eighteen, it didn't surprise me. She took adolescence in her stride, as she took everything else.

Kate's side also had the now-familiar green, black and white Devon flag, only approved as recently as 2003 in a public vote. The whole thing was a striking representation of the union of these two young people, with a centrepiece which represented (again, as I found out later; they were all good conversational points to overcome the awkwardness of weddings) the Coat of Arms of the Inns of Court, of which both Kate and Robert were members.

It was almost as if the couple, whom I knew had remained largely in charge of this whole business themselves, were saying to us that even if the traditional religious side of weddings was not going to figure in this one, there would still be a strong acknowledgement of tradition in it, which I think some of the slightly bewildered older members of the company were appreciating.

However, there was also a kind of unease, both as we filed into the Coleridge Suite and as people took up their places. Once again, the nod to tradition was to place the waiting bridegroom with his best man on the right, with the left side awaiting the bride and her father. Behind the bridegroom and best man were the Harrington principals, Robert's father, mother and grandmother; Mary and I were in the second row behind the chairs for the bride and her father, along with Helen, Kate's brother Tom and his girlfriend Claudette. I had already spoken to Tom, who was now actively involved in the whole strategy compiled by the two families at short notice, but at closer quarters, I was again taken aback at the change in him and struck by the dark-eyed beauty of Claudette. The Tom of old would never have been looked at twice by the likes of Claudette, and the boy's rehabilitation was gratifying; I have always thought he had more in him than we had so far seen.

'You know what you're doing, then, Tom,' I said, having nodded and smiled at Claudette again and received the same beautiful smile in return as I had the first time. I suppose I couldn't resist being the uncle with him, but he smiled quietly himself, another innovation in my extensive knowledge of him, and whispered an answer.

'Sort of bouncer,' he said, which discomfited me a little. 'The other lads have been tipped off. If it comes to it.'

'Which we sincerely hope it won't,' I said quickly.

'Oh, absolutely,' he said, but there was that quiet new smile of confidence again. My unease ratcheted up another notch, and I realised that I was not alone in such feelings. As the number of people entering the room increased, the hum of noise was rather louder than one might expect in a gathering of people waiting for a wedding to happen. There were several people amongst us whom I didn't recognise, which isn't unusual in a sizeable wedding, but it seemed to be becoming clearer that no-one else recognised them either. In the foyer outside the suite, which connected to the main hotel entrance, there were a few other men, specifically men, whom the hotel staff were eyeing uneasily themselves. They were perfectly acceptably dressed; it's just that nobody seemed to know who they were and why they were interested in a wedding taking place which was none of their business.

However, I'd seen Tony, Ben and Russell around the main foyer area before I came in to the wedding suite, and I knew Ben was an expert at taking concealed photos; many of these unknowns gathered around will already have had images of themselves taken to the hotel's office area by young Russell and sent on to the paper. Robert's friend Simon, though now in the suite with us, was in the hotel business himself and had managed to wangle the use of the hotel's scanning and sending facilities with the easy diplomacy which I gather is one of his professional assets.

The groom and his best man now joined us, and their wide grins and nods to people as they passed them reassured us. Both Robert and Giles scrubbed up well in their immaculate dark morning suits. Some men, most of them Italian, will manage to look reasonably good in just about anything, but these two were both athletically built and good-looking; most female eyes and a few male ones as well watched their progress to their waiting place. But I noticed Giles also looked thoughtfully at one or two people in the gathering. Giles, I knew even on the briefest of acquaintance, was a smooth and subtle operator, and I strongly suspected he had a few guys of his own in the hotel, though he wouldn't be so unsubtle as to plant them right there in the wedding room.

The appearance of the groom and best man seemed to soothe the company, and the relaxation rippled through the rows of celebrants again as 'Here Comes the Bride', the Wagner march, struck up, and everyone realised that Kate had appeared through a door at the back of the room, presumably a staircase connecting directly to the Bridal Suite. However, whoever expected that such music would be matched by a traditional bridal outfit was to be disabused. There was no veil, no spectacular white dress, no bridesmaids carrying her train. Kate, I knew, was twenty-seven, and whereas there may probably still be places where twenty-seven-year-old virgins are still in abundance, I suspect modern London is not one of them. Kate and Robert clearly regarded tradition as a series of options, some usable, some not, but if bridal white was still taken as a statement of purity and virginity, she was having none of it. While I sympathised – the two of them were a modern professional couple who had been living together for some time – an uncle has a whole boatload of memories of the girl and the child, and while I rejoiced at her growing up into such a beautiful and successful woman, fond memories of the growing will always remain.

Peter stepped back, Kate stepped forward, Robert moved to her and the two of them exchanged great big conspiratorial grins.

My heart went out to them, but that also served to aggravate my pangs of unease.

Celia

The groom's family are not traditionally the decision makers at weddings, and I didn't expect this one to be any different; Devon is not a place I've generally associated with rampant radicalism, limited as my experience of it is. When I first understood that this do was largely financed by the happy couple, I began to have visions of lots of touchy-feely stuff, or loud rock music, or everyone crammed into tents – hippie-ish things. Then I reflected that the couple concerned were both lawyers in their late twenties, and kaftans and flowers in the hair were rather more my era than theirs. My teenage years were in the fifties, when everything, including the food, was green, brown or grey and teenagers per se hadn't actually been invented. But the sixties and my twenties did allow me to let my hair down rather more and the rules concerning relationships between the sexes loosened a little, though nothing like as much as the popular images of the sixties would have you believe. Derek and I found it excruciatingly difficult to arrange time when we could be alone together, and even when we did manage it, I still experienced anxieties about my mother suddenly appearing behind the pillar of a dance hall or emerging from the kitchen of the restaurant to occupy an adjoining pillar or table while her hawk-like eyes followed our every move.

In short, I didn't really know what to expect, and had more or less resigned myself to go with the flow. When the flow grew gradually more bizarre, I found myself resigned to each new peculiarity as it appeared.

At the appointed time, we all trooped down to what was apparently known as the Coleridge Suite. Of course, I am aware of the poet concerned; 'Rhyme of the Ancient Mariner' was one of the less turgid items featured in my literary education. However, the man's connection with the matrimonial process is perhaps more obscure. I gather he comes from Devon, which I hadn't known before, but that doesn't really make anything much clearer. I grew up in what Betjeman described as 'Metroland'; however, I wouldn't necessarily have been pleased to get married in a room with pictures of Sir John and his works, perhaps Miss Joan Hunter-Dunn or, God help us, Death in Leamington Spa.

A place less connected with weddings or romance would be difficult to imagine, and I couldn't help wondering why they didn't just do the ceremony in a registry office; the décor uninspiring enough, yes, but at least connected fairly securely with weddings.

We filed in without any general direction as to who should sit where, but fortunately I was with Malcolm and Barbara, who were obviously more au fait with the proceedings than I was, and when we were settled in our places, some of my anxieties subsided. We were, as tradition would have it, in the row immediately behind the front row on the right side, the customary spot for the waiting groom and best man. I was also very taken with the beautiful presentation in front of us, which was at least connected with the lives of the young people concerned, rather than garlanded with hundreds of flowers which would undoubtedly have set my hay fever off and would probably go to waste afterwards, probably chucked on the hotel's manure heap, because I don't doubt a place with as much garden as this one would have a manure heap.

I was also securely in the company of Malcolm and Barbara. We had a row of seats – I can't really call it a pew, it was a row of seats, and if anyone should take it into their heads to sink to their knees in prayer, they would either dislocate their kneecaps on the hard wooden floor or pitch themselves forward into a prostrate position which is probably a little over the top for an English country wedding, especially when there is no-one to prostrate oneself to.

Not long after the room had filled, which took a little while because it was quite a hefty turnout, probably at least 200, and more expected for the evening do, I understand, Robert and his best man Giles appeared, and my traditionalist hackles were soothed again when I saw they were both beautifully and appropriately suited. I have heard men complain of the restrictions placed on them in the matter of wedding attire, but I think such complainants are in the minority. Being properly suited does at least take away from them the agonies of choice which brides have to go through, when in almost every case in history, she and her mother will disagree, quite possibly fundamentally, over what she should wear. My mother wanted me to wear her late mother's wedding dress, a bizarre monstrosity of frills, curls and unpredictable lace appendages. 'Let in stay in the family, dear, and think of all the money saved!' I remarked that perhaps I should also put on seventeen petticoats, a big hat with a garland of flowers in it and arrive at the church on a penny-farthing, but she wasn't amused. It took me several weeks before I put my foot down finally, declared that Derek and I would buy the thing ourselves, and the choice would be mine and only mine. I'm not sure the relationship with her ever recovered.

Suddenly, the room was full of the 'Here Comes the Bride' march; I can never remember whether it's the Mendelssohn one or not; not, I think. This additional nod to tradition provided further reassurance, or at least it did until I caught sight of the approaching bride. She was actually dressed in light blue; her hair, which I remember last night being bunned up, had been dropped and was cascading down over her shoulders. She was suddenly caught in a beam of sunlight, and with the breeze entering the room enough to gently move her hair, she was, by anyone's standards and in any age, quite stunningly beautiful. She was also wearing a curious-looking brooch, the shape of which I only managed to make out when she was quite near to us. It seemed to be a pair of scales, which momentarily mystified me; perhaps quite the thing for a woman about to marry a grocer or butcher or something, but in a ceremony of this kind? Then, of course, I called myself a dunderhead and realised it was the scales of justice, done in solid gold, by the look of it, and I am quite a reliable judge in these things. Gold objects, usually watches, tended to be presented to Derek's employees on their retirement or sometimes weddings, and arranging these gifts generally fell to me, one of the many duties which devolve upon the wife of an owner and managing director. No employee of ours was ever going to find, should they be suspicious enough to want it checked, that their watch or whatever was gold-plated or cunningly disguised brass. I knew of two reliable tests; firstly, gold is not magnetic, and if there's anything in your object which isn't gold, it will react to a magnet. Secondly, dragging the gold across an unglazed ceramic plate will leave a gold mark if it's gold and a black mark if it isn't, though the size of some of the objects I was dealing with could make that difficult. In any case, I always backed up my own assessments with an expert. We had one, dear old Jake Reynolds, whom we knew we could trust because he was an old friend of Derek's father, and we were in any case personal as well as commercial customers.

As she approached her place on the left of the main table, I saw that the brooch was also distinctly glistening, and I realised it had been fixed on a bed of little diamonds. I found out subsequently that it was one of a number of wedding presents from her parents. Quite, quite charming, and it, plus the fact that she did look very good in blue, allowed me on balance to exonerate her for not appearing in bridal white. I don't know how seriously anyone takes the whole business of virginal white these days, but in the days when it was taken quite seriously, the vulgar guffaws which greeted some girls' all-white appearance are mercifully past us. She'd also backed out of carrying a bunch of flowers, I gather on the basis of hay fever. Plighting the troth while sneezing one's head off between every two words, while one's beloved looks askance at one's streaming eyes and reddened nose, does not appeal, and I applaud her common sense rather than otherwise.

Attention is usually so focussed on the bride that the accompanying daddy doesn't usually get much attention. Of course, there's no certainty these days about it being Daddy, with so many marriages going phut; it could just as well be Stepdaddy, Uncle John or the nice man from the library. But today it was bona fide Daddy, and looking at the two of them together, the relationship was all too clear. The man is in his fifties and the woman is in her late twenties, but the eyes are strikingly similar, as is the facial bone structure, and even the slow walk is similar. There are also echoes of her mother in the mouth and the swimmer's shoulders, so whatever the malignant rumours going about concerning Mummy's proclivities, the fact that Kate is a product of the Densham union is visually indisputable, as it is with the bride's brother, a fine figure of a young man whose fraternity is very obvious.

I don't cry at weddings; I never have done, even at Malcolm and Barbara's, and if I had cried at that one, it would have been more about frustration and irritation than about my joy for the happy couple. I belong to a generation which has always been, rightly in my opinion, reticent about public blubbing, and those of us who are left are likely to have become more rather than less doubtful about it after the increasing emotional flatulence which has become characteristic of public life now. Contestants in meaningless, contrived television competitions, people being given some fatuous award or other, sports persons, male and female, after both winning and losing, we live surrounded by the legions of the weeping like some gargantuan, pink-strewn Barbara Cartland extravaganza.

Apart from the 'I dos', 'I now proclaim you man and wife' and a kiss, the subsequent ceremony was completely indecipherable to me, though neither God nor Jesus seemed fated to feature in it at any point. I am a long way from being a religious fanatic, and unlike many of my generation, I believe in a certain amount of give and take on such matters. Derek always believed religion was 'pretty much myths and fairy stories', but he was quite content to rumble on in that slightly off-key baritone of his if the occasion demanded. The master of ceremonies, as I suppose he should be called in this context – he's certainly not a vicar, with that benign but fairly dotty manner they all seem to have about them – looked genuinely as if he was enjoying it, with broad smiles and nods at bride and groom alike, even if he was wearing a tie which men like my ex-husband would only ever have worn for a 'dare'.

However, it all seemed done and dusted within about twenty minutes with a commendable lack of fuss and an even more commendable lack of standing up and sitting down. People do rather forget that those of us well struck in years no longer find it easy to keep shifting up and down like so many geriatric pistons, and are quite likely to find ourselves incapable of the up movement on about the fifth or sixth attempt.

It was all unconventional but perfectly acceptable as far as I was concerned, and when the bride and groom simultaneously turned to face us, apparently to make an announcement, I was no longer batting either eyelid at it.

'Thanks to one and all for giving us your time and good wishes, ladies and gentlemen,' said Robert, and there was a remarkable power and carrying tone to his voice, which even those at the very rear would be able to catch. I was momentarily startled, but then Robert has never had any occasion to address me as if I were a public meeting in the past, and of course, he now needs to be heard in large public courtrooms. M'learned friend is unlikely to impress the jury by standing at his lectern mumbling and stumbling through his case.

'We are now going to adjourn for the wedding lunch, which is to be held in the Christie Banqueting Suite; you'll see clear directions as you leave here. We would like to be there to greet everyone as they come in, so please bear with us for five to ten minutes and then make your way to us.'

'Those of us, including Robert and me, who don't eat meat will find there are vegetarian alternatives available,' the bride added, in the same clear and ringing tone as her husband. It's only to be hoped they remain as row-free as possible, because I suspect a row between these two would be likely to be heard several streets away.

'Likewise any of the company who prefer beer to wine will be accommodated, as will those who don't care for alcohol at all,' Robert said. 'Kate and I believe in celebrating diversity, even if it does make life more complicated.' His smile was so warm and infectious that many people couldn't help but return it, though in the case of some of the gentlemen, that may have had something to do with the availability of beer. I do sympathise, as a matter of fact. On a warm day such as this – warm, though mercifully not hot – cold beer is a more practical proposition than the much stronger wine, which, if drunk in beer-like quantities, is likely to find some of the happy celebrants in sorry states by the evening, which I always think rather lowers the tone.

A music background – Vivaldi, I think it was – struck up as the bride and groom left the room with their parents and the best man. Our arrangement was that I would follow them at my own pace, and since it wasn't practical politics for me to stand at the entrance greeting two hundred people in ones and twos, I was to make my way straight to the top table, where the bride's brother Tom and his girlfriend Claudette were to take care of me until the rest of the table joins us.

So I stood up and gave my legs a moment or two to adjust to the fact of not being seated any more, then, with a polite nod to one or two Harrington acquaintances – we kept the invitations on our side fairly restrained; London is a long way from Devon – I followed the lead party, managing to resist the temptation to do the little celebratory jig which the cheerful Vivaldi suggested. The news that Granny is flat on her face in the Coleridge Suite and about to be taken into intensive care would not be an auspicious start to the wedding feast.

Phyllis

We only just about made it into the room where the wedding is to be held, both a bit breathless and startled at what had just happened. For me, a fairly simple and straightforward ceremony is fine. I've been to weddings where people are dropping off all around me and the announcement of yet another hymn causes an audible rumble of dissent around the place, still usually a church, as we all heave ourselves up yet again. I had one, a good time ago now, where the vicar decided to give a sermon tracing the history of marriage back to almost the Stone Age. I was struggling to retain any feeling in my bum and I distinctly heard a man in the pew in front of me muttering 'sit the fuck down'; disgraceful as such an uttering is in a church, the dirty look he got from his wife was definitely token.

They were a striking young couple, and the 'what's happening next' announcement thing they did at the end showed just how at ease they are now speaking in public. Kate always has been an outward-looking girl, never lacking in confidence, and it looked like she's met a man literally after her own heart. I'd liked what I've seen of him so far, but the male in the company who'd attracted most of my attention was Kate's brother Tom. I hadn't seen him for a while; he flew the nest some time ago. It took me several glances before I realised it was him; the first two only registered that there was a tall, good-looking young guy in our midst. Now the chins and the incipient gut have gone, he really is quite a babe, as is the girl with him. He also looked about two or three inches taller, which is probably an anatomical impossibility, but maybe it was because he didn't slouch around like he did.

So, off to the Christie Banqueting Suite, with a big portrait of the lady herself and her archaeological husband – not Christie, the one after him, Max Mallowan, eventually Sir Max. The house where they lived in Devon, Greenway, is less than twenty miles away from where we were now. There were pictures from various Christie films and a few Mallowan digs, not to mention some lovely studies of Greenway and the countryside around it. It wasn't the most obvious accompaniment in a room dedicated to feasting, but it did get across to us where we were and it had a curiously relaxing effect. Agatha wasn't Max's first wife and Max wasn't Agatha's first husband, but it did remind us all that marriage can be a wonderful condition, even if you don't ring the bell first time around.

We all filed in, to kisses or embraces from the bride and groom according to gender, age and temperament, and we collected a glass of bubbly en route. 'So glad you could come, Phyllis,' said Kate, and why should I have doubted it; not so long ago she called me Aunt Phyllis, a kind of grace and favour aunt, and I would drive Helen crazy by giving her daughter little treats. 'So kind of you, Phyll, and she adores chocolate, of course, though I do have to remember her young teeth.' God, I thought, not seven days a week, twenty-four seven you don't, she's a kid. Tom I didn't treat so much, since he seemed quite capable of sourcing treats himself.

My favourable impression of the groom was confirmed at close quarters; the boy exuded health and well-being, and to catch one who comes with a brain as well is one to Kate. Beautiful as she is, so much so that she could get away with that toned-down dress that almost made her look like one of the bridesmaids, had there been any bridesmaids, many men are intrinsically suspicious of clever women. Kate being Kate, I can't see her ever playing the brainless bimbo to allay their suspicions, and she seems to have found a guy with the wherewithal to make her a suitable mate.

The scramble around to find who was seated where was lessened by a board with a plan big enough for everyone to see without having to creep up to it amongst the crowd and peer from about six inches away.

We were not on the main table, of course, but we were on the one nearest to them on their right. But, while the position was fine, my heart sank at the allocation of names. The company had been arranged in pally little tables of fives and sixes; ours, in addition to Colin and me, had Helen's friend, the creature Judi, ousted from the top table, it seemed; Peter's foot doesn't go down very often, but it had there; some kind of a deal being done, I suspected. The names Simon Roche and Duncan Allen initially puzzled me, then I remembered from last night that Simon was the gay mate of the groom's, who went back with him further than the appointed best man, but perhaps his gayness got in the way of him getting the gig; does the groom want a big kiss from his best man at the stag night? The tall man with him was his civil partner and mysteriously connected with cybersecurity, says the grapevine.

And the sixth name in our happy party? Why, of course, none other than Professor David Bennett, my erstwhile heartthrob, who had already had a few choice words with my husband. Of course, the table planners' thinking was all too obvious; Professor Bennett, single man, Judi Curzon, single woman, both scientists in their different ways, click, click, click.

I was struck with gloom from the start. What a happy time is in prospect, I thought, sat between my teenage boyfriend and my husband, the two of them glowering at each other over their pints, no doubt, with every probability that one or both of them would finish up with a drink emptied over the top of their heads before we got to the speeches. Meanwhile, the other three would have established a mini-gay mafia and be spending their entire time talking Prides and Coming Outs and a few of the more let's say specialised sexual activities.

Being of a pessimistic disposition means you can rarely be surprised, but this time, I really was. As we were sitting down,

Colin found David Bennett on his right, and instead of looking daggers at him, he held out his hand.

'Professor Bennett,' he said, loud enough for David and me to hear, if not the rest of the gathering assembly, 'I was very rude to you last night, having sadly misinterpreted the situation. My only excuse is that I was very tired after a long and demanding day, and I wasn't thinking as sensibly as I might have been. Please accept my apologies.'

David of-coursed and think-nothing-of-ited prettily, and insisted on being addressed as David, meaning as soon as we sat down, my husband and ex-lover were on first-name terms, which feels odd, but they hadn't been husbands and lovers simultaneously, so there was no reason why there should be tension between them.

The idea behind the table seems to be that, if it had to be to have four men and two women on the table, the two ladies should at least have the company of each other, which might be a kindly thought, but it left me with Helen's Judi on my left and Colin and David on my right. On Helen's left are Simon and Duncan, meaning Duncan is next to David. But then again, a table of six meant conversation was just as likely to be general as localised.

Localised was how it started. Unlike some wedding lunches I'd been to, this one actually offered a menu, without everyone having to order in advance or take what was coming. The choice wasn't huge, but the fact that there was a choice at all was quite impressive and another proof of Helen's organisational abilities, not to mention a decent budget for the whole thing.

Going through the whole business of ordering food and drinks set the talk going. If Judi was seriously miffed about missing out on the top table, she was making a good job of concealing it. As we contemplated the starters, I took a chance of addressing her as if we were just re-starting a conversation, which works with people who want it to work.

'I'm always tempted to opt for the soup to be on the safe side. Unenterprising, but better safe than sorry, I think.'

'Oh, absolutely,' she said, with a slightly forced smile; willing to make an effort, obviously.

'Button mushrooms with garlic sauce – tasty, I dare say, but a little anti-social at close quarters. And smoked salmon, posh or not, I just can't make myself a fan.'

It seemed we had bottles of white and red wine already on the table, not to mention carafes of water. Menu preferences are always an interesting guide to people you don't know much about. Duncan and Colin were red meat, beef on this occasion, though Colin was red wine and Duncan was pale lager. I was chicken and red wine; people keep telling me I 'should' drink white wine with poultry, and I tell them, as politely as possible, that white wine is too acidic for me and that there is no 'should' about any wine; everyone should drink what the hell they like. Simon and Judi were fish, hake on this occasion, and white wine. David, interestingly, had opted vegetarian, a mushroom stroganoff, and he was only drinking water.

'The only virtuous one on the table, I see,' I said to him, and he looked momentarily puzzled, as if I'd accused him of something.

'Oh, the sobriety, you mean. Practicality more than virtue, to be honest. I'm going to be saying something later on, and it's the sort of thing you need a clear head for.'

I found that rather cryptic; wedding speeches these days usually tend to be cut down rather than elongated, and he wasn't even on the top table. When it comes to order of speaking, a new colleague and ex-student friend of the bride's father doesn't usually figure in the proceedings, but the fact that this wasn't a normal wedding had, I think, seeped through to most of us by now.

And not necessarily in a good way. I tried to do my bit to keep conversation and conviviality going, but that didn't mean I was blind to what's happening on the wider scene, and there were aspects of this thing which were beginning to unsettle most of us. We'd all seen Councillor Needham settled on the table nearest to the top table on the other side from us, with Councillor Fawning Creep – I can never remember his name, but FC will do – his perpetual bagman, beside him, the other four consisting of three very suited and very tough-looking males and a dark-haired woman with a daring V-neck line and a black dress which makes her look like something out of *Cabaret*.

'What is Needham even doing here at all?' was the unspoken question which I thought was going through many people's minds, let alone accompanied by his henchmen and Cruella de Vil there. He was also looking insufferably smug, but I thought with him that was permanent.

There were also other background accompaniments to this business which were making people nervous. A set of double doors had been left open to allow the waiting staff to bring in food and take away dishes, and while this was obviously part of a direct route to the kitchens, the hanging about and toing and froing in the wider hotel could be seen and heard, and the noise could probably best described as an aggressive mutter. Many of the individuals apparently hanging around out there didn't resemble standard family holidaymakers; there did seem to be a preponderance of men, and not necessarily nice-looking men, on the premises not far from this suite. Occasional little groups formed out there to have conversations while looking in our direction. It came across as a highly inappropriate form of intimidation, and the noise inside the suite was beginning to move beyond a natural buzz typical of what was supposed to be a happy event.

Finally, when everyone was drinking tea or coffee, or just sticking with their standard tipple, an air of resignation settled over the company in anticipation of the speechifying. Given the top table on this do, it was not unreasonable to expect that the speeches would not be too ropey. It's usually the best man, bridegroom and father of the bride – all men, of course – who do the honours, if that's a fair way to describe some of the poignant disasters I'd witnessed at this stage over the years.

So it came as something of a surprise to most that the guy who seemed to be first to his feet was none other than Councillor Joe Needham. It also registered with me that three of the people sitting at this table didn't appear to be surprised – Simon Roche, Duncan Allen and David Bennett.

'Ladies and gentlemen,' said Joe, and that was enough to get him heard; all those big council chamber years have given him a carrying voice. I should think they could hear him in the loos.

Simon

I ate my wedding lunch with a sense of anticipation at the approaching fun and games. We found ourselves at one of the tables nearest to the top one, which was useful in some ways, though it made it a bit difficult for me to exit surreptitiously. All the same, I'm chief assistant manager in a good London hotel; entering and exiting surreptitiously is almost part of the job description. But it applies to the guests, to the public; being chief assistant manager means I do need to be noticed by the staff. Hotel assistant manager can cover a multitude of sins; I've known places where the guy whose main functions are checking the loos every hour or so or seeing that the goods deliveries go to the right door is termed an assistant manager, even though he (it's usually a he; for some reason, women have to start at the bottom) might well be weeks away from his A level results and not so many years away from his balls dropping. Even allowing for a posh part of London, I'd notched up a fair bit of experience, not to mention a whole skip load of chutzpah, by the time I applied for the post, and I insisted that if they didn't like deputy manager, then it would have to be chief assistant manager, because I wasn't about to stand in foyers arguing the toss with some posh-voiced public-school adolescent about who's entitled to order who about.

Duncan found himself a member of the little cabal organising Our Side, all at the last minute, of course, and he asked me whether or not I'd be prepared to play a part in it 'which would make use of your professional expertise, dear boy'. Or would I rather just sit and watch my old school buddy get married? I told him that if I understood correctly what Our Side is about, Robert and his bride-to-be are well and truly up to their neck in what Their Side might be able to do, so yes, I would do my bit, as long as it wasn't checking out the loos.

So I found myself having a conversation with my counterpart in this hotel, a lovely lady called Joyce Firth, who may not be in the first flush of youth, but has a no-nonsense manner about her and obeys my most basic rules in being scrupulously clean and neatly but not ostentatiously well-dressed.

We pretty much took to each other from the start. She was impressed with where I work, which always goes down well with an incurable hotel-snob like me.

'You'll be thinking yourself slumming it in a place out in the sticks, Simon,' she said, as we're sipping a couple of very dry sherries in her office, which, irritatingly, is bigger than mine.

'Hotels are hotels, Joyce. I doubt whether you have too many hookers or drug dealers trying to function on your premises, but then, we don't have people coming back at tea time trailing sand on your carpets and smelling of fish.'

She laughed, a kind of deepish guffaw which wouldn't be out of place at a rugger do. 'Don't be so sure about the hookers and drug dealers, Simon. It's that much easier for young ladies, and for that matter young gentlemen, to display their wares freely around indoor and outdoor pools, and the south-west smuggling habit hasn't all gone away. There are lots of quiet coves to land stuff, if you're prepared to risk your boat being battered to bits on the rocks. Twenty or thirty million in the way of profits makes them brave.'

We spent a little more time comparing London and Devon notes, but time was getting short. The planning itself was straightforward enough, but there seemed to me to be a danger that she might feel her authority in her hotel compromised. She had, like me, a manager whose main raison d'être was PR and finances, meaning the day-to-day running of the place fell to his assistant.

On the day of the wedding, the hotel manager, Christophe Clauvier, was attending a meeting of the hotel chain in Paris. Joyce didn't have much trouble persuading him to co-operate with the general strategy.

'He spends almost as much time at head office as he does here,' she said. 'The last thing he wants is any grief breaking out in his own backyard. Whatever tactics I feel I need to adopt is OK with him, which will be fine unless something goes drastically wrong, in which case he'll deny all knowledge of it and it'll be *la guillotine pour moi. C'est la vie*, Simon. But if we work together, we can bring it off without too much trouble.'

By the time Councillor Needham climbed to his feet, we were pretty much all set. I'd had a good meal, but not too much, and a drink or two, but not too much, and I noted Duncan and this guy Bennett were taking it fairly easy as well. Bennett worked with the bride's father, it seemed, and they were old university buddies, so I didn't doubt he was in on the act.

This wedding hadn't as yet been the most conventional one in the world, but it hadn't been the most bizarre either – the tales I could tell, both personally and professionally, about Weddings I Have Known – and the fact that Councillor Needham seemed to be the first one to be making a speech at this do was obviously boggling the minds of about three quarters of the assembled company; the rest knew what was going on.

I can reproduce verbatim what Councillor Needham said, because both the hotel's CCTV cameras and one of the staff of the local paper, whose editor is the bride's uncle, was recording it all as well with a concealed camera as he sat not far from the councillor himself.

'I thought it might make a stir,' said Needham, projecting his smarmy voice right round the room, 'to see a chap who's not in any way related to either the bride or groom be the first to get to his feet for this wedding. Though I don't think it too outrageous for me to claim family friendship, and I've known the bride since she was a little girl. Some wedding arrangers can be very inflexible about guest speeches, but then compromise is what life is all about, isn't it, and I'm glad we've been able to come to a compromise in this case.'

Glances from all round the room at Peter and Helen Densham, both being as inscrutable as a couple of Chinese emperors.

'All the same, it is exceptional for family friends to be muscling in, but then again, we are looking at an exceptional couple. Kate, we all know well enough, is a brilliant young lawyer and Devonian born and bred; Robert the Londoner, I knew nothing about until quite recently, but bringing them together has not only resulted in a happy couple, it has also brought about a formidable partnership, and as an elected representative of local people and the appointed chairman of the local planning committee, I felt I really needed to congratulate and commend them for pulling off the spectacular deal they've managed for the people and prosperity of Devon.'

A ripple of applause, and optimistic looks were exchanged that he might leave it at that and sit down, but they were probably not people much acquainted with Councillor Needham.

'There is, of course, many a slip between cup and lip,' he continued, and I thought it would probably be possible at this stage to start taking bets on how many clichés can be squeezed into one wedding speech. 'People can lose their nerve, people can get cold feet, people can, regrettably, be weak enough to allow their resolve to fade away as soon as one or two obstacles present themselves. In my now quite extensive experience of planning processes, I can say that bringing to mind examples of occasions when obstacles didn't present themselves is difficult indeed. But I'm already well enough acquainted with Kate and Robert to know that, for them, every obstacle just presents a new and interesting challenge.'

A rather thinner ripple of applause this time, largely confined to Councillor Needham's table, where Councillor FC was beaming round on everyone, and the bandits, which was what I strongly suspected they were, were trying and failing to look less like bandits.

'I have an idea, though they've never said as much, that Kate and Robert have deliberately sought to bring this property deal to fruition to correspond with their big day and make it an even bigger day. Well, I say, why not? Most of the people who could seal the deal, so to speak, are with us, and those who aren't can easily be contacted. Let's do it, ladies and gentlemen, let's set this happy couple off on their life's journey with a great triumph, an opportunity to significantly add to the retail and housing resources of Kate's home county.'

A larger ripple, perhaps in the forlorn hope that Joe has finally shot his bolt, but no such luck, and his features had suddenly hardened.

'Of course, life isn't necessarily always the way we would like it to be, and I know there is negativity amongst us, which has been evident to me since my arrival yesterday afternoon, at the kind invitation of Professor and Mrs Densham. They are always, regrettably, there, the naysayers, the carping critics, the destroyers. Which is why I'm all the more relieved that some of my friends and I are here, so that we can do our best to ensure that this opportunity is taken and those who would want to pour cold water on Kate and Robert's big day are encouraged to give their best consideration to consequences as well as prizes. Such things as breach of contract, underhanded business practices, spreading false information, peddling fake news.'

Now the room was very conscious that an atmosphere had been created, and it was one of menace and tension. Another very necessary piece of the hotel management unspoken manual is understanding atmosphere. And no imagination was needed in this situation to see the source of the tension, with Needham's men – almost all men – gathered in the spaces outside the Banqueting Suite. A few were actually in it; Needham's table could now be perceived as not the only one his followers, henchmen, whoever they were – no-one was quite sure – were occupying. Their unsmiling eyes were sweeping around the room. When Needham had twisted Peter Densham's arm into inviting him, he'd obviously managed to include a few extra tickets, as it were.

But I knew now, and that makes all the difference. I knew it all, right down to the point of letting Needham bring all these guys with him. I couldn't claim to be the bravest man in the world. There have been occasions when I've had to deal with obstreperous or intoxicated guests when my heart has been pounding away so heavily I wondered how the whole hotel couldn't hear it. Hospitality is a bit of a hit-and-miss trade. The great majority of people were no bother; most of them were a pleasure to serve. But there were some, and then some, and then some more, and it has to be said that it's often the ones with the most money or power or status who are the worst.

Needham suddenly smiled, a gruesome sight, like a tiger licking its chops after the final remains of a gazelle or something have gone down very nicely. 'But this is not the tone we should be striking at an event of this kind,' he said, the benign pick up after the slap down. His sentence had two issues for me; one, the word 'we' should actually be 'I'; two, no it isn't, and you know it, you weasel.

'Some couples celebrate with spectacular honeymoons, perhaps spectacular in more ways than one.' His jokey voice made clear this was supposed to be a vaguely smutty weddingish pleasantry, but he was a long way past amusing anyone but his clique.

'Others rely on really slap-up celebrations, and certainly we've had nothing to complain of in that respect.' A vague smattering of half-hearted applause. 'But, for Robert and Kate, it is the deal, the very big deal, which even in their youth, they've managed to accomplish, and both their legal futures and the prospects for the people of Devon will be so much the better for it. And it's on behalf of the people of Devon that I thank the families concerned for letting me say my piece. More power to their and your elbow, Robert and Kate Harrington, and may this great day be the prelude to a long and happy life together.'

His guys managed to make a vaguely convincing noise, and as they were doing that and people were exchanging glances, knowing from Our Side, embarrassed and bewildered by the majority, I took my cue. I nodded to Duncan, who nodded back, and then I nodded again to the top table, in particular Peter Densham and Giles Cavendish, as I took the opportunity to leave the room. As I did, I notice Needham had seen and noticed this exchange, and for the first time, he didn't look quite so comfortable.

The Christie Suite had its own sort of foyer area behind it, with a broad corridor leading down to the reception area and main foyer to the right and another not quite so broad heading off to the rooms to the right. There were more people milling about in the Christie foyer than there ought to be, and it was clearly making life difficult for the staff moving between the suite and the kitchens. People hanging around or plonking themselves down in areas which should be about transit is a constant problem in hotels. Most customers are, of course, working people, and they usually visit hotels in their leisure time, meaning they find themselves in the unfamiliar situation of having nothing to do. But most of the people hanging around at the moment were not temporarily bewildered hotel guests at a loose end. I've not worked in these places without developing antennae for this stuff, and Giles Cavendish, in the last pow-wow of Our Side, made clear enough the kind of people we were dealing with.

'I'm not going into nationality details; there are limits on what I can and can't tell you. But when these organisations are working on their home ground, they tend to fix on family events because they know how important family is to the people they're dealing with. In many cases, they have existing arrangements with the police – occasionally, they are the police. They know that people are never as susceptible as when they know something unpleasant might happen to members of their families, and they also know that promises made in front of family members are particularly unlikely to be broken. That's why they tend to pick on these sorts of events to lean on the people they need to sanction the deal, and the bigger the deal, the more the leaning. Someone has probably said to them that Britain isn't like that; you can't buy the police, and if you muck about 'creating a disturbance' at a private function, you will be arrested before you can put the deal to bed, but that doesn't necessarily bother them, as long as their message of intimidation has got across. Everyone knows the police can't be around all the time.'

Joyce was keeping a watching brief from about halfway down the corridor to the main foyer, and she beckoned to me, taking something from her pocket as I got to her. 'Here, pin this on, Simon.'

A neat badge, self-adhesive and large enough to be seen from several feet away, said 'Simon Roche, Assistant Manager', in matching style to Joyce's 'Joyce Firth, Events Manager', giving both of us public credentials, which didn't guarantee, of course, that anyone would take any notice of them, especially in view of the sort of people we might be dealing with. We would need back-up if things started getting nasty. I couldn't deny there were very distinct and insistent butterflies circulating my insides, but I knew something of what Cavendish had in mind, and that made me a little more comfortable.

What Cavendish was planning was going to happen anyway – I've met enough fixers in my time to know one when I see one – but Joyce and I had it in our power to help it along. We both took a few deep breaths and headed towards some of the characters in the Christie foyer.

Matthew

Simon made his exit well; he was obviously used to moving around hotels unobtrusively, but I wasn't sure even such a rapid and quiet withdrawal had gone unnoticed by Needham, who was turning to one of his flunkeys almost as soon as he'd sat down. It's said that some paranoiacs really do have people gunning for them, and that might well sum up his situation. I'd noticed him glancing at Giles Cavendish just a little nervously; I think he'd already worked out that Cavendish might be more than just the best man. The air of authority and organisation Giles carries around with him is unusual for such a relatively young man, and it was pretty certain to give food for thought to such a man as Needham.

The last unobtrusive text I had from my guys in the foyers suggests that they were hoovering up a lot of photos of the people hanging about. Tony also told me that we were no longer the only publication represented in the environs of the hotel; word about the supposed approaching big deal and the sort of tactics being used to secure it had spread, and he reckoned there was at least one national daily sniffing around.

The order of speaking had been cooked up between Peter and Kate, their theory being that once the councillor has kicked off, apparently by invitation of the family, people were not going to be too surprised about whoever now got to their feet. Perhaps they have a point, because when it became obvious that the next person to speak was going to be the bride, the reaction was little more than a kind of shimmering murmur and a few raised eyebrows. For all the huge amount of time, planning and care women put into weddings, it remains rare to see any of them actually get to say anything, but the murmur had a more interrogative than disapproving sound to it, and perhaps there was even a note of appreciation that here, at last, was a wedding determined to do things the way it wanted them done, which took on the traditions it saw as appropriate to the occasion and discarded the others.

Any notion that Kate won't have the volume or command to her voice to induce the company to listen to her were instantly dispelled by the assertive courtroom tone which now broke upon the room and rebounded from the walls.

'Thank you, Councillor Needham. I have always found your take on the world interesting at the very least, and I suspect that, in your take on the world, the last person you'd expect to be following your speech would be the bride. Brides are about looking pretty, demure, even virginal, if the bride in question thinks she can get away with it; if they are expected to open their mouths at all, it is to gush their shy thanks, usually to the caterers or someone similar.

'However, this particular bride is also the legal representative of the concern which Councillor Needham believes will bring such prosperity and prestige to our part of the West Country woods, and the legal representative with the local knowledge which Councillor Needham and his friends think so essential to the success of the Big Deal. In a few minutes, I'm going to hand you over to the best man, perhaps a more traditional wedding speech maker, but before that, there are a few myths which need dealing with and a few points concerning the Big Deal which need clarification.'

Now we had reached the point where a pin dropping from anyone's table would have resounded like a veritable cacophony.

I've never yet seen Kate at work professionally, and my mind was already boggling somewhat at the adult presence of this girl who was once so used to taking a backseat, usually to her much bigger and louder brother. I'm not sure Tom had seen his sister in court either; he was gazing towards her as if struck by a revelation, not least at the sheer voice projection she can manage; it wouldn't surprise me if most of the people in the foyer could hear her.

'It is a shame that occasions like this always come with some baggage, as if it's suddenly necessary to throw the affairs of both families into the limelight, whether or not they have anything to do with the wedding itself. This is often simply gossip, but some gossip can be malicious. Who has been circulating malicious gossip and why is a subject I think the best man will be returning to, but both my family and Robert's feel that much of it is what lawyers might call "of bad motive" and the real position should be made clear in front of so many people here who do genuinely care for our families.

'I have been authorised – another dreadful lawyer's phrase, I know, but very necessary on this occasion – to speak on behalf of both families, in this matter at least. Firstly, it has been put about that Robert's parents are about to divorce; why this should be seen as immediately relevant to our wedding, neither of us can understand, nor why such stories should emerge at what should be a happy time for the family. I can tell you categorically that no such divorce is going to happen, and the family want me to add that they would be quite happy to take legal action against anyone who is proved to be the source of such stories. Since the family contains at least two highly competent and experienced lawyers, it would be as well for them to take such a warning seriously.'

Now Needham was starting to look a little unsettled, which he expresses, as I know from previous experience, by a kind of hurt exasperation, as if he was struggling to credit what appeared to be happening in front of him. But, more significantly, he was also whispering something to one of his henchmen, causing the latter to make his exit, though because this was in the middle of someone's speech rather than at the end of it, the departure was noticed. Giles Cavendish had certainly noticed it, and it seemed to be the cue for him to text a message to someone. I was close enough to him to see what he was doing, but to most of the hall, he'd made it look as if he was just thinking over what the speaker was saying.

The speaker herself remained entirely undaunted by the departure. She had already changed the atmosphere in the hall by seizing control of the proceedings back from Needham, and the great majority of the assembled company were fully behind her in that.

'There are also some silly stories about my own parents circulating, and again it's difficult to believe the people behind them are anything else but evilly motivated. As it's already clear that the stories are not being taken seriously, I won't even dignify them by repeating them in public. I will simply say this, and I say it again with legal resources in support if they have to be, that neither my parents nor Robert's are in public service, and even if they were, their relationships are totally and entirely their business and no-one else's.'

A few people in the Christie Banqueting Suite were now sitting up straight, as if they'd been told to sit nicely. I suspected that Kate could now tell some of them to stand to attention and they'd do it like a shot. I've known her and her parents since she was born, and it's not too difficult to see what Peter and Helen have given her; she has a lot of Peter's eloquence and public presence, and equal amounts of Helen's powers of organisation and control. But there was something else now. I think it takes until adulthood for those qualities which are entirely individual and distinctive in a person to emerge, and Kate communicates a kind of seriousness of purpose, almost a crusading spirit, which is really hers alone.

I sneaked a glance at her husband; I still didn't know the guy very well, and if there was in him some quality of suppressed caveman or downtrodden doormat, he certainly wasn't showing any sign of it. He looked attentive, but totally relaxed, and the state of his eyes as he looked at his new wife left no doubt whatsoever about his feelings for her.

'But now we come to the matter which Councillor Needham has named as the great triumph of our wedding day, the spectacular property deal which the organisation Councillor Needham supports and recommends is about to do with the university authorities for a development generally described as "leisure housing", a development which is, allegedly, going to bring new prosperity and distinction to us all in our part of the world. It will also provide the university with funds enough to expand their provision right across the board. Robert and I were flattered and honoured to be approached by Councillor Needham's associates to handle this deal for them, especially in view of our relative youth.'

She paused for long enough to gaze directly at Needham, who managed a kind of self-deprecating shrug which registered no reaction in Kate at all. Then we found out what the pause was in aid of.

'It therefore grieves me, Councillor, to have to tell you that Robert and I will be unable to continue representing your associates as of today. I also have to tell you that we have passed on to the relevant authorities substantial evidence of malpractice and illegal associations concerning both them and you. Yes, my dear new husband and I did seek to bring a triumph to our wedding day, and we believe we have, insofar as I believe we might well have succeeded in putting you and the kind of people you work with permanently out of business. I hand over now to Mr Giles Cavendish, who will eventually be addressing us in his wedding-day role of best man but has to begin by speaking in his more professional capacity. Giles?'

As Giles was getting to his feet, a light flashed on the phone in my lap and a text appeared from Tony: 'Uniformed and plainclothes police arriving. Four carloads of them. Showing identity cards at reception.' If this was an example of Cavendish's timing and organisation, it couldn't have happened much more neatly than it had.

A ripple of dazed but impressed applause rippled around the hall as Kate sat down, and all eyes turned to the immaculately dressed and coolly authoritative Mr Cavendish. All except those on Needham's table; all of them were on their feet, and their very menacing aspect was not being lost on the rest of the company.

'Thank you, Kate. I'm deeply sensible of the honour I've been accorded in being chosen as best man, and I wouldn't normally dream of usurping such an occasion as this by talking shop. Unfortunately, the shop in question is extremely relevant to both the bride and the bridegroom, and if I can contribute modestly to their considerable recent achievements, I'm only too happy to do so.'

Two of the men on Needham's table, specifically the two largest, had left their table and were walking towards Cavendish. Tom Densham, Duncan Allen and several other men on or around the top table were also on their feet. At this precise moment, a rustle of surprise right across the room caused everyone to turn in the direction of the foyer connecting to the rest of the hotel, where something in the region of a dozen uniformed police personnel, three of them women, had appeared, accompanied by three men in suits carrying papers and folders, and a fourth suited man who was, clearly enough, in charge of the whole group.

For a moment, the whole hall froze, as if performing a tableau. Then the officer in charge, a man in late middle age with occasional streaks of grey in the temples of his hair whose age, and somehow also presence, set him apart from the other police personnel, nodded at Giles, and the cool public-school tones asserted themselves over the hall again.

'I think Detective Superintendent Conroy would appreciate it if you gentlemen would resume your seats. DS Conroy and I would both also be very grateful if no-one leaves this room until I have finished speaking; we have had enough disturbance during what should have been a happy family occasion as it is.'

No-one seemed inclined to argue, and by the time Giles resumed, we were back at the pin-drop stage, though this time, the silence was enhanced by the quietness which seemed to have taken over throughout the nearby areas.

'I should say at this stage that I am attached to a government department; I cannot say which department, nor can I say what my role is, but I do want everyone to understand that I am acting with that authority behind me, as, of course, is DS Conroy.

'We have for some time been following the activities of Councillor Needham and his associates, and my department were notified some time ago on the basis that their actions could be endangering the lives and liberties of British citizens. I know a good deal, from research and from personal experience, about international trends in illegality, and we know that it is not unusual, in totalitarian countries where distinguishing between the police and the criminals is sometimes very difficult, for gangs wishing to further their own interests to descend upon family gatherings like this to intimidate some person or persons into co-operating with whatever the persecuting organisation wishes to achieve. No-one is more vulnerable than when the safety and security of their nearest and dearest is a stake. We were first alerted to the nature of Councillor Needham's associates by the combination of Professor Peter Densham, his daughter Kate and his prospective son-in-law Robert Harrington, an ex-student friend of mine. Through Robert, they all reported their concerns that a very substantial, multi-million-pound property deal between Professor Densham's university and the company whose proposals Councillor Needham was supporting was being advocated in rather an aggressive fashion, with each successive contact including vague but unspecified threats. Kate and Robert had accepted the brief of Needham's associates partly to gain greater knowledge and experience of this organisation which seemed to act in such an odd way. Before I arrived here yesterday, my department had already garnered a good deal of information about Councillor Needham's associates, some of it directly from Kate, Robert and Peter. Since I arrived, our knowledge has been considerably enhanced by contributions from Peter's brother Matthew, editor of the leading local newspaper; Professor David Bennett, an environmentalist and colleague of Peter's; and Duncan Allen, a widely acknowledged expert on internet security, especially as it bears upon commercial companies. I will now summarise briefly – I've already been on my feet too long and DS Conroy is a busy man – what we know now to have been going on.'

I'd been glancing towards Needham from time to time, answering his murderous glare when my name was mentioned with a happy smile, and it was something of a miracle that he'd remained quiet to this point, but he now looked about ready to burst, and the inevitable interruption arrived.

'Is this some kind of kangaroo court? This is a wedding, for God's sake. I hope you, whoever you are, have got good lawyers—'

He was interrupted by DS Conroy, whose laser eyes and well-built frame had now become more obvious as he moved towards Needham and was closer to us.

'Mr Needham, sir, I can arrest you publicly now or more privately later. It is your choice, sir, but if your preference is for more privately later, I would advise you to resume your seat.'

Needham, with a wide-armed gesture of outrage, did just that, but his attempt to share his outrage with the other men on the table found them visibly ignoring him.

'So we can now make clear what has been happening before and since we gathered at this hotel, supposedly for a happy family occasion. Professor Densham, on my advice, conceded to Councillor Needham all he asked, including the right for the councillor to book representatives of his associated company into the hotel, and even the right for the councillor to be the first to address the wedding ceremony. All these negotiations were carried out with implicit background threats. Needham and his associates wanted the deal to be signed before the wedding, so the wedding could be used as a publicity vehicle; they made unspecified threats as the date approached, and when it was clear that the deal was not going to be signed before the wedding, several things happened. An ex-colleague of Malcolm Harrington QC, Robert's father, was bribed to reveal what he thought were details of Mr and Mrs Harrington's relationship, and these details were released to the media on the very day, yesterday, when we were assembling at this hotel. When Professor Densham made clear that a signing deal was not going to happen during the wedding either, attempts were made to compromise his own relationship, but the national media were not interested and the local media refused to see it as a news matter.

'Needham's associates not only booked into the wedding hotel, they also maintained a vigil of illegal surveillance of the hotel, in order to establish who was where if further more personal intimidations should be needed. We also now have incontrovertible evidence of Councillor Needham's personal involvement with the organisation which was acting illegally in these many ways, because an IT expert with highly sophisticated security equipment who Robert Harrington knew would be attending the wedding intercepted incoming messages addressed to Councillor Needham in which direct references were made to the fees Needham was expecting to receive, even if the deal were not signed, and Needham's participation in the intimidation campaign directed at this occasion was specifically and undeniably acknowledged.'

All eyes were now directed towards Needham, and some of the others on his table had even actually physically pulled away from him. He seemed to recognise this as the moment when it was all over. He made an odd open-armed gesture of resigned hopelessness, got up and moved towards Conroy. For a moment, Conroy tensed, but then he recognised that the movement was one of surrender, not confrontation, and it became obvious that, public arrest or not, all Joe Needham wanted to do was get out of the building as soon as possible.

As Needham left the room and his companions trailed off after him, DS Conroy turned back to the top table. 'We'll speak later, Mr Cavendish. And my congratulations to you, sir.'

As the company in general realised that the atmosphere of tension and intimidation had just been adroitly wafted away, spontaneous applause broke out, and it soon became clear that it was likely to continue for some time. Cavendish at first nodded and smiled, but standing alone in the spotlight didn't seem to suit him too well, and when the ovation had continued for upwards of ninety seconds, he called on the bride and bridegroom to stand with him. He also tried to raise one or two more of his fellow 'conspirators', but no-one wanted to be seen to take attention away from the couple at the centre of the whole event. Giles Cavendish eventually resumed his seat and left the newly married Mr and Mrs Harrington to have the floor to themselves. When the applause finally died away, Kate also sat down and her husband was standing alone. He held up his hands and eventually achieved something like silence.

'Ladies and gentlemen, I suspect you've had as much speechifying as you can live with for one day, but I do have one or two things which need saying. Kate and I will be appearing during the evening, but not for very long, I'm afraid. We are both exhausted, after an anxious and demanding period, and we intend to leave early tomorrow for London to wrap up what we need to do before our honeymoon.

'And now, I have one last duty to perform. We can hardly claim this event as the most traditional wedding in the world, but it usually falls to the groom to say the thank-yous on behalf of the couple concerned, and I am more than happy to do so. If I went through the entire list of the people who are due thanks for rescuing this event from the pit of trouble which threatened to engulf it, we would be sitting here until the evening and we are already imposing on the hotel staff who have to clear this room for the evening's purposes. I will, of course, signal my gratitude to the best man, whose best man's contribution went above and beyond what most grooms might reasonably expect. I would also like to mention both my parents and Kate's parents, who were the unfortunate targets of some of the wrecking tactics of Councillor Needham's friends and who have taken that into their stride as well as all the other crises bringing up Kate and myself have thrown into their path. We are grateful to the hotel staff for providing us with such a wonderful do, and I thank my dear friend Simon Roche, a hotel professional himself, for pitching in with that on an occasion when he might reasonably have expected to be off-duty.'

Simon was now standing at the side of the room and at this, he blew a kiss in Robert's direction and bowed.

'But most of all, I want to give my love and thanks to the beautiful and brilliant woman who, by some benign miracle, has been prepared to become my wife. We wanted to give the marriage a memorable send-off, and I rather think we have; I suspect those of you here present are not going to forget this wedding in a good while! Ladies and gentlemen, please be outstanding for Mrs Kate Harrington!'

The hotel staff had been steadily maintaining the supply of drinks through the speeches, and at this, the room rose as one.

The boy was right, of course. Very little about this wedding will drift from my memory in a long time, and as young Robert sat down, flushed and smiling with sheer delight, I looked from him to my dear niece and back again, and a great feeling of pride and satisfaction rose within me at the sight of them. May they always be as happy as they are at this moment.

Celia

As the guests began to file out of this splendid Christie room, or whatever they call it, I knew that the lump in my throat was not, as I might have suspected, the lingering effects of that final profiterole. What a marvellous and extraordinary experience, and how startling for it all to be happening here. My eyes have been opened; we Londoners, who pride ourselves at always being in the thick of things, can learn a lot from these supposed West Country backwaters. Perhaps it's a bit much to still call myself a Londoner, having moved myself to a quiet place in the country where a bare-torsoed young gardener can provide the major source of interest on a summer morning, but London will always be 'where I come from'.

I was quite proud, not only of my own family, but these redoubtable Devonians my grandson has appeared to have married into, who have systematically brought to justice a rogue in their midst. They'd also managed to reassure me that I wasn't slowly going round the bend last night as a result of excessive alcoholic consumption; there really were odd characters inhabiting the hotel grounds, and as far as I can gather from what's been said, they were deliberately attempting to inhibit and intimidate the people who had come to the hotel for the purposes of enjoying a wedding. I only hope they got thoroughly cold and had at least seventeen species of insects invading their clothing.

I made my way gradually in the direction of a lift; I was finally beginning to understand the topography of this hotel. Some of the guests were already heading for the bars, I see, at just going on for quarter to five in the afternoon, meaning there would be those amongst us who would be well whiffled by this evening, and especially the late evening, which is usually embarrassing and creates an unpleasant atmosphere. Fortunately, I am not in the business of late evenings these days, and if I don't get a fair dollop of rest this afternoon, I might not be in the business of early evenings either.

I supposed it behoved me to show up, for at least some of the time; I thought Malcolm and Barbara, not to mention the bridegroom himself, might be a little hurt were I to go completely AWOL. However, the prospect was a little daunting, not least because of the assumptions people make of the understanding of old people, which was, I suppose, the group in which I must now find myself. I anticipated a number of people, few of whom I either knew or was related to, would assume that I hadn't been able to follow the complexities of 'the case', as it were. I would be offered, mostly but not necessarily exclusively, by men, patient explanations of the Needham plot, the bad lot he was associating with, or perhaps more accurately, being used by, and the various nuances involving the spies and the police, etc. Happily, I am neither deaf nor demented – well, not yet anyway – and my condition will probably ensure that I've gone before having had the chance to get either.

I made it back to my suite without incident and gratefully so. I was tired, and taking a little time out on my splendid balcony on what is now a correspondingly splendid day might have changed my mind about venturing down into the lion's den this evening.

The facilities provided by the hotel included a little teapot, which I appreciated; all this fooling about with tea bags in mugs is not my cup of tea, nor will it ever be. Tea needs to come out of teapots. Why I wanted any kind of beverage, I wasn't sure, having been gulping down liquids of various kinds all day long, but there was a different quality about having tea on one's own. It suddenly occurred to me that, much as I criticised my retirement village from time to time, I was actually quite content there, and a bit wary of alternatives which people might dream up for me. I was wondering about the consequences of Malcolm and Barbara's separation, because I didn't doubt it would be a separation, whatever the talk about trial periods. They are incompatible; in my opinion, they always have been, but they gave it every chance and they did manage to produce a remarkably gifted and charming boy, who rounded off the proceedings today, I thought, with great charm and elegance. And no, my traditionalist instincts were not outraged by the bride's oration. In my younger days, brides were required to say little more than 'I do', and like most brides, I could have had a lot more to say if the opportunity had been given to me.

It didn't take me long to have my little teapot and the normal accoutrements out on the balcony table, and it seemed I had timed everything to neatly correspond with the departure of Councillor Needham from the hotel, I suspect in a rather less bumptious mood than when he arrived. Even in the teeth of quite a considerable body of evidence to the contrary, I've never really believed that anyone is intrinsically evil; there is almost always an explanation for those who stray from the straight and narrow. What went wrong in Needham's case, I have no idea; perhaps an alcoholic parent or parents, perhaps being bullied at school, perhaps an inflated ego from being given power he couldn't handle. My experience of men like Needham, and it is quite extensive after a long life, is that their main problem is that they are not as clever as they think they are. And, of course, there are always those whose brains tend to be contained in other parts of their anatomy, and there are always, if I'm trying to be even-handed about it, women around who are prepared to take advantage of that strain of fellow.

I could almost have felt sorry for Needham, as I saw him doing a sort of half-slumped walk on his way to a marked police car. He was surrounded by three men, all of them clearly bigger than him, and the chutzpah had been well and truly taken out of him. They had, at least, spared him the handcuffs. He didn't look to be a particularly old man – mid-forties, I'd say – so perhaps he might yet find some kind of redemption. I would like to think so. If we're being honest, I think the great majority of us, certainly including me, have had something of a dance with the devil at some stage of our lives.

Which, of course, made me think about mine, and my own naughty-girl moments. Which, of course, led me to the realisation that, whatever I've done or been, none of it is going to go on for much longer. Tea is supposed to put new life into one, or calm the troubled mind, but it didn't seem to work on this occasion. Life is a peculiar beast, rocking horse, tiger, big dipper, whatever, but it's the only thing we know, and the nearer one gets to losing it, the more apprehensive one becomes about what, if anything, will follow.

Thinking this wasn't, perhaps, the most suitable mood for my only grandchild's wedding, I tried to wrench myself back to some determination that, as long as there was a little left in the tank, I would continue to move the vehicle forward. Then someone knocked at the door, and I only had a few seconds to think about suitable retorts, with, I'm afraid to say, 'sod off' quite high in the running, before a voice followed the knock, and it was immediately recognisable as the voice of the aforesaid solitary grandchild Robert, even though only one word was uttered.

'Gran?'

I got up and moved towards the door, not without some difficulty, and realising that he might have decided I'm not in and gone away by the time I actually got to the door, I relied on a little vocal delivery, which he and his wife had given us admirable examples of earlier.

'It's open, Robert! Do come in, dear!'

And so he did, and he was already out of his wedding finery, though perfectly respectably dressed in a short-sleeved shirt and proper trousers, not these ubiquitous tatty jeans so many men go in for now.

'I was just taking the air on the balcony, having been indoors for so long,' I said.

'Well, I'm happy to join you with that, Gran,' he said. 'I haven't had too much of it myself today, what with this, that and the other.'

We'd settled ourselves on the balcony and exchanged a few comments and observations about the wedding before he got to the main purpose of his visit, though even when he did, I still had an inkling it wasn't the really main main purpose, as it were.

'It's all been rather more exciting that we would perhaps have wanted, and I'm hoping you won't feel too tired to join us this evening. As you know, evening dos at weddings can get to be rather noisy, and we wanted you to know we've made arrangements concerning that. Music and dancing will be going on in the Christie Suite where we were, but the hotel also has a lounge called the Williamson Lounge, which we've booked as well as the Christie Suite so that people who aren't so keen on the noise, heat, etc. of the suite will have somewhere peaceful for a quiet drink and conversation.'

'Catering for all age groups. How very considerate of you and your wife, Robert; a phrase which you're going to have to get used to. But it must be costing an awful lot of money.' I regretted the words even as they left my mouth; it was no business of mine, after all.

'Oh, we all decided to push the boat out, especially when it became clear how – well, let's say, individual – the thing was going to be. It's mainly Kate and I, but both sets of parents have chipped in.'

He said this with a detectable note of embarrassment that I should have mentioned the vulgar subject of money. I would have chipped in myself, of course, but that was water under the bridge now, and an offer at this stage would embarrass him.

'Well, thank you, Robert, darling, and I do think the Williamson Lounge will be the place for me. Why Williamson? Is this another Devon literary link?'

'Yes, Henry Williamson, who wrote *Tarka the Otter*, though I can't, in all honesty, look smug and claim I knew that before coming here. The lounge is about comfortable armchairs and pictures of Devon wildlife and scenery, calculated to be relaxing.'

'Splendid,' I said, and a realisation immediately came to me as I gazed at him. I'd known this boy since the day that he was born, and that did give me a certain intuition about what he's saying and what he's not saying.

'But that isn't all, Robert, is it?' I said.

His eyes had temporarily fallen to the floor, and when they returned to me, while no actual tears were there, a rather different expression had taken over.

'Gran, how ill are you?' The voice was very quiet now.

'Oh,' I said, and for a moment, that was all I could manage. I could be angry; this could be a rather sly attempt to use him, the particular apple of my eye, as fisher-in-chief to get some kind of straight answer out of the stubborn old so-and-so, i.e., me. But here he was, on perhaps the greatest day of his life, marriage to a beautiful and talented young woman and a truly enormous professional coup, worrying himself about me. A churlish or fob-off response simply wouldn't do, not here, not now.

'I am ill, Robbie,' I said, thinking I probably haven't called him that since he was about twelve. 'I know it, and the consultant knows it. But we are still in the business of doing tests, and until they've all been finished, we don't know what the full story is. I know people think I'm being stubborn or secretive or something, but I can't give people information I don't have. Even when we have all the test results, it's extremely unlikely that we will get to the point of talking about how long in terms of specific times. They don't do that now, because of legal and insurance stuff, policies being invalidated, people likely to sue them and what have you. But I'm an old woman, darling. Nothing lasts for ever.'

'More's the pity.'

His head went down again. I suppose I was a little taken aback. I'd always known that Robert was fond of me, and there was an element of self-congratulation about it, but in all honesty, if you can't develop a close and loving relationship with a grandchild when you've only got one, you're not doing very well, are you? I tried from the start not to indulge him too much; I know grandparents are supposed to be in the business of spoiling their grandkids with little treats which their parents don't give them, but Derek and I tried to avoid that, with the possible exception of Christmas. Mostly for Robert's sake, I wanted to steer clear of confrontations with his parents, or more specifically his mother, which might have resulted in limiting Robert's access to us. Well into his teens, Robert liked to come and stay with us for a few days every now and then. He would help us in the garden and Derek would take him to the local pool sometimes, when Derek was still able to do a few lengths. Robert was a keen swimmer from babyhood onwards, but his father lacked the time and energy to spend as much time with him as he would have liked; you don't get to Malcolm's level of career success without putting in a great deal of hard work.

He also liked 'the atmosphere' of our house. He spent the great majority of his time either in his school, with all that testosterone and competition sloshing about, or at home, when the tensions between Barbara and Malcolm would be all too evident at times, I suspect. He said to me once, 'You're so relaxed here, you and Grandad,' which is as close as he would ever get to criticising his parents, in front of us anyway. I looked at him with his head bent, a just-married up-and-coming London lawyer, and I thought, this has to stop – today, at least.

I took both his hands in mine, as I used to do when he was a child. 'Look at me, Robert,' I said, and he did; no tears, just a slightly ruddy flush to the cheeks, which could be robust good health as much as emotion.

'Generations, Robert. People come and go. One day, and I hope it's still a very long way away, you may well be having the same sort of conversation with your own grandchild. By then, I hope you will have had a long and successful life, and after today, I suspect you probably will. But until such time as eternal life comes along, and we will all have to think long and hard if it ever does, people's times come and they go. Mine probably hasn't got long to go, but we've had a happy time of it, you and I, and we've got a whole stack of nice memories, perhaps all nice apart from when your grandad had to leave us.

'This is your wedding day, darling. It's unhappy that all this business with your parents had to come along, but they will find a way; I've spoken to them both, and they've already started. Love the past, retain it in your mind and memories, but don't let it sour the present, and especially not the future. Enjoy the rest of the day. Make the most of it, now and always. What is Kate doing now?'

I've always known when something I've said to Robert has registered, which is more than I can say for some men. He took it all in, processed it and extracted what he needed.

'She's resting; she'll be starting shortly to get herself dressed and ready for the evening, but for the moment, she's kind of mentally preparing. As am I; we're both tired. It would have been pressurised coming up to the wedding anyway, even if all this Needham business hadn't come along. But she wanted people to know about the Williamson Lounge, in case those who don't like sitting with noisy music got the wrong impression. And she especially wanted you to know. Her own grandparents are no longer with us; I suppose you could say that you're the matriarch of this do, Gran.'

He smiled. This sort of intrigued and terrified me at the same time. I almost felt inclined to go down wrapped in a shawl and carrying an ear trumpet, so I could park myself in a prominent position and pretend to be deaf.

'Bless you, darling, and if it's true, I'm happy to have had the chance to be. Now go to your wife, my darling, and tell her I'll be down matriarching away in the Williamson Lounge, keeping them all in order, though I'm not sure many of the Williamson loungers will be much in the business of doing anything else.'

He laughed, rose, kissed me lightly on both cheeks and was gone. As always, even before Derek died, his departure left me with a huge vacancy, and made me reflect that a huge permanent vacancy may soon be coming down the line.

But the time for that stuff had gone, for the moment at least. I was going to just slop on down in my daytime wedding gear, but I did bring a change for the evening which is a little less formal and a little less old lady. Matriarchs can't exactly turn up in T-shirts and shimmering mini-skirts, but they don't have to be doled up like old Queen Mary either.

'One more time, old girl,' said Derek in my ear, and I could remember the time and care he always took to 'dress for the occasion', within the restrictive parameters of what men can and can't get away with, parameters which might well be tested this evening, though not necessarily, I suspect, in the Williamson Lounge.

Phyllis

Perhaps it was the sudden onset of such unforeseen passion between us, or perhaps it was the bizarre ceremony we'd just gone through. Maybe a combination of the two, the physical fatigue following our bath-time romp combined with the mental mind-stretching involved in the wedding, though 'the wedding' seems an inadequate, under-nourished word for what had gone off in that room. I've never been to a wedding which didn't have its dramatic side, perhaps most obviously my own; I'd spent the previous three days in a state of agitation and pathetic indecision. I worried that I didn't feel much for Colin then beyond lust; he was a real hunk in those days. As I said, even now he doesn't carry much spare flesh; then, he had a body like an Adonis, and the fact that he wasn't a pretty boy was as much in his favour rather than otherwise. I knew I didn't have much in common with him, but men being from Mars and women from Venus, spending your life waiting for a man to come along who shares your work and leisure interests could leave you in old maidhood with no energy left for the interests which are really interesting. Sharing a table at the wedding with both Colin and David and the knowledge that my initial attraction to both of them was pure and simple lust was somehow a bit demeaning, but then I reflected that getting the real hots for two men in over twenty years is not exactly galloping nymphomania.

We made it back to our room, not without some difficulty; folk were wandering about either dazed or still hyper, chattering loudly and oo-ahing. Someone had pushed a note under our door about the evening options, basically the youthie dance room or the oldie quiet lounge, and in spite of our earlier activities, or maybe because of them, Colin and I had no doubts about which scenario would suit us best. The bathroom physicals had made demands on places where I didn't know I still had places, and much as I would like to think of myself as immune to the passage of time – wouldn't we all – anything like even an hour's bopping on the dance floor would almost certainly leave me in someone's treatment room with several physios seeking to unlock my limbs from paralysis.

But we both knew something had changed between us, and perhaps permanently. As soon as we were back in our room and enjoying those vistas of the hotel car park, Colin set about making a pot of tea unasked; tiny as the provided teapots were, they were still proper teapots. We sat down around our little table like two soldiers just returned from the battlefield, and if we couldn't pick up the passion from where we were, we could revive the spirit. The notion of a common purpose had a genuine attraction, as if opening a door to a place where the exhausting conflicts and tensions of our relationship might just fade away.

After two or three restorative sips, Colin broke the silence. 'Now then, Mrs Drayton, let us review the recent and present proceedings and see how we stand, going forward.'

He sounded so like a pompous boss that I couldn't help a giggle, but he was meaning the caricature, so he giggled too.

He resumed in his normal Colin voice. 'We could just go home. This isn't a wedding connected with either of our families, and I don't know about you, but I'm pretty much fagged out.'

'Colin Drayton, are you telling me that you came here just for a few shenanigans in the bathroom? Shame on you. In any case, the room is paid for tonight.'

This was the answer he seemed to be expecting. 'Righto. Well, what I suggest is a leisurely walk to that village you can see from most windows of the hotel, just to get a bit of fresh air and leave the hothouse of this place before braving the what's-it lounge for the evening. Tea rooms, pub or something. We've done more talking, more real talking, today than we've done for some time, Phyllis. OK, we're both still a long way from retirement, but we've only got each other to look after, and I think it's each other we should be taking care of. I don't want anyone else but you, Phyll; maybe I should have been making that clearer recently, but I've had a feeling for a while of being trapped in my mincing machine of a job with no way out, and it's taken just a few well-chosen words from you to make me see that I'm not trapped in anything. We have no need of this, Phyll; the mortgage was paid a while ago, the house is ours, we both have entitlements from our working years.'

His hand, still warm from his tea mug, was on mine. Maybe not the most steamily romantic gesture a girl could experience, but just at that moment, good enough for me.

'There isn't a word of that I could disagree with, Colin. Let's get out of the wedding stuff and take the afternoon Devon air.'

The afternoon, quite late afternoon now, was beautifully still, with that striking mix of rural airs, both delicately scented and more earthy, which characterised this part of the world. It was perhaps slightly more than half a mile to the nearby village, but neither of us cared very much; my arm was in his, and even if this was proved to be more of a truce, a hiatus between two exhausted combatants, than a permanent change, it still needed to be enjoyed while it lasted, for me and, I think, for him.

There was a pub open on the outskirts of the village, quite a traditional-looking number, not thatched but low-roofed, with an obviously cared-for garden and a few people dotted about at wooden tables, but we'd both done ourselves fairly well at the wedding lunch and a pub wasn't really what we had in mind. We found a tearoom, underneath a roof which really was thatched. It apparently did coffee as well, and oddly enough, a coffee pot between us seemed strangely appealing, in spite of all the other beverages we'd consumed that day. I suspected that I might finish up spending half the night on the loo, but this harmony between us was just too good for either of us to break the spell.

They had a sign up saying 'waitress service only', so we went through the café to a garden they had at the rear, with table arrangements much as the pub. I'd no sooner sat down and looked around to get my bearings than I realised that sitting no more than three tables away were Helen and Judi.

For a few brief moments, they didn't see us; they were, as I suspect they usually are, engrossed in each other, and people were coming in and going out of the place at regular intervals. Then Judi, who was facing us, saw us and I could see her making a rapid calculation along the lines of 'can I get away with pretending not to know them?'. However, before she made up her mind, Helen looked across to see what Judi was looking at, and Helen being Helen, she was entirely up to the situation.

'Phyllis and Colin, wonderful! Why don't you join us, there's room enough for four?'

Judi's smile was somewhat on the rictus side, a kind of open-mouthed gape, and Colin's was initially much the same, but this was a renewed Colin, for the moment at least, and he, surprisingly enough, was the next person to speak.

'Just thought we'd take a little time out before the evening do. It's been quite a day,' he said, and once again, I thought, he finds exactly the right words, as he did with David Bennett. Maybe I should have realised some time ago how much he needed a break.

'Hasn't it just,' said Helen, and I detected a certain ruefulness in her tone.

'Much the most exciting wedding I've ever been to. I'm not sure whether anything else will quite match up. Except, perhaps, my own,' Judi said.

She looked straight at Helen, who smiled rather awkwardly. This was intriguing on a number of levels, but at this exact moment, a middle-aged, hawk-eyed woman suddenly appeared at the table and wanted to know our requirements. Colin ordered a latte and I opted for a hot chocolate; I had a feeling that heat and sugar might be an antidote to any further shocks coming my way on this day so given to them.

We didn't wait for the drinks to arrive.

'So you're getting married, Judi? To whom, might one ask?'

Now Judi had a rare moment of being discomfited. She seemed to be struck dumb, her eyes resting on Helen. The pause only lasted about five seconds; Helen rarely has any problem with making up her mind.

'To me, Phyll. You might as well know; everyone else will shortly. We deliberately delayed it until after the wedding; Peter had agreed the thing, but only on condition that we saw this wedding through first. We will separate amicably enough, with the gracious help of Kate's new father-in-law, who knows how to do these things with minimum fuss. And expense.'

'Sorry if you find this awkward,' Judi said, or more accurately muttered, to Colin. My husband was as unerringly correct as ever. I made a silent vow to share more bath nights with him. Amongst other things.

'I don't find it awkward at all. Who, how and why people choose to love is their business. It certainly isn't mine.'

'Thank you, Colin. I would have expected you to understand.'

At this point, the drinks arrived, and I took a stunned sip at my chocolate. If Helen had taken literally some of the stuff I'd told her about my relationship with Colin in recent months, she would have concluded he was a workaholic sex-maniac; perhaps it's rather plainer to other people than me that those two terms are pretty much mutually exclusive.

'What will Peter do?' I said, after my very necessary chocolate and sugar hit.

'Well, Peter is heading at a rate of knots towards being university vice-chancellor. The old boy who currently is vice-chancellor is stepping down, or more accurately, stepping up. Don't run away with the idea that chancellors are above vice-chancellors; chancellors are figureheads, not uncommonly showbizzy people, who don't do much more than go to prize presentations and degree ceremonies and make speeches. It's the vice-chancellor who runs the place. This whole episode with Needham has more or less sealed it for Peter. He was seen to be a bit of an "academic"; he needed to prove he knew his way around with the bad guys, in the big wide world which universities need to deal with these days. Now he's seen off Needham and his mates, saving the university a hell of a lot of money and even more local and possibly national notoriety, he's everyone's blue-eyed boy.'

'Does he have an… arrangement with anyone?' I said.

'Helen,' Judi whispered, decidedly jumpy now, by the sound of her.

'It's OK, Judi,' said Helen, following it up with these marvellous words which will live in my memory for a long time. 'Phyll is an old friend now; without her neighbourly support, I don't think I'd have survived recent years.'

'I've always thought that it was you who was doing the propping up,' I said. Colin's look over his latte had something of reproach, or maybe regret, about it.

'It's always worked both ways for me, Phyll. Anyway, what can I say? Peter's had five affairs I know about and I dare say a few more I don't, but I'm not really blaming him too much. After we'd had Kate and Tom, I did kind of lose interest, I suppose for pretty obvious reasons. As soon as he gets to be vice-chancellor, they'll be coming at him from all directions; he can take his pick of the best of the bunch for who he wants as the trophy wife I suppose he'll need. He's leaving me the house, bless him, as I understand being VC comes with a pretty nifty gaff of its own. But no more questions on that, Phyll. This is Kate's wedding day, let's see it out with a bit of blast, even if quite a subdued blast in the Williamson Lounge. We can talk about what everyone's doing over a G&T or several. Do you and Colin have any news, because I've been thinking ever since you walked in that you both look – well, invigorated?'

I looked towards Colin and he nodded back.

'Well, Helen is being as honest as you could possibly expect from a friend, Phyll. There's nothing to stop you being as frank back. I can always sit here and blush.'

We all giggled; once again, the man was being disarming. But, for the moment, it was straight talking we needed.

'Yes, well, I suppose a change of surroundings and a little leisure time for Colin has given us a lot to think about. And we're intending to prolong the leisure time. Colin is owed a lot of leave because of the hours he's put in, and we're going to take a proper holiday and talk about our options. After the length of time he's worked for his company, he does have options, and I think we would both rather that he got out or found some less demanding alternative, so we could have more time to… well, do what we want to do.' Adventures in the bath returned, and I found I was the one blushing.

Judi, of all people, came to the rescue. 'Good for you. Too many people spend their time flogging on when a few changes to their lives could make them so much easier. Helen and I have been living a lie for so long that I think it was beginning to exhaust both of us.'

That seemed to settle a silence over the four of us, but it was more of a silence of relaxation than tension. Shortly afterwards, Helen insisted on paying for us all, and we wandered back in easy company, exchanging no more than a few remarks about the scenery, which was striking, and the coming evening. None of us had any doubt about the venue we would choose, and it wouldn't be the noisy one.

Our preparations for the evening do had rather less of the passion of the wedding preparations, but we were both, by now, beginning to understand how much easier a relationship is when it remains in harmony rather than two people bouncing off each other, and when we'd done what we needed to do, which wasn't much – we'd been promised quite an informal evening – we spared ourselves further views of the car park and wandered down to the hotel's grounds, to sample the delights of an early Devon evening.

Simon

I did my bit, and I've been in sticky hotel situations before; people who think working in hotels doesn't amount to much more than being nice to people and carrying out some not too demanding domestic tasks are displaying their ignorance and naivety about the business. I've dealt with situations where people, both male and female, were trying to sell their sexual services on hotel premises; where journalists, trying to disguise themselves as something else, were getting into the hotel, sometimes even aiming to infiltrate the rooms or suites of their targets; where groups or individuals were planning robberies or blackmail attempts in the hotel, and, of course, there are the bomb scares, and various other kinds of terrorist scares. People out of their mind on something or other destroying their rooms; people walking off with fixtures and fittings, and, of course, the runners, aiming to sneak off without paying their bills, and generally ignoring the rather obvious fact that they'd registered contact details when they arrived. Perhaps the most disturbing of all is the occasional case of someone using a high-rise hotel to do away with themselves. Sir David Attenborough has studied all kinds of species in all kinds of detail; I've been exposed to the human one in all its fascinating, wonderful and incredible diversity, but some of the diversity can be very much on the negative side.

After joining Joyce in the foyer, the pair of us knew what our part of the business amounted to, which was to remove from the premises people who were not bona fide guests of the hotel. At the time of day we were dealing with, the only people entitled to be in the hotel were either residents or guests at the wedding. Some hotels have bars or lounges open to non-residents, but this one didn't except when they were attached to some 'do' or other. Joyce and I looked around us at the people in the main foyer and other individuals apparently hanging round between the foyer and we both knew that a good proportion of them shouldn't be there. We exchanged glances, a sort of professional 'oh, here we go again', and I looked at my watch and said, 'Ten minutes, Joyce,' which was how long we now had until Giles Cavendish's guys arrived, including a senior policeman. Even if we could only shift some of these intruders, we could perhaps avoid what Giles called 'a major incident', when things might get out of hand, perhaps allowing Needham and his immediate associates to get away and start trouble again as soon as another opportunity came along.

Heart in mouth, I went towards the most thug-like and the tallest of our 'guests'; I have an inbuilt sort of 'courage switch' which has stood me in good stead since I realised it didn't need a large intake of alcohol to switch it on. It just needed a certain amount of personal and professional necessity. It's what caused me to approach a gigantic figure like Duncan in a hotel he was attending as a conference-goer, on no more than a hunch or a whisper that he was gay. I knew there was every chance that, rather than agreeing to some kind of a date, he might heave me through the nearest plate-glass window. He who dares, etc.

But now I very much needed to stay in the present, and the formidable guy facing me.

'Excuse me, sir,' I said, in my poshest hotel tones, 'may I ask, are you a guest at the hotel?'

He looked me up and down, and for a crazy moment, I thought he might be about to make me a proposition, but then I realised it was a contemptuous look up and down, the kind one might direct at a showing-off child being tedious in adult company.

I think he might have just brushed me off, but Joyce's best megaphone tones were not too far away, confirming I was acting under hotel instructions.

'I am a guest for this evening's celebrations.'

'I see,' I said, in my best Basil Fawlty manner. 'Well, may I ask, sir, that you withdraw from the hotel until they start, particularly in view of the fact that a substantial number of people are going to need to be moving through here quite soon, and our catering staff have to get a lot of meals and drinks in and out?'

He gave me another up and down. Another guy near him, shorter and stouter but with an even more unfriendly expression on his face, took two steps in my direction. My instinct was to back away, but I saw in the corner of my eye a couple of our security guys and I felt bold, or foolhardy, enough to actually move nearer to them.

I dropped both my voice and the posh tone. 'There are three carloads of policemen arriving in' – I looked at my watch – 'less than five minutes, gents, with a detective superintendent in charge, and unless you can prove you have a reason to be where you are doing what you're doing, there's every chance that you will be arrested. This has become a governmental as well as a local issue.'

The last sentence, even if it did creep a little out of my brief, did register with them, and set me wondering whether they were actually legally in the country, never mind Devon.

While I'd been dealing with a mere two of our miscreants, Joyce had been herding people out like a loud, aggressive cowboy moving them along. The bride's uncle, an editor, it seemed, had already told his men to move outside, where a set of interesting pictures could be on their way and were, and that, alongside Joyce's efforts, made it clear that a general exodus was in progress. The hotel had also contrived to add a few more personnel to its security group, from where I don't know, maintenance staff or lads from the kitchens, perhaps, and 'we' were beginning to outnumber 'them'.

The guy I'd first spoken to realised he was losing the argument, but before he moved away, he came close enough to me for me to sense the animal warmth of him, like a wild creature cheated out of its kill.

'I'll remember you,' he said quietly. 'That face of yours. I'll remember it.'

Growing up gay and working in some of the places I'd worked in, I'd come across this kind of thing many times before. Brute-beast intimidation, the last refuge of the cornered.

'And I yours, sir, I do assure you. Except that I'm the one who will shortly be talking to the detective superintendent. And one or two other official gentlemen. And since you will now be featured on the hotel's security cameras approaching me with menace, as I believe the phrase is, quite a few people will be remembering your face. Sir.'

With something like a kind of sub-growl, he started to move, and at that moment, the noise and fuss at the main foyer made clear that the police had arrived, mob-handed as predicted. Giles Cavendish clearly has a lot of clout. Gratifyingly, my friends decided to get a wiggle on, but it wasn't enough of a wiggle to stop them running into the incoming police. As I went off to help Joyce and her team with the last of the catering, I saw my thuggie friend engaged in an intense conversation with what looked like a plain-clothed officer.

I made it back into the wedding suite when Robert was making what looked like a winding-up speech. He looked and sounded triumphant; even though I wasn't actually in the room, I could hear much of what was happening and it didn't take too many powers of detection to work out why Needham and his pals were being escorted out of the place and into police cars. I always knew Robert was made for great things, and hopefully this was just the beginning of it, though it did worry me that he'd set himself against some very bad guys who might well aim to take a pop at him sooner or later.

By the time Duncan and I had settled back in our suite, I was deadbeat and even action man himself looked like a snooze would do him good. Our day had included a vigorous bout of mildly sado-masochistic sex before breakfast, immediately followed by both of us being lugged in to a complex operation, heavily dependent on good timing and determination, to bust up an operation conceived and almost executed by a large, ruthless organisation. We both knew any further strenuous activity, sexual or otherwise, would well and truly destroy our chances of getting much out of the evening. We felt we had to at least put in an appearance at the youth end of the do and manage a token bop or two, after Robert and Kate had kicked off proceedings. Whatever that would be, I suspected it probably wouldn't be a waltz. I've seen the two of them dance before, and it's as near sexual intercourse as two fully dressed people who wish to remain within the law can get away with.

I stripped completely and got into a satisfyingly warm bath. Halfway through, I heard a mysterious but quite interesting noise. Duncan was, he really was, having a snooze.

SATURDAY EVENING AND NIGHT, June 15th

Matthew

I am not exactly a stranger to weddings, including both personal and professional occasions. In my early days at the paper, it was largely a question of 'Matthew, you go there', regardless of whether 'there' was a local courthouse, a launch of something, a local fete or carnival and, of course, local weddings, especially the bigger ones. Even at such a level as a cub reporter, there is a sense of anti-climax mingled with relief. No wedding I've ever attended, including my own, goes like clockwork, but the slip-ups and faux pas are generally all part of the fun, ready to enter family folklore for ever afterwards.

This one was different, very different indeed. I knew pretty much from the minute we arrived that this one had so many strings attached, it was going to be a very big and very mysterious parcel we were all unpacking. Proud as I was that we managed to forge an alliance of the 'good guys' and thwart Needham's dastardly plans, and all in a matter of hours, not even days, the come down after the main event left me feeling drained, and a few questions hanging in the air. In journalism, as in police work, it generally pays dividends to be suspicious, and it's easy enough to accept that all of us 'good guys' were acting in the name of what is legal and reasonable, but in my experience, nothing is ever as simple as it looks. In this hothouse atmosphere of people familiar with each other, and most of the legitimate guests were of or connected with our family, anything newsy spreads in hours, sometimes even minutes, and the news that my brother was now more or less a shoo-in for vice-chancellor of the university was already widely being bandied about even before people started turning up for the evening do. So were the rumours about Peter's marriage, apparently now about to go as kaput as that of the groom's parents. The latter wasn't really my concern, apart from what it would do to the mental health and career prospects of Kate's chosen guy, but the first was very much my concern. I needed another fraternal chat, and it needed to be just me and him, whatever else the evening demanded of him.

But before that, and in any case more important than that, we had the question of what Mary wanted to do for the evening. She hadn't been feeling too well since we arrived, and by the time we got back to our room after that unique wedding ceremony, she looked ashen. Mary isn't and never has been a conspirator or intriguer; she has had to acquire some coping strategies to deal with the sometimes incredibly complicated internal school politics, and she has developed useful antennae for people trying to involve her in whatever plots they might have brewing, but being rid of all that was one of the reasons why retirement and withdrawal has come to be so attractive to her.

We headed for the balcony again; that place of fresh air and privacy combined has been very useful since we arrived, and having such a quality suite has helped too. Superficial as it may be to enjoy being looked after and pampered, all of us need a bit of it from time to time, or as near to it as life is prepared to allow us.

The hotel was in that lull the places tend to go through between lunch and dinner. Only a few die-hards were still in the bars, and because of the weekend, the businessmen and conference attenders were not in situ. Rural Devon was no great noise creator either, and we sat with our cups of tea – some things English just carry on being English – taking in the superb air and blessed peace.

'I'm afraid I may have to disappoint you again, Matt,' she said.

This statement, plus her pallor and weariness, touched me to the core. I put down my tea and went over to hold her hands in mine. 'You don't disappoint me, Mary. You've never disappointed me. How could you?'

She smiled and closed her eyes momentarily. I suspected another headache had arrived.

'I have a kind of sense of never being there when you need me to be, of being constantly out of my depth, which this business has intensified rather than relieved. I've still only half grabbed everything that this case – because it's more of a case than a wedding, isn't it, Matt? – is about. I don't doubt our oldies' lounge will be a good deal more peaceful than the dance floor, but everyone will be talking about what's happened and expecting me to do likewise, and I'm really too tired, Matt, as I always seem to be now. And as for eating anything like a full-scale dinner, I just couldn't manage it at all.'

'No, neither could I,' I said. 'I'm only intending to go down for a couple of hours myself, but if I have anything, it'll be a sandwich. At a rather more normal wedding, I might be going down to wave off the bride and groom, but Kate and Robert have chosen to make a brief appearance during the evening and stay here for the night to re-charge the batteries.'

She smiled, which was gratifying to see. 'That's one way of putting it,' she said.

'Oh, no, I'm not sure much of that will be going on. They've had a long and incredibly demanding day.'

'So had you, all those years ago. But I seem to remember you managed.' She smiled again, and a host of flashbacks came to mind, of a different me, a different her, a different time, but perhaps not so different as all that.

'Yes, but our wedding night really was the first "all the way", as it was called at the time, wasn't it? We'd done a bit of this and that, but that wedding night was the real deal.'

'Yes, it was, and I've never forgotten it. I was so touched by your gentleness and consideration. Some of my old girls' school pals had been on at me about what pigs men can be, but during the "this and that", I'd been picking up different feelings.'

'Yes, me too. Young men like it to be known that they've "been around"; I had a bit, but not much. I knew enough to be sure it had to be both people to really mean anything. But Kate and Robert have been living together for some time, and I suspect they went through those experiences some time ago.'

'Yes, I imagine so. And they are a very attractive couple.'

'As we were and are, my love. I suggest that you put your feet up and take it easy. Most of what I want to do is have a conversation with Peter, preferably on our own.'

She gave me the kind of look she gives me when she thinks what I have in mind could be a mistake. We've been together for so long now that she doesn't have to articulate it.

'Yes, I know. Fraternal confrontation. The path of true fraternity never runs smooth.'

'When you talk about seeing him on your own, it's usually something like confrontation or crisis, Matt. And while he may be feeling triumphant over Needham and the land deal, he is simultaneously facing the collapse of his marriage and what some men call "the loss of a daughter". I don't want to sound like an old school ma'am, though I suppose that's what I am, but weddings and funerals are notoriously the best times for family rifts, and irritating as Peter can be on occasions, he is a very able and worthwhile man who has been a help to us on more than one occasion. He's also Kate and Tom's father, so be careful how you go, Matt, though I know you will anyway.'

I looked at her, still the voice of reason and sanity in my life.

My walks on the wild side have been rather fewer as I've got older, and just about died away ever since I became an editor. There are editors who treat their publications like totalitarian states with them as dictators, but they don't tend to last long. I knew she was right, as she usually is; I could well catch Peter on the raw, and whatever he's done or plans to do, he is my brother and about to become vice-chancellor of one of the oldest and most respected universities in the country. And if the circumstances of his marriage are as they are rumoured to be, his serial infidelities might reasonably be seen in a rather different light.

I left Mary resting, and now dozing, on the balcony and called Peter, using his private phone number rather than his room. I know what silly games hotels can get up to with room-to-room communications, the same intrusive methods favoured by some types of journalist.

'I just wondered if there was any chance of a pow-wow just between you and me. All the material we now have on Needham and the whole deal is available for the public domain, and I'm not saying I'll do whatever you tell me to do, but I will listen and co-operate as much as I think I can.'

'Come over now, Matt, if you can. Helen is taking Judi to the station, and we will put a face on it for the evening. In the meantime, I confess I'm having a glass of decent wine. I was very wary about indulging too much earlier on; if I'd escorted Kate down the aisle, or the equivalent thereof, hiccupping and threatening to topple over at every step, I don't think she would ever have forgiven me. How's Mary coped with it all?'

'She's managed, but I think the evening do might be a step too far. She is very tired. She's made some decisions about her work, which I think make a lot of sense. Shall we say about ten minutes? Save me some of that bottle?'

He chuckled briefly, a good sign. 'Done, but there's more where this bottle came from. See you soon.'

I went back to Mary and saw she was now asleep. I scribbled a note saying when I'd be back to see her again before the evening, then I walked the whole distance of next door but one to Peter's elegant suite.

I expected to find him lording it on his balcony, but no – he was alone in the generous living room of his suite, with not one but two bottles of very nice red wine in front of him. He was about halfway through what looked like his first glass. He'd discarded the wedding finery, of course, but even his casual wear was elegant enough, with a neat light blue shirt and grey trousers which certainly weren't off the high street peg. Peter also has been a bit of a clothes horse, more so than I've ever managed, and I've always suspected that my feelings about him have perhaps more than just an iota of jealousy, maybe even enhanced now when his elevation to vice-chancellor seems so imminent.

But brothers are not in the habit of being too formal with each other, and with a brief nod and a handshake, we settled down with a glass each, he with his legs crossed and one arm draped across the back of an immense sofa, while I leaned forward towards him, unwilling to descend into the enveloping softness of an equally spectacular armchair.

'Which do I do first, Peter, commiserate or congratulate? And that isn't, I assure you, intended to be facetious.'

He smiled, if rather wearily, and I saw something of what the day had taken out of him. 'The first isn't really necessary, and the second probably a bit premature, Matt,' he said. 'Helen and I are parting amicably enough. Like many gay people who grew up in circumstances very much less tolerant than they are now, she gave it her best shot. She wanted children and she had them, but it always seemed to me that she was forcing herself to it, the necessary means to the desirable end. After Tom, she largely lost interest, but she's always been robustly fair-minded, and when I looked elsewhere, she genuinely didn't feel she had much to complain about. I told her I would be as discreet as anyone in my position could be, and she said, simply enough, "Yes, Peter, so will I," and that's how things stood, though as it turned out, she was better at the discretion than I was.'

'She was hardly as exposed, Peter. I'm just impatient with myself for misunderstanding the situation as completely as I did, and perhaps I'm a little bit disappointed that you didn't feel able to confide in me.'

'Part of the deal, I'm afraid. I see members of her family quite regularly, and it was obvious to me that they didn't know anything about it. I concluded that, if she was prepared to respect our confidentiality, I could do no less myself. A touch more? I know two bottles seems a little excessive at the beginning of the evening, but I won't be having much more when I'm with Helen. I don't really want it to end like that.'

And then, a sudden and very transient display of emotion, covering by a strategic cough or two. I just waited. He has always been more easily hurt than he's prepared to let anyone see, but that's hardly unique in men.

He recovered himself and immediately asked me about Mary. As he had been so frank with me about his relationship, and as Mary hadn't stipulated that her decisions should be treated as confidential, I told him the gist of what Mary had in mind.

'Eminently sensible, I'd say, as much as it has anything to do with me. I don't intend to bash on indefinitely.'

'Oh, really? Rumour has it that you're heading for great things.'

Now he was leaning forward, and it needed another generous sip before he continued. 'Matt, I'm fifty-two years old. Well, you know that. Yes, it seems highly probable that I'll become vice-chancellor, but in these days of fierce competition and stingy government, it's not exactly a sinecure. Needham isn't the first and won't be the last hard nut I'll have to deal with. Fifty-eight is my absolute limit, and I'd much prefer fifty-five. Assuming I keep the job that long.'

'And you'll find someone in the meantime? I don't think you're cut out for being a lonely old man, Peter.'

He smiled rather ruefully. 'Oh, for that fraternal frankness. I don't doubt you're right, however.'

'Is there someone? Now that is one you don't have to answer, fraternal or not.'

'No, it's a day for getting it off my chest, I think. I've had and I'm having affairs, though as soon as Helen and I have split, they will stop being affairs, of course, and I really don't know what effects that will have. I'm happy to play it by ear, as that glorious English phrase has it. There is a lot going on professionally. David Bennett, an old university mate who's now a colleague, has been working on a new housing scheme to put to the planning committee, now bereft of Needham, of course, which will include extra student accommodation and affordable housing, all built to the best of environmental and ecological principles. David knows what he's doing and when the planning committee become aware that his proposals, to be contracted out to local builders, have my full backing and that of the board, I suspect we'll be in business. I have friends on that planning committee, most of them no friends of Joe Needham. They've always been as keen on getting rid of Needham as I am.'

A glimmer of doubt crept into my mind, probably another example of my disloyalty, but something didn't quite gel here.

'So, when push comes to shove, it was about getting rid of Joe Needham? Weren't you sort of friends at one time?'

This seemed to necessitate re-filling both his glass and mine.

'I set out to befriend him, certainly, in the early stages. I had an idea then of where I was probably heading, and being in with the chairman of the planning committee could not but be useful in the university's interests.'

And yours, I thought, but allowed it to remain as a thought.

'It didn't take long to discover that he was not only a man who was nowhere near as clever as he thought himself, he also had a few serious problems, including compulsive gambling. He seemed to think that he could exploit the weaknesses of others as ruthlessly as he liked – one member of the planning committee was a closet married homosexual, another had a fraud conviction in his record, and there were others – without anyone cottoning on to his own. One or two of his pretend friends or blackmail victims hit back by encouraging his habit as much as they could. And, of course, he started drifting into debt. The main reason why he took up with the people who were putting forward their land development proposals was to get rid of his debts before drastic steps were taken to recoup them from him, which would probably have included selling the house he lived in.'

'If you knew so much, couldn't you have stopped him?'

'I did stop him, Matt. If you mean, could I have managed to bail him out somehow, no, I couldn't. I don't have the kind of money he needed, and even if I did, I could think of at least a thousand better ways to spend it than giving to Joe Needham.'

'I don't think that's what I mean. If not quietly warn him off, then perhaps launch a media campaign against him which would cause him to walk away from the lot he'd got involved with and seek to deal with his problems with proper professional support.'

'I've a feeling that this scenario might have included you at some point, Matt.'

This is the kind of remark, always accompanied with a smile but making no secret of its agenda, which is characteristic of Peter, especially in my direction. A quiet dig at my eagerness, which he knows is quite likely to get up my nose, but he does it anyway, presumably to amuse himself. It's one of those brotherhood routines, ever-repeating and which have the effect of re-affirming the relationship, mildly irritating as they may be.

'Yes, OK, Peter, but there isn't much that the media doesn't get dragged into now. If we'd known about this, we could have perhaps forced him out of office and saved everyone a lot of bother.'

A long sigh, and another sip of wine.

'The bother had to happen, unfortunately. Before this deal happened along, Matt, I spent a good deal of time doing some background research and investigating other university land deals, and land deals in the area generally when I could get access to the records. There's not much I can tell you, I dare say, you've seen enough of them in your time. Unlike the south-east, the south-west has more room and isn't asking astronomic prices, though how much longer that will go on is debatable. In comes the developer, maybe home-grown, maybe with investors from all over the place. Benign undertakings are given about affordable housing, community facilities and all the rest of it. Agreement is reached, considerable sums of money have exchanged hands and then the screws go on. The developer is suddenly not so keen on so much affordable housing, maybe none at all, because they won't make any profits out of it, and the community facilities start moving in the direction of optional extras – optional, that is, as far as the developer is concerned. The seller of the land, frequently local authorities, educational institutions, pension funds, could perhaps sue for breach of contract, which would not only cost them a fortune, they might also lose the case – where in the contract, says the developer, does it say that we have to take a loss on this deal? So new deals are done, the affordable housing – affordable being a dubious word anyway – somehow fades away, and another batch of executive houses or rich people's apartments go up, with the developer not worrying too much about whether they actually sell or not; if they sit there empty for a few years, they are accumulating money and represent better returns than any bank is offering.

Somehow, a way has to be found to break the weary inevitability of it, and proving the developers are crooks with crooks from other organisations on their payroll is one of the most effective ways. It also warns developers that people selling the land have teeth too, and they're sometimes prepared to use them. Whoever we do contract with now will treat us with kid gloves, and there are always some, usually connected with housing associations or environmental organisations, who are on the level, even if they do generally operate on a rather smaller scale. We don't necessarily need to work just with one huge corporation; in fact, it's better spread about a bit.'

I looked at him long and hard; he refilled the glasses to cover an awkward silence. Yes, it was all plausible and in some ways honourable; it's just that it came over to me as just a bit too cold-blooded and perhaps even ruthless, in its way, as if the media have any room to tut-tut in that respect.

'So it's all a means to an end, Peter, in the last analysis. You plot to throw the vulnerable and already perjured Joe Needham, who might have got the idea that you were a friend, under a bus big-time, at the same time as dragging your daughter and her fiancé into dealing with a bunch of seriously bad guys who might well have hit back in some pretty uncompromising ways. And lo and behold, you finish up the king of the castle.'

He didn't have to say anything, and for the moment he wasn't. I was kind of gulping inside. Peter has always had a long tether; he's worked on being as suave and smooth as possible. But before adulthood knocked at least some of the rough edges off both of us, we had some truly spectacular rows, and it usually worked around what I saw as his arrogance and capacity for exploitation, and what he saw as my holier-than-thou sniper on the sidelines, who was quite capable of dirty tricks himself but evangelically disapproving of anyone else doing likewise. And perhaps we both had a case. We'd lived with it for a long time, but as yet, physical violence, beyond kiddie pretend fights, had never got into it. But as I looked into his face, flushed with anger and wine, I thought there could be a first time for anything.

One more sip of wine went down, and it seemed as if a Rubicon had been crossed. Peter the angry man had gone, maybe never to return. Peter the high-ranking fixer, the smoother of feathers, the easy socialite, was here, probably for ever.

'I'm sorry if that's how you see it, Matt. In some ways, I wish I was as competent or as ruthless a planner as you imagine me to be, but I can assure you that it's more seat-of-the-pants stuff a lot of the time – isn't it with you? How do you know what's coming at you on the news waves next week, or even tomorrow? And I can also assure you that this whole thing was as much Kate's initiative and Kate's venture as it was mine; "dragging my daughter into it" is a gross mis-characterisation of the whole business, and if you don't realise that, then you don't understand Kate as well as perhaps you thought you did.'

It penetrated through to my brain, tired after Mary and the draining experiences of the last few days, that however difficult it would be for me to leave it at that, any permanent splits in the family wouldn't do any of us, including Mary, much good. And certain escapades I have undertaken in the journalistic business both before and since I became an editor were whispering in my ear that the moral high ground was maybe not the territory I can most easily occupy. In fact, my brother knows this well enough, even though he has as yet tactfully not said so.

My head went down and I momentarily stared into the hypnotic deep red of the wine. When it came up and I met his eyes again, I knew fences needed mending.

'Peter, it sounds feeble, perhaps, but I am anxious about Mary and things I say at the moment tend to come out more aggressively that I really intend them to be. The last few days have also left me feeling drained, to be honest. In my line of work, the occasional dirty trick is inevitable for survival; I have no moral pedestal to perch on. We've worked well together over this time; let's try and conclude it with a relaxed evening.'

He could have picked up on several things there; he chose to pick up on Mary. And if there was any simulation about the concern on his face, it was a very good act. He and Mary, perhaps improbably in some ways, have always got on pretty well.

'You're thinking Mary's problems are beyond fatigue and the demands of the job?'

'I think it might be. She seems to have headaches, and I mean bad headaches, not just something you get at the end of a noisy day, on a regular basis. I'd like her to go and get checked over, but I don't know whether that might just worry her all the more.'

Now he was leaning forward. 'If they continue after she's left the job, I don't think she'll need much persuading, Matt. Thank you for what you said. I would hate the idea of parting angrily after all we've been through this week. If you feel you need to stay with Mary this evening, I'm sure everyone will understand. If you can join us, your company will be appreciated. This is the night when Helen and I can drop all the camouflages and pretences and finish our life as a couple with a bit of dignity and maybe even style.'

There wasn't much to be said after that. Helen was due back within ten minutes; we shook hands, having averted, perhaps by the skin of our teeth, a potentially major fraternal bust-up. When I got back to my own suite, Mary was still snoozing on the balcony, but her colour had improved. I had a couple of messages from my lads at the paper, all by now returned to the office or their homes, and they all had reassuring tales to tell about the wealth of material they had, both written and pictorial.

'Could even be worth a supplement, Matt,' said Tony. 'Maybe "Devon's Big Wedding Exposes Controversial Councillor" – "Downfall of Planning Committee Boss".'

'Oh, yes, it's going to be worth a splash, Tony, especially with all the pictures. If you start putting it together while Ken Slater's still holding the fort, we'll work the whole thing out. In the meantime, it's still my niece and her partner who are the married couple, and the family intend to have a bit of post-nuptial taking it easy tonight before anything else happens. But if any of the nationals start sniffing about, and one or two of them will, let me know in the morning as soon as possible. Cheers, Tony.'

I left Mary a note to say I wouldn't be too long, and I determined not to be. Anxiety and fatigue were setting in fast, and like most middle-aged men, going so far as to admit the age thing by adjusting my habits accordingly didn't come easily. But I'd drunk the best part of a bottle of wine during my visit to Peter, on top of the wedding lunch intake, and while my head for alcohol had always been pretty good – for a journalist, it's just about a job requirement – it's when I'm on or near capacity that I am more likely to make tactical or sociable mistakes, as I'd almost done with Peter.

But the way I'd envisaged him, now and the future, was confirmed rather than otherwise by his performance during the evening. He and Helen were playing the game they'd played for so long with the same dedication and faultlessness, and the surroundings were ideal for the purpose. The Williamson Lounge, decorated with prints and paintings of the scenery and wildlife of Devon and furnished with comfortable armchairs which support the body rather than consume it like a fly trap, did lend itself to sociable conversation. The thud thud thud of the dance area was audible but not too audible; having a conversation in a normal tone of voice with the person sitting next to you was entirely possible, and with neatly jacketed waiters serving people at the tables, nothing as vulgar as queueing at the bar was necessary. I found myself wondering again how much this do had cost, but the fact that the Harringtons were loaded had been obvious from the moment I saw them – press men get an instinct for these things – and Kate and Robert would by now be earning astronomical amounts of money, so I didn't waste too much time thinking about it.

During the course of the couple of hours I was down there, I spoke to various people, but the ones who particularly stuck in my mind were my rehabilitated nephew Tom and his French girlfriend. I'd known Tom since he'd been born, of course, and close relatives who go somewhat off the rails tend to be patiently, if a little tersely, accepted for what they are. But people rarely stay the same, and Tom in his late twenties was hardly recognisable even from Tom in his early twenties. The dull, downcast eyes and awkward lumpen slouch in his chair had well and truly disappeared; he had the bright eyes, athletic figure and easy posture of a man in his prime, and I doubt whether there's a heterosexual man in the world who could be untouched by the graceful and beautiful Claudette. Or, for that matter, a homosexual man in the world who'd find himself indifferent to Tom.

I thought he might be downcast, since this night was going to be followed by the disintegration of his parents' marriage, but none of it.

'We've all been living with it for some time, Matt,' he said. I had at long last managed to get rid of the 'uncle'. 'Now it's out in the open, everyone can get on with their lives.'

'Once you know who you love, who you really love, it's foolish to blind yourself to it. Foolish and perhaps a little perverse.' Such words, delivered by a clever and beautiful woman with a noticeable if not overpowering French accent, can have an impact greater than their simple linguistic meanings, and Tom's eyes while she was saying them made it abundantly clear that he had no remaining doubt about who he really loved.

Shortly after nine o'clock, Kate and Robert appeared, and it became apparent very quickly that their decision to make their visit fairly brief was justified. They're both too young and active to let much fatigue show, but they'd already been to the youthful gathering and their body language spoke volumes of a need to have a bit of time to themselves. I think the intention was to retreat to a corner bay with both sets of parents, Robert's grandmother and, as it turned out, me, and we would chat to whoever happened to be near, but it didn't work out like that. By the time their drinks were brought to them, the set-up had started to resemble an edition of *Question Time*, with most of those present gathered in a semi-circle beyond 'the family bay' to pretty much shoot questions at the bride and groom.

People wanted to know where they were going for the honeymoon; they bravely but entirely adamantly refused to say, Kate handling the business firmly but fairly.

'Some time before today, we've been working with some security people provided by Mr Harrington's chambers, and their advice has been to keep our destinations to ourselves, certainly for the foreseeable future. Of course, I know perfectly well that we can trust everyone here' – clever girl, I thought, as looks were exchanged and some glances rested on certain family-connected people whom many would not trust as far as they could throw them, not to mention those who might be too absent-minded or careless to keep such information to themselves – 'but this is a public place, in effect, and word can get round.'

She had effectively marked their cards, however, and the conversation turned more towards general banter, with Robert being asked what he thought of Devon, Kate being asked about life in London, and the parents fending off jokey enquiries about Kate and Robert's younger years. Perhaps because it was so late, the imbroglio of the Needham case and the issues arising from it didn't feature at all; maybe people were all resigned to what was classified as 'hush-hush'. It often occurs to me that the British as a nation are just a little too prepared to be told things are 'hush-hush' and not to be talked about.

Eventually, Kate whispered to her father – I think she'd overheard some Densham aunt was on the way to asking about how many children the couple were intending to have, which might well push Kate beyond her tolerance level – and Peter stood up with all the magisterial authority which presumably he would now be lavishing on the university board.

Silence fell immediately. It is strange for brothers who have known each other almost since babyhood to see the effects they now have on people as adults; in Peter's case, it can't fail to be impressive. I thought once again that, for all the close relationship I have with him, I still haven't entirely worked him out.

'Ladies and gentlemen,' he said. 'My daughter and my excellent new son-in-law are, not surprisingly after the experiences of recent days, rather in need of rest before heading off for their honeymoon tomorrow, and don't get on to me about it after they've gone, because I don't know either. Here's to the beginning of what we all hope will be a wonderful marriage, and may they have a splendid time wherever they're going.'

The bride and groom then left carefully but as rapidly as they decently could, and just before they left the room, I saw them exchange a glance which suggested that perhaps they weren't as tired as all that. The night may yet have a traditional conclusion.

I got back to the room not long after ten. Mary had added a little note of her own to mine to say that she'd gone to bed, but she was feeling better and much restored compared to earlier on. I had a long glass of the hotel's chilled mineral water, sitting on the balcony in the extraordinary tranquillity of a Devon summer night, which even the thuds of the dance room could not seriously disturb, and then I went to bed.

Celia

It's a little bit shabby to doubt the word of your own nearest and dearest, but I confess that I am at the stage of life when I ultimately only trust the evidence of my own eyes. Very reprehensible and cynical, no doubt, but there's not much point in living for extraordinarily long periods of time if you don't learn a thing or two along the way. In my retirement haven, one of the residents is an ex-priest. I don't mean ex in the sense of him being defrocked, or whatever they call it now, for gallivanting with the choirboys or something; I mean he's retired, though you never can, it seems, retire from God. He has somehow got wind of my health issues, or some garbled version of them; the village is full of old gossips both male and female, who fill up parts of the huge amounts of leisure time now available to them by tittle-tattling about all and sundry. He thinks I should be preparing for the 'hereafter,' as he calls it, and he urges me to pay regular visits to the chapel in the grounds of the village. I do go occasionally, just to throw him a bone, as it were; he is a good man in essence, who does help people from time to time in very practical and useful ways, including helping them make their way through the labyrinthine application forms which the government uses to ensure people don't get the benefits they're entitled to. Not everyone can just phone a lawyer who happens to be their son. But the priest and I have yet to see eye to eye about the hereafter, and it's on the same principle as I mentioned earlier, of only trusting the evidence of my own eyes. 'I have never seen the hereafter, Vicar,' I say – I never can remember his name – 'or even seen any tangible evidence that such a state exists, and neither, with all due respect to your profession, have you. If it does exist, presumably my husband Derek will be there, and that means everything will be suitably arranged.'

'Once again, dear lady,' he says – I don't think he can remember my name either – 'you weave a sort of protection of flippancy around yourself.'

'You never met my husband Derek, did you?' I say. 'If you ever had, you would know I speak of reality, not flippancy.'

So I was grateful when the evidence showed the Williamson Lounge was very much as it had been cracked up to be; tastefully decorated with local wildlife and scenic images, and equipped with armchairs which are high-bottomed enough to ensure that hoists and winches would not be needed at the end of the evening to extricate the elderly guests.

Malcolm and Barbara had rather cleverly cornered a comfortable table near one of the picturesque windows as Harrington territory, and for the purposes of this 'do', the Harrington contingent included Giles Cavendish, having discharged his best-man duties; Simon Roche, who would have been best man, had things been different, and whom I've known since Robert's schooldays; and Duncan Allen, Simon's partner and lover, and no, I have no problems with either of those terms.

Malcolm started by explaining to me tomorrow's arrangements, which were pleasing enough. Barbara, it seemed, was to take a recreational detour to meet up with an old artist friend of hers, a woman who lives in Cornwall, and once upon a time, I would probably have had a terribly inappropriate, even sarcastic, reaction to such news, but I no longer bore any animosity towards Barbara, especially in view of the fact that her ill-fated liaison with my son was to come to an end.

Consequently, Ron was to drive Malcolm back to London and drop me off at the retirement village on the way. The Ron bit was predictable, and pleasant enough, but to have Malcolm to myself is something of a bonus, and I flattered myself that this was a time of his life when I could still make a helpful contribution. Re-starting in middle age after a broken relationship isn't easy.

Once parked in a comfortable chair with drinks served to the table, with a reasonable certainty that no-one will have the nerve/ be allowed to park themselves in the matriarchal chair should she find herself facing an urgent call of nature, I was able to have three meaningful conversations, above and beyond conventional sociable noises, during the course of the evening.

The first was with Giles Cavendish, at close quarters rather an intimidating young man. At my age, virtually all young men look, from a distance, like big boys, but this one, at close quarters, was clearly more formidable. He was strikingly good-looking, it's true, with perfect skin, well-groomed very dark hair and meditative brown eyes which you could see all too clearly could and would flash with anger if the need arises. He also had a 'minder' here, obvious even to an aged observer such as myself, a huge man sitting as unobtrusively as a huge man can, beside the door separating the Williamson Lounge from the rest of the hotel.

Important men, and especially important young men, can often convey within a sentence or two their true feelings towards old people – an old person is what I am, despite all the flowery euphemisms. A louder, bantering tone, a tendency to smile or laugh agreement with what the old dear has said, even sometimes a kind of grotesque flirting, such as admiring the person's appearance or clothing, are all familiar parts of the repertoire.

None of these items were in Giles Cavendish's old-person repertoire. It occurred to me afterwards that some of his superiors were probably old people themselves, or verging on the acquisition of that venerable status, so such inter-generational communication is not as unusual to him as it might be to others of his age.

He was sitting on my right and for a while engaged in a long and mostly indecipherable legal exchange with Malcolm, before Malcolm got up to pay a visit. Young Cavendish didn't sit there fidgeting and signalling oh so clearly, 'God help me, now I'm landed with the old dear.' He smiled at me and said, 'My apologies, Mrs Harrington, I've been neglecting you. The law features a lot in my business, as you can imagine, and I suspect there are few people in the world who know more about British law than your son.'

There are few better ways to an old lady's heart than nice remarks about her darling boy, even if she privately thinks her darling boy is an amoral, witless waste of space who would be better off liquidated, which is nothing like how I think of dear Malcolm, of course. My answering smile to young Cavendish was entirely unforced.

'Very true, Mr Cavendish, and I suspect my grandson is very much heading in a similar direction. I couldn't help wondering how you and Robert became friends, but before you answer that, perhaps we could avoid sounding like an extract from a Jane Austen book by you calling me Celia and allowing me to call you Giles.'

'Of course, Celia, and please do call me Giles. As a close friend of Robert's, I hope we'll meet again. I met Robert in the context of swimming, as a matter of fact. We both belonged to the university swimming club, and we seemed to find talking to each other very easy, even in the not-too-promising context of sitting dripping away by the side of a pool.'

I couldn't deny that this created an image in my mind that was worth toying with for a minute or two, and while I was so toying, he resumed.

'I suppose praising your grandson just after having praised your son probably puts me in danger of ingratiation, but Robert is in many ways the perfect companion. He has decided opinions, of course, but he doesn't express them in a pompous or narrow-minded way and he knows how to get away from work and enjoy himself when he needs to. He and I took part in several of the debating society's functions, and he could frequently get people on his side by humour as well as insight.'

'You know him well, Giles, I can see that. So, between you and me and the hush-hush outfit you work for, just how much danger is he likely to finish up getting himself into?'

Such a direct question could well stymie a less balanced man, but, of course, it did not so much as bat the Cavendish eyelid.

'Well, not much at the moment. The outfit Needham got caught up with are perfectly happy to see Needham carry the can. It can be proved easily enough that Needham was breaking all sorts of rules in terms of his planning committee job, but when it comes to a foreign corporation, proof becomes more difficult, especially when most of what they're doing is outside UK jurisdiction. They will also want to make further attempts at getting into the UK market, and while they're not too hot on UK standards and practices, they will know well enough that an assault on a UK citizen would turn the business from a domestic legal matter to an international incident likely to embarrass their own governments, and the governments we're talking about do not like being embarrassed to the point where they would be inclined to take quite drastic recriminations. Robert is brave, but he's not reckless, and the same can be said of his wife.'

'That's very reassuring, Giles. You have obviously acquired a very thorough knowledge of the world for such a relatively young man.'

Again, I've known young men who would have found this a bit of a googly, but young Cavendish whacked it for six.

'Very kind of you to say so, Celia. My father was a diplomat and my mother a translator, and while they obviously decided against dragging me round the world with them in order to let me have a settled schooling, they inevitably tended to think globally rather than locally and I think a fair bit of that had rubbed off on me even before I went to university.'

'Well, it seems to me that you are a very loyal and useful friend to Robert, and as a grandmother who loves him very much, I appreciate that and hope it will continue.'

'It certainly will as long as I have anything to do with it, Celia.'

Malcolm returned at this moment, and I would have had a pang of anxiety about him taking so long to relieve himself – ridiculous as it may seem to some, a mother's anxiety about even the most basic of her offspring's functions does not disappear with the years – had I not seen him in animated conversation with Peter Densham, the father of the bride. Every marriage I've ever been to has had its distinguishing characteristics, and this one already had one of the main guests being arrested and carted off, the main wedding speech delivered by the bride and a concerted effort made to intimidate and coerce the entire company, so adding to it all the disintegration of the marriages of both the bride's parents and the groom's parents becomes almost a commonplace. However, I know my men well enough to realise that the conversation was much more likely to centre on Peter Densham's widely rumoured elevation to vice-chancellor, and the careful way men in power have of sounding out whether they are likely to be of much use to each other.

Pleasantries continued between Giles and myself for a few minutes, before he was once again locked into conversation with my son, but it wasn't long before I found Simon Roche seemed to have secured the chair on my right.

'Hello, Robert's gran,' he said. 'I suppose you don't remember me after all this time.'

'Don't be silly, Simon. I remember you very well. You were not the kind of boy one easily forgets. I seem to recall you spent four successive summer holidays, or most of them, with Robert at his parents' house, and I was close enough to them then to visit frequently, along with my husband Derek, Robert's grandfather.'

'Yes, I remember. No doubt you all thought I was leading Robert up the garden path.'

It took me a moment to place what he meant, but of course he was talking about their respective sexual identities, and I admit I did have some anxiety. Simon was never overtly effeminate, then or, apparently, now, but there were undoubtedly a few signals which I picked up on. I mentioned it to Derek.

'Yes, I think he probably is gay,' he said. 'But I don't think it's of any great consequence. It doesn't follow that Robert is, and I've certainly never had any sense of that. Friendships between hetero and homosexual schoolboys are by no means uncommon, especially in the hothouse atmosphere of boys' schools. I knew three who identified themselves that way; one changed after leaving school, but the other two are my friends to this day. If you know perfectly well you're not gay, there isn't anything you need to worry about. Which I think is where Robert is with Simon; Simon is funny, lively and highly intelligent, much as he would like you to think otherwise, on occasions; clever boys often find pretending not to be as clever as they are is a useful defence mechanism in and out of school.'

I could remember Derek's words about Simon almost verbatim, even though I'd be hard-pressed to recall what I was doing at this time last week. And Simon's cleverness has been proved as real enough; he not only has a line of work in which he's progressing well, he also has a very well-paid, attractive and successful civil partner.

'Not really, Simon,' I said, that snatch of memory having flashed by in about seven seconds. 'It was clear enough from the start that Robert was more of a leader than a follower, and his procession of girlfriends, so bewildering to his parents, was underway from the age of fifteen, I seem to recall. He befriends people he likes and gets something from, and it didn't surprise me that you came into that category. The pair of you did several sessions of digging my garden, if I remember rightly.'

'Good gracious, fancy you remembering that. I do a bit of that to this day, usually on my own; Duncan isn't what you'd call green-fingered.'

'I'm sure you manage admirably, Simon. And I think all of us, excluding Mr Needham and his friends, owes you a debt of gratitude for what you've done today. You even had to leave the wedding feast to carry out the role you so handsomely volunteered to do.'

Simon did not have quite the Cavendish insouciance, and something almost corresponding to a blush came over his features. 'There isn't much I wouldn't do for Robert Harrington,' he said quietly. 'For all sorts of reasons, and staggeringly enough, they are all what you might call honourable. He isn't the only platonic friendship I have with men, but he is the greatest and long-lasting of them.'

I reached forward and patted his hand. 'I'm an old woman and probably not going to be around for much longer, Simon. It gives me great heart and confidence that my grandson has such very good people in his camp.'

I think it was shortly after this point that the bride and groom made their appearance, and unlike most features of this wedding, I did think it could have been handled rather better. Their arrival created the sort of commotion which would have flattered a film star, and rather than pass around the room having a quiet word here and there, they were jammed into a Densham enclave and expected to answer a series of generally impertinent questions. However, young as they are, they seemed to manage this with the same sort of slickness that they manage everything else, and young Kate was entirely adamant that no-one was going to find out the honeymoon destination. Yes, they had been the stars of the day, but even so, I thought it inappropriate. So many people have become so used to this tawdry, vulgar so-called reality television shows that the atmosphere of them pollutes ordinary life.

Eventually, and quite rightly, the bride's father, who had impressed me throughout this occasion, called a stop to it and they withdrew to general affection. Catching sight of me in Harrington-land as he and his wife were leaving, Robert came over to kiss my hand.

'We'll come to see you soon, Gran, and thanks again for being there for me.'

'Goodnight, dear. And sleep well.'

At that, a truly wicked smile spread over the boy's features.

'Well, at least some of the time, darling,' I whispered, and the grin got even bigger. He turned, and Kate put her arm in his. I saw the expression their eyes exchanged, and a sudden panic button inside me asked whoever was listening to let me have long enough to meet my first great-grandchild.

My third conversation, briefer and more business-like, even allowing for the emotion with it, was with Malcolm and, rather to my surprise, Barbara.

As the evening drew on to its later stages and my watch told me it was way past my bedtime, I tried to lever myself out of what I had thought was quite a user-friendly chair with arms which would make raising myself out of it relatively easy. However, when my first three attempts failed and my embarrassment and irritation mounted, I noticed that Malcolm had noticed me. I really didn't think that I was drunk; I had taken pains to be careful and stick mostly to non-alcoholic drinks, but I was undoubtedly tired and, yet again, the tiny man with his miniature power drill was making his presence felt inside me.

Malcolm moved towards me, and I felt it might make sense for me to ease the way for him.

'I think I am going to have to retire, Malcolm,' I said. 'It's been a long, busy day.'

'Absolutely, Mum.'

He held on to me, and as we took a couple of tentative steps, I realised that, but for Malcolm's strong support, I was indeed going to fall, and I might actually do even with it. But the matriarch concluding the evening in a crumpled heap on the carpet was most definitely not on my agenda, and I sent stern warnings to my legs to behave themselves. Even so, it remained touch and go for a few minutes until another strong hand took hold of me from the other side and I realised it was Barbara. I smiled my gratitude, and turned to take a proper matriarchal leave of the company. My table and several around me had fallen quiet, no doubt a little concerned about the turn the night was taking.

'Thank you, everyone,' I said. 'This whole event has been unforgettable and a triumph; it has been the most remarkable marriage I've ever had the privilege to attend, and I hope all of you can look forward to a bright and prosperous future.'

I waved feebly and turned away, but the smattering of applause which greeted my words seemed to swell, and when I looked again, almost everyone was standing up, and not only the Harringtons and their connections, but the Denshams and theirs. I smiled and waved, feeling like the Queen herself, and then, with the essential aid of Malcolm and Barbara, I got to a relevant lift.

Away from the multitudes, we went up in the lift in silence, for me a blessed state by now, and as we emerged on my floor, Barbara spoke into my ear, her voice very loud against the new silence. 'Can I leave you to Malcolm now, Celia?'

I nodded. 'Yes, I think so, Barbara, and thank you.'

'I will visit occasionally, if I may.'

'Of course,' I said. 'I'll be happy to see you.'

And I wasn't fibbing. Now she was out of Malcolm's life, treating her as a friend will be that much easier. She kissed my cheek lightly and then departed. I wondered whether she really meant it; something instinctive was telling me that I would probably never see her again. I felt a genuine twinge of regret that the two of us had never managed to come to terms more successfully, which would at least have made life a bit easier for Malcolm.

My son took me to the door of my suite and insisted on getting me in. He placed me on the armchair nearest the bed. 'Will you be OK, Mum?' he said, and I nodded, quite truthfully.

'I think the noise and the heat of the lounge were the prime suspects for my fatigue, Malcolm,' I said. 'I'm much better now.'

The tiny maniac with the drill let loose again, just to remind me of his presence.

Malcolm had something to say before he left. 'With Ron driving, Mum, we'll have a few hours in the car to talk. I have an idea that I will find a place in the country – I don't want to spend all of my time breathing in the bad air of London. It could include your own accommodation, independent of the main house, and someone to look after you, if you wanted it to. If you'd rather stay where you are, fine, but the offer is there.'

I beckoned to him to put his face down where I could kiss it. He did, and I did.

'A beautiful offer, Malcolm, and beautifully put. Yes, I am happy to talk it through tomorrow, from the bottom of my heart.'

He left me, and I managed to get myself into bed. I've been around long enough to know the actual meaning of a 'song in the heart', but this was perhaps the first time since Derek to have one helping lull me to sleep.

Phyllis

Having spent some time taking in the hotel grounds and enjoying the evening air, we walked aimlessly back into the hotel, realising as we did so that the question of whether we attended the youth do or the more ageing specimens in the Williamson Lounge had yet to be settled. However, Colin went in for a pre-emptive strike and we found ourselves heading in the direction of the Williamson Lounge, without protest on my part. There are those who feel that the way to deal with ageing is to pretend that it's not happening, but it's not an approach that holds up too well when presented with the realities of day-to-day life. After the day we'd had, I had an uncomfortable feeling that even fairly tepid bopping about in the floor to whatever was currently the taste of the younger contingent might well dislocate something or strain something, and finishing the festivities being stretchered off to the sotto voce chortling of our youngsters was not what I had in mind, especially bearing in mind this whole occasion had contributed so handsomely to putting Colin and I back on the path of marital harmony.

So we made our way to the Williamson Lounge and were happily assimilated amongst the intelligent and realistic guests who accepted gracefully that their bopping days were behind them.

The room was ideally suited to the purpose; not as large as a grand hall, with people's conversations echoing around and bouncing off the walls, and not so small that you would find yourself listening to about a dozen other conversations apart from your own.

A few faces were more noticeable by their absence that their presence. Judi, it seemed, had disappeared altogether; once the arrangements regarding her future with Helen had been settled, she was happy enough to withdraw, presumably not wanting her future with the younger members of the Densham family to be clouded by memories of an overstay at Kate's wedding. Helen and Peter were also amongst those not present at first, the information being that they had put in a token appearance at the youth do, bearing in mind their son and his girlfriend, rapidly becoming his intended, were there. I just hoped that they weren't going to be so misguided as to step out too strenuously on the dance floor, though Helen, I know, is sickeningly fit from all her swimming, and Peter is likely to be pretty fit too, though his exercise might better be defined as horizontal jogging.

The groom himself had announced that he and his bride were going to put in a late appearance, making yet another departure from the usual routines for this wedding, though people were growing so accustomed to it now that hardly any remark was passed. They had decided, several voices confirmed, not to leave the hotel on the night of the wedding, for various reasons, some practical, some undoubtedly amorous. And perhaps not so revolutionary as all that; after all, the traditional practice on wedding nights had always been about a generous indulgence in rumpy-pumpy, and the fact that the couple may have rumpy-pumpied on many previous occasions didn't necessarily mean that the bridal suite shouldn't be used for a similar purpose, perhaps to the extent of a mega-rumpy-pumpy, the four-poster bed shaking to its foundations and the champagne flutes wobbling precariously on the bedside tables.

Colin and I found ourselves amongst a gathering of what I suppose you could call Densham associates, which undoubtedly includes us. The rather outnumbered Harrington contingent, having made their way quite sociably through the day, to be fair, had obviously decided to gather round and take their ease after a demanding day, and they still had quite a lot to talk about, when all's said and done. I found myself with Colin on one side of me and David Bennett on the other; an odd sense of déjà vu crept over me. I glanced uneasily at Colin, but we had all gathered into a kind of semi-circle and one would have to have a fairly advanced state of paranoia to imagine I'd organised the entire circle so as to be next to David. Peter and Helen had arrived by now, and they were gathered around the table next door, alongside Peter's brother Matthew, his son Tom and Tom's girlfriend Claudette, and a couple of Helen's relatives, looking a little shell-shocked, it has to be said, but Helen herself was the life and soul of the party; perhaps emerging from an increasingly oppressive closet had liberated her in more ways than one.

At first, Colin and I shared our conversation with David. As soon as he saw who his neighbour was, David leaned over to me a little conspiratorially and my heart started tapping a bit, but his eyes gathered in Colin as well.

'I've had some good news, this very evening,' he said, and there was a happy gleam in his eyes which returned yet more memories to me. 'Most of the people at this gathering don't know me from Adam, but I'm bursting to tell someone and you two probably know me better than anyone here apart from Peter, and I've told him. The lady I asked some time ago to live with me has just decided she will go along with the idea. So we intend to set up home together, you might say, possibly until she gets sick of the sight of me, but that's part of what it's about. If and when we do get married, we want to be sure that we can stand the sight of each other; we've both been around the houses once or twice, and this time we'll come to it without too much pressure.'

'Congratulations, David,' I said. 'I'm happy for you.'

'Good for you, David,' Colin said, and the man-to-man handshake followed. David then gave me a light peck on the cheek, without Colin so much as narrowing his eyes. Maybe now David is spoken for, his anxieties will fade away. I reflect that it's touching that he still does want me with him, and it took a trip away from home to point this out to me.

Even if relief figured in there as well, I was genuinely happy for him, but I couldn't resist a little fishing. 'I don't suppose I know the lucky lady?'

He smiled. 'A lovely way to put it, Phyllis, but I'm still thinking that the luck is mostly mine. Her name is Denise Walters, Professor Denise Walters, if we want to be formal about it. She's been helping me in the new scheme we're getting together to present to the local planning committee regarding the tender for the university land and what our expectations will be before we ask for bids. I suppose you might say she's an expert on social and working spaces, how they can best be used to satisfy diverse demands, including work, leisure, culture, etc. She has a very wide imagination and a practical intelligence.'

I was momentarily speechless, perhaps returning to our adventures behind the Pavilion, when David's wide imagination was very much in evidence, introducing me to one or two things which I hadn't previously known people did to each other.

Colin once again stepped into the silence, and the two of them started talking about the practicalities of the new housing scheme, Professor Walters already receding into the conversational distance. It took me a while to insinuate myself back into the chat, because my capricious memory, good at remembering things I didn't need to remember while regularly obliterating things I did, returned the name Denise Walters to me as included in the lengthy list of Peter Densham's old flings. However, I reflected that it might well be difficult to find any female member of the university staff whose work was likely to bring them into contact with Peter who hadn't had some kind of a fling with him somewhere along the way. I almost felt a little slighted that I hadn't crept on to the list at some point, though I suspect Peter, whatever his faults, does have sense enough not to crap in his own nest, as it were, and with two kids as sharp as Kate and Tom, it would have been sailing pretty close to the wind.

The bride and groom duly arrived after their own visit to the youthful party; they looked a little warm, but by no means worn out. It all turned into a kind of press conference, with the happy couple jammed in a corner with both sets of parents fielding questions. I saw Kate's face turning more set and tight-lipped; I don't think this was what they'd expected, the pattern of these dos usually being they would circulate gradually, or even just be left alone to have a quiet drink with their family. I don't pretend to be any expert on social etiquette or taste, but it struck both Colin and me as a bit distasteful and we moved away to the further reaches of the room while it was going on. I suppose they were sort of victim of their own success; if you're going to get yourself up as the star of the show, you can't expect everyone else to drop the role just because you've decided you want to.

Even at the distance we were, we saw Kate's whisper, almost resembling a hiss, in her father's ear and he stood up and curtailed the proceedings. We got a wave and a smile from both of them as they made their way out, and we moved back towards Densham HQ.

Later in the evening, Colin and Malcolm Harrington found themselves straddling the Densham/Harrington border, and soon seemed to be getting themselves into quite an intense conversation. It is just a little bit worrying when your husband suddenly forms a close acquaintance with a man acknowledged to be a leading divorce lawyer. I had also suddenly found myself next to an ancient Densham aunt called Myrtle, Peter's mother's older sister, apparently, who had an obsession with roses and other horticultural topics and who was also, unfortunately, somewhat hard of hearing. Our conversation was following a pattern of her roaring various comments at me about the foliage which had graced the wedding room and which was also, it seemed, abundant in her own garden, me roaring back the best I could do in terms of an intelligible response, her saying pardon and instantly setting off on another roaring session about a few hundred more reliable blooms. This would be fairly trying in any ordinary circumstance, but it was happening while my ex-school friend David had withdrawn to get involved in another intense male exchange with Peter Densham and my husband seemed to be in a lengthy seminar with a divorce lawyer.

I had just about reached the point where my two most attractive courses of action seemed to be (a) use one of the many empty pint glasses around to murder Aunt Myrtle with a swift blow to the head, and (b) loudly interrupt Colin and Mr Harrington with a remark to the effect that we couldn't afford his fees, when the whole do suddenly disintegrated. Cheeks were being kissed, hands shaken, 'must keep in touch's echoing around the premises, and before I knew it, Colin and I were making our way slowly up the stairs, with me steadfastly refusing the lift on even the vaguest chance that Aunt Myrtle might be in it.

'Have you enjoyed your exchanges with the divorce man, Colin?' I said, a little haughtily. 'Will we be able to take out a second mortgage to secure a decree nisi?'

He seemed now to be able to tell when I was joking, though it occurred to me that my sardonic wit might well have been misinterpreted on more than one occasion in the past.

He chuckled, a noise still not too familiar in our relationship recently. 'Oh, I wasn't talking to him about that,' he said. 'I was talking to him about workers' rights, related in particular to occupational pensions.'

This needed further investigation. Back in the room, I didn't waste time. 'He's a divorce lawyer, Colin, isn't he?'

'He is now, yes, but you don't get to be a specialist lawyer until you've got at least a smattering of the rest of it, and in any case, he has a personal interest. He's the kind of age when the subject starts becoming relevant in your life, as I am.'

He suddenly started looking a little coy, or something vaguely similar. I had just started thinking that if he really thought another bath-time frolic was on the cards at this end of the day, and particularly this day, then he should be so lucky, or words to that effect, but then he sat down at our little table and said it like it was. 'Maybe it was violating the privacy of our marriage, Phyll, but I thought that if he was seriously willing to help me, I thought he might need to know something of my situation. I told him I believed my obsession with my work had almost destroyed my marriage. I certainly didn't expect the reaction I got.'

'Which was?'

'He said his obsession with his work *had* destroyed his marriage.'

'What?'

'Yes, it took me aback. Ever since we got here, we've been hearing all sorts of rumours about him and his wife, though we know now some were deliberately being bandied about to put pressure on him and his family. We made a mutual agreement, sort of wordlessly, that whatever the difficulties were, they would stay confidential. "I'm now interested in solutions," he said, "not complications." So we talked about solutions. I hope you don't mind, Phyllis.'

'Mind? That you're picking the brains of a top London lawyer to help us with our situation? No, Colin, I don't mind. I think it's a stroke of opportunist genius. So what did he say?'

Reassured, he settled back in his chair and off he went. 'He said quite a lot. He said he thought that my employers have been taking injurious and probably illegal advantage of me for some time. He said the situation wasn't so far out of his line of work as I might think, because divorce settlements tended to involve going into the working situations and entitlements of both parties. He advised me to get in touch with the company and demand three weeks of my leave immediately, using him as a reference.'

'Using him as a reference? You mean him acting for us? It would cost us a fortune, Colin.'

'No, quite specifically no. That bit was quite touching. He said this day will be remembered by his only son as his marriage day, but also the day when his parents' marriage disintegrated, and in spite of his son, the groom's, professional triumph, that marriage situation will always be a stain on the day. He described you and me as "innocent bystanders", behaving decently even without any direct family connections to either party. He said that, in any case, he didn't think it would involve him in a lot of work. If I could send him details of my contractual terms and conditions of work, including pension entitlements, etc., and the name of my union man he could liaise with, he doubted whether it would take more than a letter with his company's heading on it to make my company fulfil their obligations to the letter, and as his son had used his wedding to bring about something beneficial and worthwhile, so he would like to do something similar himself, even if on a smaller scale, and save someone else's marriage as well. If it finishes up in court, well, so be it, he will act for me. I think we're just about home and dry, Phyll.'

We joined hands and walked through to the bedroom. We both knew that fervent love-making was not on the cards; it had been a long and very demanding day, during which we'd both probably consumed at least three times as much booze and rich food as we would normally do even on an indulgent day, so we just lay together, hand in hand for a while, then with arms around each other for a while, and then, just as we both realised we were slowly dropping off, we got up, prepared to go to bed and did.

Simon

We did make the effort. We really did. Being of the bride and groom's generation, and seeing that they were both there to do their bopping duty, we felt sort of obliged to back them up and fly the youthie flag. In spite of, or perhaps because of, the day they'd had, they were moving about quite credibly and easily; I remembered Robert being quite into this kind of thing in student days. But we'd only been up on the floor a few times before we realised that, firstly, we didn't recognise what we were dancing to, always a bad sign for those who imagine their finger is still on the now pulse, and secondly, we were both moving with what might be termed an economy of energy. Duncan was doing a sort of Cyberman jerk, as if making his way cunningly up to someone to liquidate them, and my dance felt and probably looked like an annoying little bunch of wasps had invaded my clothing. It became pretty clear pretty quickly that, far from being the mega boogie-masters laying it down to the kids, we were actually becoming more a source of mirth as we watched the bride and groom bop dominantly on.

Eventually, we sat down to get some breath back and stop sweating, and we exchanged a few pleasantries with some of the boys and girls, who occasionally gave us the impression of being about fourteen. They were mostly a bit bemused about the events of the day, and we realised that much of this company had not actually been at the wedding lunch; they were amongst the further-flung family and friends of the Denshams mostly, with a smattering of Londoners who'd come along largely to spend a few days in Devon on a trip financed by their parents.

We got chatting, or as near as it's possible to chatting when there's the noise equivalent of the Vietnam War going on in both your ears, with the guy we recognised as the bride's brother, Tom, the kind of hetero male calculated to make gay men sigh, with the words 'if only' never far away, and Tom's girlfriend Claudette, the kind of hetero female calculated to make straight men sigh, with the words 'if only' never far away from them either.

Shortly after getting chatting to them, we were joined by the happy couple, their dance-floor triumph a little mitigated by a certain shortness of breath and two unusually red faces.

After about twenty minutes of roaring at each other over the cacophony of music, we were willing enough to go along Tom and Claudette's suggestion that we withdraw to the hotel's main bar for a drink or two to calm ourselves down, decide honour had been satisfied in doing our Duty by the Young and credibly sneak into the Williamson Lounge.

Rob said they would head straight there, because 'we don't want to be too late going up'. How he expected his audience to react to this remark I don't know, but it gave rise to a rather disgraceful outburst of giggles amongst us all which was perhaps an even more convincing bit of revisiting youth than the dancing had been. We said goodbye to them in the entrance to youth HQ, in case they would have gone by the time we got to the Williamson Lounge, and it was one of those moments when speech was mercifully redundant beside a series of very genuine embraces. One exit remark from Rob was directed at me: 'You'll probably always carry the prize for the best man who wasn't,' and I almost blubbed, but Duncan grabbed my hand in time to stop such an exhibition.

The main bar was about half full, very classy and mercifully music-free. I realised once again how totally away with the birdies my images of Devon had been, the groups of ruddy-faced farmers chewing on bits of straw and expectorating into the nearest spittoon with unerring accuracy rather different from the reality of the suited, booted and evening-dressed clientele with hardly a single Devon accent in earshot.

Even allowing for the drama which had played out during the day in relation to the wicked Councillor Needham and his sinister allies, the hotel guests, or at least the adult part of them, were mainly abuzz with marriage issues, sadly more about the disintegration of both the parental marriages than the one the day aimed to celebrate. I had to establish how sensitive Tom was on the subject before I went steaming in with my hobnail boots on.

'Tom, if it isn't something you want to talk about, don't, but did you and Kate know?'

He looked at me a little doubtfully, but I got the impression that now we were away from the main family gathering, he had it in mind to get it off his chest.

'We knew about it eighteen months ago, or thereabouts. Much as she seems so cool and in charge a lot of the time, my mother had a hell of a job persuading herself to come out. We knew also that nothing much in the amorous line was happening between them at home; Kate had worked that out before she went to London. It was Kate who solved it, of course. Until fairly recently, when I kind of came to my senses with the aid of Claudette, I was wondering about in an alcoholic haze most of the time, locked into the rugby sub-culture, if you can call it that. Kate knew Mum was spending a lot of time with Judi, and she knew Dad was having affairs; Dad is the kind of guy who very much needs the physical side of love, and doesn't get on too well without it.'

'More or less like you, Tom, I think,' said Claudette brightly, and Tom actually flushed.

He grinned shyly at her, and pressed on. 'Kate talked me into helping her bring about – well, not exactly a confrontation, but at least putting cards down on the table. It would be going too far into family business to reveal who said what and when, I think, but arrangements were made, and they've worked out pretty well, I think. I suppose coming out is never easy, is it, even now?'

'That's more one for Duncan than me, I think,' I said. 'No-one was ever in any doubt about me. They worked me out in school; some lads wouldn't let me near them in the shower.

It's not that I'm screamingly camp, or at least I don't think I am, but I suppose I send out signals, especially in rooms full of naked males. I'm made like it; there was never much point in persuading people otherwise. That's why Robert was always such a good pal. He knew it, and he didn't care. But for a six-foot-something Scotsman like Duncan, that's not such a straightforward proposition.'

'There again, I never came across anyone who particularly wanted to argue about it,' Duncan said. He pulled a fierce face, and we all laughed.

'But, unlike Simon, I had a choice, and I stayed right there in my closet until school was over. I knew university would be much easier, and it was. So Simon's really the brave one.'

At this point, he kissed me, right there in a crowded bar. A lavishly dressed old lady pulled a horrified face; apart from that, not a flicker.

'My cousin Georges is gay,' Claudette said; her French accent is slight but detectable, and it, added to a further use of the word 'gay', brought forward an audible tut from the old lady. We ignored her.

'The nearest city to us is Lyon, which has a whole gay life of its own, not to mention a lot of very nice food. Georges is thirty-five now, and he's been with his partner Rene for seven years; they say they are more interested in the cuisine than the sex. What they do at home, of course, is another matter. When Tom went to France with me, I introduced him to them. I won't repeat everything they said, but I think they approved.'

We smiled. She was a delight, this girl, with her wide-awake eyes and open friendliness.

Then she was suddenly serious. 'But there never are – what's the English word – guarantees? People at twenty are not the same as people at forty; whatever beauty you have will never last for ever. If you love, truly love, you have to adapt, you have to let the relationship develop, and whatever happens, you have to find a way of working it out, as I think we have all done today.'

A general enthusiastic agreement which started some old-lady tutting off stage again, and then, of course, Duncan being sensible. 'Well, I think I'm about ready to show my face in the Williamson Lounge amongst the otters and dams. Anyone else?'

So we made our way over to the lounge and socialised generally with the Denshams and the Harringtons, though by now booze and fatigue were taking their toll. All the same, there were precious few wedding-goers left standing by the time we decided to call it a day.

'I think I may need to find out what happens to a naughty boy sometime tomorrow, perhaps,' I said to Duncan as we started getting ready for bed.

'You haven't been a naughty boy; you've been a dear boy, dear boy. And sometimes, finding out what happens to dear boys can be even more fun than finding out what happens to naughty boys. But at the moment, I couldn't raise a cheer. There will be time enough.'

The last five words were not a bad collection to fall asleep to, so I did.

SUNDAY MORNING, June 16th

Matthew

We both woke up feeling better than we expected to feel; Mary had made the right move by ducking out of the evening's activities, and I was conscious, for the time being at least, of business done.

In fact, an odd calm seemed to have fallen over us. We were keen to get away, not because the hotel or its inhabitants were intolerable to us, but the last few days had plunged us into an unfamiliar world, to Mary particularly, and we wanted to be back in the one we normally inhabit. Times and places arise occasionally in people's lives when the whole pace and breadth of what's happening accelerates to a bewildering intensity, and neither of us was used to it. I suppose we felt as if we'd been through some high-powered health cure aimed more at the mind than the body. Mary had been in need of a quieter and less demanding time for a while, and investigations were needed into her health situation which we had both been putting off for too long. I needed to take stock of where I was and how much the whole 'Densham Do', as it was already beginning to be called (and it didn't just mean the wedding!) would inform the future of the paper and my role in it. I think I had probably managed to acquire several very useful and powerful allies, and come to a better understanding of my brother in particular; I could see now that part of my image of him, the one that saw him as a feckless libertine, was not only superficial but fundamentally unfair. Now that his affairs had also 'been to the cleaner's', as it were, we might look forward to a more constructive and understanding relationship between us.

We copped out of the hotel breakfast room and a succession of long, wearisome goodbyes. Most of the Densham contingent, in any case, we were likely to be seeing again in a matter of weeks if not days. Kate and Robert were off on their honeymoon and would be concentrating on picking up their careers when they came back, but Kate will always be a Devon girl at heart and her partner has made the kind of impression which is going to see him welcomed in these parts for a good while.

We had two smallish suitcases with us and at shortly after eight o'clock, having just had a pot of tea in our suite, we took the cases to the car, which was tucked away in the smaller car park at the side of the hotel. Thanking our luck, we were about to get in when a voice hailed us from above. For a moment, our hearts sank, but it was Phyllis Drayton hanging out of her window so far that we feared she might fall out, and it seemed churlish not to wave back with similar enthusiasm.

'See you soon!' said Phyllis, and we could see Colin waving behind her. It's good, and I have to say quite rare, to see the two of them so much in harmony with each other; as with so many of the rest of us, the Densham Do seems to have provided them with a kind of catharsis, though exactly what form it's taken in their case I don't know. But something has happened for them, and it's good to see.

On the quiet Sunday roads, we were home in just over half an hour, and we decided then that we were ready for a proper breakfast, in our dining room looking out through the French windows on to the garden both of us, but especially Mary, have put a lot of time and effort into to make it the neat, ordered but relaxing place it is.

We felt we were home in more than one sense, home as in returned to the true, unsensational but satisfying reality of our lives as if waking from a long, intricate dream. For the rest of the day, we talked, read occasionally and gave the garden some attention. It was Sunday as Sunday is intended to be.

Celia

I woke up, to a kind of light grey half-light. The clock beside my bed said that it was just after six, meaning I had actually managed, for once, to almost sleep the night through. The most irritating awakenings happen right in the middle of the night, when I know I have little chance of going back to sleep and there are still hours until daylight to somehow occupy myself. And then there's the little bastard with his drill, and excuse my French, but I do have to give him his true name from time to time. He respects no times or moods, and my dread is that it won't be much longer before he's permanently in residence.

The warm glow inside me that Malcolm had chosen to say what he did now inevitably gave way to looking at the practicalities of the situation. My retirement village was comfortable enough; I had several good friends there and everything was done for me. Did it really make sense to parachute myself into Malcolm's life? I don't doubt for one minute that the offer was made sincerely; ever since childhood, Malcolm doesn't make offers or promises lightly, particularly to people close to him. And if he says he will ensure comfortable quarters for me separate from the main house, with someone to look after me – my own establishment, in fact – that's what he means.

But there are always questions. If he chooses to marry again, and he should, in my opinion, is the lady in question likely to be impressed that his mummy is pretty much parked on the premises, even if a little distance away from the main house? And if Malcolm chooses to play the biological trump card which men in middle age always have over their female contemporaries, i.e. the ability to go on having children for as long as they like, is the child's mother, presumably with parents of her own, going to take kindly to the rival grandmother being always on campus, as it were, and in a position to treat and babysit the infant to her heart's content? And, given Malcolm will be spending quite a lot of his time in London, am I going to be rattling around the premises with no-one but whoever it is 'looking after me' to talk to? Am I going to miss for ever the chance to tell Stephanie Holston, a woman who takes hypochondria to new and uncharted levels, not to be so bloody silly? Am I going to regret 'the girls', the four of us, all well over seventy-five, having our occasional whist drives or hilarious bingo sessions?

The dawn had already passed, it seemed, and I decided to get out of bed and wrap the hotel's monumental dressing gown, which could easily insulate a heavyweight boxer, around myself, before spending a last session on my magnificent balcony.

It was very June, crisp with a roaming breeze but sunshine frequently breaking through. Take the questions one at a time, Derek would say. You might not even have to get through them all; there could well be one which tells you the answer all on its own.

So I lined them up to shoot them down like ducks on a fairground stall. Malcolm is a bit of a catch, middle-aged or not; he is a top lawyer, very comfortably off, and still attractive enough in terms of looks and personality; the older he gets, the more he reminds me of Derek. A woman who has got as far as visiting his home is unlikely to be put off by Mummy being nearby; she's more likely to take it on as part of the deal, especially as we are all very much beyond the stage where I am likely to walk in on them cavorting on the sofa in their knickers. And if she is put off by my presence on the same estate, she probably wouldn't amount to much as a life partner anyway.

Second, if the lady does conceive, it will double the number of my grandchildren and enable me to see something of the child's growing up; yes, I did see a fair bit of Robert's, but not actually on the premises, as it were. It might also help me to get closer to the new Mrs Harrington, and even present her and Malcolm with a useful baby-sitting option, at least until the child begins on the booby-trapped rink of adolescence.

As for rattling around the premises on my own, the sale of my retirement apartment and whatever largesse Malcolm might want to put my way will equip me very well to make myself a local Lady Bountiful, giving her time and effort generously to local good causes and making friends amongst my fellow Bountifuls. As for the girls, with our whist drives and bingo sessions, they are to some extent done with sheer frustration at the regime we all live under, which purports to be a 'management' and yet seems to 'manage' everything much more to their own convenience than ours. As for Stephanie Holston, if I am determined enough to keep telling her not to be so bloody silly, I could invite her to my splendour and spend entire weekends telling her not to be so bloody silly.

At this point, little so-and-so started up with his drill again, and I decided, on not terribly good medical assumptions, that a pot of tea might well drown the bugger. And as I was doing so, what has been rightly called the cold douche of reality came over me.

It might well be something which Stephanie could be prone to saying, but what we are almost certainly talking about here is somewhere to die in. There are only so many self-delusions one can feasibly carry around in a situation like mine. Whether the time will be granted to me to be Lady Bountiful or babysitter number one is unlikely. If I'm going to die, and I am, probably sooner rather than later, I want it to be in the bosom of what remains of my family, not in a semi-institution all too practised in wrapping the stiffs up and carrying them off. I want to die a Harrington, not a resident; a mother, not old lady no. 5,643.

Curiously enough, a pot of tea in one of the hotel's pert little teapots, producing two mugs at most, did seem to quieten down my little friend as if a touch of hot liquid has got into his drill's workings.

Back on my balcony, with my tea slipping down nicely, I watched Devon beginning to wake up, and it suddenly dawned on me, just about literally, that having things like balconies or terraces could well now be in my gift. True, they won't come with views of bare-torsoed young beauties, but then again, a sprightly young gardener might even be on the cards too. And each day, however many there are left, will be spent with me deciding for myself what to do with each day, with no concessions to institutional demands for cleaning, meals, etc. according to their convenience rather than mine.

By twenty past eight, I found myself catching up on a smidgeon of lost morning sleep, until wakened by the phone. It was Malcolm.

'Morning, Mum. Will you join me for a bit of breakfast?'

'Certainly, dear. Will Barbara be with us?'

'Barbara booked a hire car yesterday and she left early to drive home. By home I mean the house we currently inhabit. Well, to be entirely accurate, the house she now currently inhabits. I'll be driving back to the London flat for the moment.'

There was something in that voice, which I could detect because the normal voice is so familiar to me; something of desperation and indignation, something that says to me that the final separation wasn't so terribly stiff upper lip English as they would both like me to think.

'Yes, of course; breakfast would be lovely. Give me fifteen minutes, dear.'

However many children you have and however old you get, don't imagine your parental duties will ever be over. They won't.

One hour later, almost to the minute, Malcolm and I were comfortably settled on the back seat of the palatial Harrington motor, with the admirable Ron taking us steadily and comfortably London-wards. We chatted easily, about the lovely countryside we were driving through and about the new arrangements we would soon be making, with Ron making occasional contributions. Ron was far from being the obediently silent servant.

I will remember dear Robert's wedding for all sorts of reasons. It might even divide my life into BRW and ARW. The latter will probably be a good deal shorter, but having finally attained the ultimate distinction of wealthy and acknowledged matriarch, I intend to make it last as long as is humanly possible.

Phyllis

I woke up before Colin, which isn't exactly unusual. It was only just after dawn. I suppose I could have gathered the duvet about me and slept on, but waking up early seemed to present the ideal opportunity to cast my mind back over what is certainly one of the most extraordinary days my life is likely to produce.

I looked across at Colin. On the relatively rare occasions when we stay in hotels, we settled for twin beds some time ago; he isn't the most restful sleeper in the world, and one bony foot banged itself into my shin once too often.

His duvet had drifted down; he doesn't take kindly to heat, and the combination of warm night and duvet had probably made him a little uncomfortable. The duvet's drift left him only just about decent, with the entire torso exposed almost to the groin.

I'm not, as a general rule, a great fan of the male nude, but if something presents itself to me in the flesh, I'll take a peep. There have been occasions on Spanish and French beaches when my peep has included a certain quickening of breath and a realisation that I wouldn't be entirely averse to seeing the rest of the story, as it were. I've been familiar with Colin's body for a long time, but in that silvery light, there was a kind of combined power and economy which hadn't registered with me for a while; a total absence of extraneous flesh as well as prominent biceps and shoulder blades. He looked, and there was a spasm of guilt in my heart as I saw it, like a man who worked hard, perhaps too hard.

And then the startling thought occurred to me that for years now, I seem to have become used to seeing him as belonging to someone else, more a creature of whoever he worked for than a partner of mine. One of the problems with long-term marriages is that both partners tend to assume that they will get to know each other better over the years and therefore become closer and more comfortable with each other. It often doesn't happen like that, because when the more hidden and complicated aspects of what the other person amounts to become clearer, they can have the effect of forcing apart rather than growing together. I didn't really understand when I met Colin how work-orientated he was and how much his work is central to his self-esteem. If he is working hard and making a good living, that satisfies him, partly because he sees that as what he brings to the relationship. When his efforts don't seem to be making me happy, his reaction is to work all the harder. If I'd realised that early on, it might have made things easier between us. But, equally, if he'd realised then that a higher and higher income is not my be all and end all, because I know well enough that both partners working flat out means they have no kind of life with each other and all the money coming in is therefore pointless.

Now it seemed that I'm about to see off the competitors and make a real partner of him. Now we were going to live in a new world where our time was ours and we were each other's. I wouldn't be moaning to Helen about Colin and she wouldn't be moaning to me about Peter, although that kind of conversation was much more on my side that it was on hers.

So it further dawned on me, on this dawn of dawnings, that Helen was actually the only real link I had with the whole Densham crowd, who would now all drift off in various directions. Like Colin was losing his employer and his long hours of work, I was losing the family I seemed to have attached myself to compensate for having a husband who belonged to someone else. Not anymore. We would make a new life for ourselves, with our friends, meaning the friends of both of us.

I realised that the day was now fully alight and my husband was watching me, and he was still as half-naked as he was when asleep. He looked at me and I looked at him, and we both realised simultaneously what we both had in mind, in spite of all the food and drink intake and excitement of yesterday.

'OK, Colin. I'll have a shower, then you have a shower, and then maybe we'll see how sturdy the hotel furniture is.'

He just nodded, his face flushed.

A veil over the next however long it took us after the showers to engage in a little morning exercise; suffice it to say we both needed another shower afterwards. Then, dressed and clean as new pins, he revealed that he'd pre-empted the whole breakfast room thing and ordered us a fairly innocuous continental-type breakfast which was due to arrive at quarter to nine, as in twenty minutes' time.

Just before breakfast arrived, I was looking out of the window for no particular reason and I saw Peter's brother Matthew and his wife Mary packing their car ready to move off. It occurred to me that this might well be the last time I ever see them, and I've always liked what I've known of them, so I waved their way, and Colin joined me when he realised what I was doing.

After that, it was all easy. We had a decent breakfast on a table in the privacy of our room, Colin went and paid the bill, without a queue, to his great surprise, and then we packed and enjoyed the sole advantage of being in a room overlooking the car park, which is getting your cases to your car easily and rapidly. We were spared any long, drawn-out farewells to either Denshams or Harringtons, which I hate, and as we drew away from the hotel, I was still feeling that the world as it was when we arrived was not the same as it was now we were leaving.

I probably will see a Densham or two now and then, but my farewell to Matthew and Mary was now fixed in my mind as a farewell to them all. For some reason, I am absolutely positive that Malcolm Harrington's offer of help will prove valuable, that Colin will shortly be leaving the company who have threatened to gobble up his life with everything due to him, amounting to a lot, and that we have reached that point in our lives when all our yesterdays become all our futures.

Simon

We decided to brave the breakfast room fairly early on. Neither of us was at his most pristine; it had been quite a long and boozy do, with more twists and turns than an animated Kamasutra. Duncan mentioned it being a long way to London, and how we'd probably need to stop on the way, which sounds like an uncontroversial statement about a stop at a motorway services, but I know the range of expressions even an enigmatic Northumbrian can command, and this one suggested a SAFF was more on his mind than the coffee and sandwich, though I dare say we'd get both in before London loomed on the horizon. I wasn't arguing; a full-blooded SAFF seemed a suitable way to round off the weekend. The coffee and sandwich; well, whatever.

We've long ago ceased to take pleasure in the pathetic fist some people make of putting themselves a hotel breakfast together. It was a pretty standard buffet; on the upmarket side, yes; rocket science, no. I work in a hotel and Duncan spends half his life in them, so it takes a particularly fiendish number to put us out.

We vaguely recognised a few of the Densham diaspora in the room, but a civil nod sufficed for people only vaguely recognised, especially at this time of the morning.

I was getting outside of a surprisingly tasty piece of Gouda when I detected a female presence in my vicinity and immediately recognised Joyce.

'Joyce, my love, good to see you. Pull up a pew. Are you allowed a pew at this time of the morning, or will the kitchen descend into a chaos of crushed croissants and jam?'

It seemed she had a minute or two to pew. Duncan nodded and smiled, then, being the good trencherman he is, he continued his encounter with a place of scrambled eggs and beans on toast, a contest which was only ever going to have one winner.

'I just wanted to say how much I appreciated your help yesterday, Simon, a sentiment I know is shared by the hotel's owner. We could well have been in danger of some serious incident if you hadn't used your experience and weighed in on our side.'

'That's very kind of you, Joyce,' I said. 'Very flattering, too, though if one of those nasty men decided to bop me on the nose, things might have been very different.'

'Maybe, but you used your expertise in handling situations and your sense of timing to good effect, and it was mostly you who diffused the situation long enough for the police to get in and take over. You're a real professional.'

'He is that,' said Duncan, pausing in his studied demolition of the scrambled eggs. 'He's got a lot of guts, too, and he often doesn't get enough credit for it.'

I was thrilled by these words, coming from such a source, and I made an odd gushing sound before my incisive and eloquent comment on the London hotel business.

'You have to learn on your feet in the Smoke,' I said.

'I don't doubt it,' said Joyce. 'Down here in Devon, we like a quieter life. London's all very well, the big metropolis and all that, but it's restless and dangerous and difficult to relax in. I like the quieter life down here, where things happen more slowly; the whole pace of life is more laid-back.'

'As in yesterday?' said Duncan.

Joyce smiled. 'I can assure you, Duncan, that yesterday was so unusual that it will be spoken of in these parts for generations, probably. It's all I can do at the moment to get the boys and girls off their mobile phones to concentrate on their work. But I know guys like you need the metropolitan buzz rather than the rural life.'

This seemed to touch off an odd reaction in me.

'I'm not so sure about that. Even allowing for all the fun and games yesterday, this is a beautiful place, and I think I could do with a lot more of it.'

Duncan glanced curiously across at me.

Joyce got to her feet. 'Well, let me tell you, Simon, if you ever decided to re-locate down to this part of the world, I suspect the Devon tourist industry would open its arms to you. And this weekend won't have done you any harm at all with that. Anyway, I must get on; they'll all be on their phones gassing again by now. Best of luck to both of you, and lovely to have met you.'

We both got to our feet, and cheek kisses were exchanged. As soon as I sat down again, I realised her words had already set me off on a train of thought.

London hotels have their weird assortments of guests, some of them very famous, well thought of and respectable people, some of them leading spirits in their line of work, including music, art, politics, nature, literature, etc., etc. But then there were the types who'd invaded our Devon hotel this weekend; here, they stuck out like a sore thumb; in London, you just have to get used to them. Yes, you are where the buzz is, but I realised I was no longer too sure about wanting to be where the buzz is.

I looked across at Duncan, who seemed thoughtful himself as he was seeing off the last of the coffee pot. 'Well, what do you think of Devon, Dunc?'

'I think you have some scheme in mind, dear boy, as you usually do when you call me "Dunc",' he said, but happily enough.

'Oh, God. Am I already that predictable, then? Can you read me like a book?'

'After Joyce has just said what she said, it wouldn't be surprising if she's put the idea of living around here in your head.'

'Stop being all northern and inscrutable. Can you ever see yourself breaking away from the Smoke, where all the big shot spooks and what have you are handing you work?'

He started to get up. 'Let's get back to the room and give this a good airing.'

Which is what we did, and a little to my surprise, I found he was quite keen on the idea.

'I don't know why it should be so much of a surprise to you, Simon,' he said. 'I grew up in one of the most beautiful counties in the country, and from what I've seen of this place, it has an intense, striking beauty of its own. Less rugged and intimidating than much of Northumberland, and with much better weather. And in all honesty, I can do what I do anywhere in the country, and there could be pluses as well as minuses to living somewhere more remote. It's occurred to me more than once that I wouldn't mind losing the bad London air and the sense of being trapped in a kind of hornet's nest. I suggest, when we get home, we start talking about the where, when and how.'

And I couldn't ask for much fairer than that. His mention of home reminded us both that, London or not, we were now quite keen on getting back to it. Duncan had further conversations to have with spooks, including Giles Cavendish, and I had plans to get my hands on the trade papers and see what was going off in Devon job-wise.

We managed a SAFF in the countryside near Winchester, which pretty much rid both of us of any remaining tensions from the weekend. In the middle of being comprehensively saffed and on my way to one of those orgasms which linger in the mind for ever, I nevertheless had two more prosaic moments, one to wonder whether the tree branch I was draped over would continue to take my weight, and two about how many locals my screeches and Duncan's roars would shortly summon to the scene. But there was also something of a revelation, as it occurred to me that SAFF opportunities in and around Devon could be many and various.

But, of course, I also knew full well that, in the fullness of time, Duncan and I couldn't and wouldn't be saffing for ever, and the case for Devon had a whole lot of other more momentous issues to be gone into and sorted out. Man cannot live by SAFF alone.

When we'd screeched and roared accordingly, and rounded the procedures off with a refreshing flask of coffee, we got back on the road, and a way to summon up the whole Densham do occurred to me when I saw one of those black and white road signs pointing in at least three directions which you see all over the English countryside, but perhaps even more so in Devon. You stand there and scratch your head, wondering which way to go and realising that sooner or later, regardless of whether you know enough to be able to compare the various directions, you are going to have to make a decision. From the moment we all arrived at the hotel to the moment we left, whatever predictions and baggage we arrived with, we all faced a serious of choices we needed to make, often with not much to go on and sometimes with some potentially very nasty consequences for getting it wrong.

For that, read my life. For that, read all of us.

.